Veer

Continuance Cycle 3

Mark McDonough

All rights reserved. This book or any portion thereof may not be reproduced or used in any manner whatsoever without the express written permission of the publisher except for the use of brief quotations in a book review.

ISBN: 979-8-4286-7578-8

First Edition, 2022

Stargon Books
https://stargonbooks.wordpress.com

Book Cover design & Logo by Ayliesha Harris @
Ayli's Offerings
http://www.aylisofferings.com/
Hopper Alien artwork and design by DrakainaQueen @
https://www.deviantart.com/drakainaqueen

This is a work of fiction. Names, characters, places, and incidents either are the products of the author's imagination or are used fictitiously. Any resemblance to actual persons, living or dead, businesses, companies, events or locales is entirely coincidental.

Acknowledgements

When I first starting writing *Shift* in 2019, I had only a vague direction of where the story would go. Yes, I knew that it'd be a trilogy and some of the plotlines, but not all of them. The plan wasn't even for the story to be told from Vic's perspective, but characters and stories often have a life of their own and I have enjoyed the ride, discovering, laughing, crying and having my heart nearly beat out of my chest at times with what was going on.

Writing isn't a solo effort, as much as writers would like to pretend it is. There are always those that are there encouraging, nagging and making sure that the story sees the light of day.

First and foremost, I want to thank the best group of writers and friends that I have been the privilege to be a part of in our Asgardian Writer's Group: Fee, Caz, Jade & Lou! Every one of you is amazing and I've needed your support to get this book finished. There were times I didn't think I'd make it. I look forward to seeing the shelf full of all of our stories.

To my boys, it's done! I've even managed to tie in a little cameo for you, just as you hoped I would. Thank you for all of your encouragement and eagerness to hold the book in your hands and to read it.

To Ayli and her amazing cover designs, getting the next book written so that I could see what you'd come up with next has helped motivate me. To the WordFam, the WordParents and their slew of Daring prompts, you've inspired me to stretch, often fueling the plot in unexpected ways. To my readers and fans. Thank you to all of you, you've helped and inspired in ways you can't imagine.

Lastly, but certainly not least, to the one person who helped keep me writing and made sure that I made the time to do so. There are scenes, subplots and even an entire chapter in here that I wouldn't have included without your insistence, and it's made the story so much better. You are an inspiration to me, more than you realise or accept. My heart thanks you.

To everyone, read, enjoy and make life what you want it to be, it's not set in stone, the future can be Shifted, it's still in Flux; Veer it onto what You want it to be.

For D.

You know the Words.

CHAPTER 1

"NO!" Vic yelled, spinning about wildly, hands outflung, eyes wide.

"Vic?" Alana asked, worry clear in her voice.

Onetwothreefourfivesix. Alana Paul Matt Ray Kadee Tolan. They were all still there. She felt her heartrate slow. Marginally.

Leaving the room right then would have been bad! Very bad! She *felt* it. There was a sharp pain in her stomach, the hairs on the back of her neck were raised, goosebumps extending all the way up her arms, and a flush of coldness sweeping her entire body. Her premonition ability was in overdrive.

She'd only felt it this bad a couple of times before but each time, she'd listened and it'd saved them from doing something stupid. Of course, she was still getting used to the idea of having the ability to predict things or, more accurately, to *feel* if something was the right or wrong course of action. Surely it hadn't just been a matter of a few weeks since she'd gained the ability?

But it had. Two weeks in this timeline and just over a week in the future. Well, one possible future. A future that would now never come to be. She hoped.

Six of them had unexpectedly been transported there, a hundred or more years into the future. They'd seen what the world looked like. Grasshopper-like aliens ruling the planet. Buildings in ruin. Nature reclaiming everything. And what few people that still survived were left hiding underground. There they'd met Kadee and discovered that their shift in time had granted them superhuman abilities.

Matt could hit anything. Paul could move things with his mind. Alana could see anything, including through things and in complete darkness. Tolan now had a pretty blue shield to protect himself. Ray could disappear into the background. And her own premonition ability.

Thankfully, they'd survived that future world, although it was close. Closer still for Kadee, having been captured by the Hoppers of the future while they were there. Together, they'd rescued her and even managed to find their way back home, bringing Kadee with them and subsequently giving her the power to create illusions along the way.

Then, having seen the future, they'd spent the last two weeks trying to prevent it, culminating in their *flying an alien spaceship into space and blowing another alien spaceship to smithereens!*

They'd thought that they'd won, that everything was now going to be alright with the world. How wrong they were.

"Your planet, your species is inferior. We have studied you. We have watched and learnt. We know all that we need to. There may be many of you but even with your guns and weapons, you are no match for us. This planet will be ours. Its resources, ours. Its land, ours. Its people, you, eradicated," the Hopper that they'd captured had told them just minutes before.

"You don't know us as well as you think you do," Tolan had growled in response. *"You'll never win! You didn't think that we could stop your ship from activating those devices, yet we did!"*

"What is coming?" Vic herself had asked.

"The Swarm! The Swarm is coming!" the Hopper had crowed. *"And when it gets here, you shall be no more and this planet shall be ours!"*

A Swarm of aliens was headed right at Earth, most likely in a fleet of spaceships. It was enough to boggle the mind, to nearly shut her down. Paul, she decided, had the right of it. At the Hopper's words, he'd used his ability to shoot the Hopper straight up to slam into the ceiling, knocking it out.

Of course, the military men hadn't liked that, this being their Army Base and all. They also weren't too enamoured by the fact that the seven of them had managed to get more intel out of the Hopper using their abilities than the trained professionals had in all the hours that they'd tried. Not that that was surprising. Vic still couldn't believe that their advice had been ignored; the three dead soldiers and two others severely wounded at least proved that the seven teens should be listened to.

"Vic? What's wrong?" Tolan asked.

"Is it your premonition thing?" Ray asked.

Vic forced her eyes to focus on them rather than darting every which way they could about the room as though searching for danger.

"Premonition, yes," she managed. "We can't go out there."

"What? Why not? What'll happen if we do?" Matt asked and she saw him reach up and around to draw an arrow from the quiver at his back.

"It's not that kind of danger," she stated, shaking her head, not that she knew *exactly* what was setting her off – one of the biggest downsides to her ability, it let her know danger or opportunity but not *why* or *what*.

"We're supposed to join General White and Colonel Jorgensen for a Press Conference, remember?" Tolan said. "The Premier, too."

That! That was where the danger was! She was sure of it.

"No! We can't!" she all but yelled.

"Um, Sweety, I don't think we have much choice," Alana said gently, beginning to rub circles on Vic's back. "You saw the crowd out there when we landed the *Scorpion*. There were already a bunch of Press there then and you can bet there'll be more here now. We need to tell them what's going on."

"Tell them what? That we flew an alien spaceship into space and destroyed *another* alien spaceship? One a hell of a lot bigger, badder and meaner? And that we stopped them setting off hundreds of alien devices hidden around the world that, if they'd gone off, would have created a massive world-wide EMP burst that would have fried every piece of tech on the planet? And that *that* was just the warm-up act? That there's now a *Swarm* of aliens in spaceships on their way here now?" she asked frantically.

"Well, yeah," Matt shrugged.

Vic stared at him incredulously.

"No," she simply replied.

"No?" he repeated, blinking at her.

"You heard her, 'no'!" Alana replied. "Haven't you watched any movies at all? What happens *every single time* some End-Of-The-World thing is approaching and the government or whoever tells ordinary people? Riots and murder and stealing and stuff!"

"Yeah, but like you said, that's in movies," Matt replied. "This is real life."

"Do you honestly think that real people would be any different?" Ray asked quietly. "People suck and are always only out for looking after number one: themselves."

"I'm leaning towards that us going out there and saying all that would be bad," Tolan stated, his eyes firmly fixed on Vic. "Vic's premonition ability has never steered us wrong yet."

Vic found all eyes on her. With each nod or sigh her body eased up more and more until it was almost back to normal, just a slight feeling of uneasiness left.

"So, what do we do? Not go out there at all? You know that's not going to work. Whether we go out there or not, some Army idiot is going to tell the world that we have what? A day? A week? A month? Left before Earth is invaded?" Paul asked.

"We can't allow that to happen!" Alana stated.

"I'm not saying I don't agree with you but what other choice do we have?" Tolan asked.

"How? How are we supposed to stop an Army General and a politician – the State Premier, no less – from saying whatever the hell they like?" Matt asked.

"Paul's already said it," Ray stated. "We don't know when this Hopper Swarm is going to arrive. We convince them that telling the world what's going on without more facts and some kind of plan is a Very Bad Idea."

"Might work, especially after that Hopper-Army guard fiasco that we had to fix," Tolan mused.

"The Press is still going to want to know something," Alana pointed out. "They saw the *Scorpion*."

"The worst of it is that they saw us getting out of the *Scorpion*, there'll be pictures and video and who knows what else," Vic added. "Honestly, I wouldn't be surprised if it's already been uploaded to YouTube or something!"

In her mind, she could already picture it: the big dark grey metal ship, the domed and glassed section at the front, the four landing struts, and its wicked looking 'tail' which curved up and over the entire ship. And the seven of them walking down its rear ramp after the ship that she'd been piloting had come back to Earth from *space*! It was ridiculous. An alien spaceship, like something straight out of a movie.

Vic's mind froze. No. Surely it couldn't be that simple. And definitely wouldn't work. Would it?

"I might have an idea," she said tentatively.

One end of the Banquet Hall – as they'd come to think of the large, open Army building, even though they were sure that it had another name or use – was filled with people. Rows and rows of chairs stretched back from the stage, a wide aisle between them. A lectern could be seen at the front of the stage, half hidden by a forest of microphones and video cameras.

"I'm guessing we're supposed to sit up there?" Ray asked, pointing to the dozen seats on the stage.

Vic wasn't surprised to see that he'd almost disappeared, his camouflage ability subconsciously swinging into effect. Ray, she knew, disliked being the centre of attention at the best of times and this, with the Press and subsequently the world, watching on, was more than even *she* was feeling comfortable with.

Still, needs must.

"This way, please."

"Vic, are you sure about this?" Alana whispered as they followed the Sergeant down the side of the hall towards the steps set into the side of the stage.

Vic glanced at her, unsure what to say. No, she wasn't sure about this at all. Yes, she had a warm feeling in her chest which she presumed was her premonition ability humming in approval. Or it could be a case of heartburn. Not that she'd eaten anything in longer than she could remember. But she could also *see* what would happen if they went through with telling the truth and it left a very bitter taste in her mouth.

"I'm sure." It was the best that she could give as an answer.

"General White isn't going to like this," Tolan stated, not for the first time. "Blindsiding him like this is not going to be pretty."

"It's not just him," Ray said. "We're going to make the *Premier* look like an idiot, too!"

"Well, it's their own fault. We *tried* to talk to them; they were both just too busy to see us," Matt reminded him.

Their trek towards the stage hadn't gone unnoticed. Heads were turning their way, more and more of them the further they walked, whispers and pointed fingers being added in for good measure. The Press was recognising them, there was no doubt about that in Vic's mind.

At the foot of the stairs, the Sergeant stopped and gestured for them to proceed. It was only a half a dozen steps but somehow, with everyone watching, those half dozen seemed to elongate into eternity. Vic stopped, staring at them. Thankfully, Tolan slid past her and began the climb, giving her the courage to follow.

They clustered together at the side of the stage, unsure what to do next.

"The seats on this end have been reserved for you," the Sergeant stated, indicating said seats.

Tolan nodded for all of them and led the way. Vic found herself sitting between Alana and Kadee but her butt had barely touched the chair when she was bouncing up once again. It was cold. Ice cold. The burst of pins and needles in the soles of her feet didn't help at all.

Wrong! Wrong! Wrong! Sitting there was wrong!

Standing, being on the stage was right – the way the cold and pins and needles in her feet instantly disappeared attested to that.

Vic sighed. She knew what had to happen, what she had to do. Didn't mean that she liked it or wanted it.

"Vic?" Tolan asked.

She looked at him, at all of them and sighed. "We need to get out ahead of this thing. We can't wait for General White and the Premier and everyone else."

Fortunately, Tolan seemed to understand instantly. "If we wait for them, then we lose, don't we?"

"Yeah," Vic nodded. "Once they're here and at that microphone, the truth will be told and panic will set in worldwide. The Hoppers will have even more free reign to take over the world."

"You're sure?" Alana asked.

Vic shrugged, shook her head and sighed. "As sure as I can be. Everything in me is telling me that we need to talk to the Press first, get them on our side with the cover story while we still have the chance."

"Yeah, that's the thing, Vic, you still haven't told *us* the cover story," Paul reminded her.

"I know," she replied. "But that's only because I'm making this up as I go along. I've really got to get more of a handle on this premonition thing!"

The last was said under her breath even as she turned towards the podium. The scrape of chairs and the sound of footsteps behind her helped ease some of the tension that she was feeling. She wasn't alone in this.

The podium was too tall for her, but what wasn't? The curse of always being one of the shortest anywhere she went. A hinge at the inside bottom of it caught her attention and she smiled. A quick squat, reach in, flip and a step appeared for her to stand on.

The next hurdle was, of course, the microphones themselves. Not only were they daunting, she had no way of knowing whether they were even on. Tentatively, she reached out and tapped one with a finger.

Tap tap tap tap TAP TAP

It'd started with the smallest of sounds that only she and her friends could hear and ended with booms that echoed around the room. Heads shot towards them and bodies shuffled quickly to seats.

"Guessing someone turned the sound on," Ray muttered.

A pointed look from Tolan reminded her that *she* was the one standing at the podium.

"Hello? Can you all hear me?" she asked tentatively.

Surprisingly, she actually got some responses; a number of calls of 'yes' were shouted back at her from the congregated Press contingent.

"Ah, Miss?" the Sergeant that had left the stage asked, having rushed back up the stairs. "You're not supposed to ..."

Vic, though, ignored him and trusted that her friends would be able to shield her from anyone trying to stop her.

"Um, hi, my name's Vic, um Victoria," she grimaced at using her whole name, ignored Paul's snigger, smiled at his 'oof', and continued. "I guess I should start with introducing my friends."

She turned, doing her best to keep her mouth close to the microphone as she pointed to each one. "This is Alana, that's Paul and Matt. And on this side of me is Ray, Tolan and Kadee. For those of you who were here and outside earlier, we're the ones that came out of that ship when it landed."

A scuffle at the far end of the hall caught her attention; it was only a pair of soldiers coming in through the door and taking up position at the very back of the room. She still had time.

"I'm sure you have questions about that but I'd ... *we'd* like to make a statement about that first," she said.

The adults before her shuffled forward in their seats. Some held phones or recorders out in front of them, she supposed in an effort to better catch her words. Others had notebooks and pens. One or two hands had shot up at the start of her statement but were quickly lowered.

"I'm guessing that many of you think you know what you saw, whether it was here in person or in photos or maybe even on-line?" she asked and the few answering nods confirmed that there was video of them landing the *Scorpion* out there. "Let me guess. You think you saw seven teenagers emerge from an alien spaceship after they'd landed it on an Army Base? Well, you're half right."

The rear doors flying open caught her attention and Vic looked up to see General White, Colonel Jorgensen, the Premier and a handful of others dressed either in military uniforms or in suits bursting in through the doors. The fact that they barely paused to stare at her and her friends before striding down the hall spurred her on. She was quickly running out of time.

"Yes, you did see us come out of the ship," she continued quickly. "And yes, you did see us land here, at the Base. But no, what you saw out there is not an alien spaceship. Really, that'd just be silly, wouldn't it? Aliens don't exist, everyone knows that!"

"If it's not an alien spaceship, what is it?" a reporter wearing a black leather jacket and with thinning grey hair called.

Vic focussed on him for a second before sweeping the rest of the reporters with her eyes. Good, they were all looking at her and not the military and politicians hurrying down the side of the hall.

"It's actually a specially outfitted military aircraft," she replied. "It's just been made to *look* as though it's alien, from another world."

"Why? Is this some kind of stunt?" an immaculately dressed female journalist asked.

"Yep," Vic replied succinctly. "That's *exactly* what it was. A stunt. A promotion if you will for a new movie that's being made that we all star in."

"Paul, hold them off!" Tolan whispered from behind her.

Vic's eyes darted to General White and the others before widening. The group was no longer moving forward. They looked like they were trying to, though – their arms and legs were definitely in motion – but they were making zero headway forwards. It was only because Vic knew what to look for that she noticed that they were hovering just above the ground where they couldn't get any traction under them.

The hand of one of the younger-looking reporters shot up, recapturing Vic's attention and she pointed to him.

"What's this new movie called? What can you tell us about it?" he asked.

A slight push on her side had Vic moving out of the way as Matt took to the podium.

"We can't tell you the real title yet, but we can give you the movie's codename: Hoppers," Matt said. "As to what it's about, most of the plot is secret, for obvious reasons. Let's just say that it involves aliens, time travel and some ordinary teens who gain superpowers."

Other hands went up and Matt pointed at the first of them.

"Dude, I can't hold them for long, they're going to be noticed!" Paul whispered.

"He's right, we need to wrap this up," Tolan agreed.

"We'll make this the last question for now," Matt told the reporters. "I'm sure that there'll be other opportunities in the future with more announcements about the movie. What's your question?"

"What's the Army's involvement in this movie?"

Vic could have laughed; it was the perfect question.

"The Australian Army actually have a fairly extensive role," Matt replied. "Obviously, they're heavily involved in a number of the visual scenes: the mock-up of the spaceship that utilizes a modified aircraft; flights over and around the city; transports on the ground; weapons control for the visual sets, just to name a few. The movie has hired General Adrian White as Lead Consultant, which I, for one, think was a genius idea – he really gets into the role and has treated the movie and cast as though the *events are really happening*! That has definitely helped us get into character."

"Kadee, be ready," Tolan breathed.

An elbow to the ribs from Vic had Matt stepping to the side to allow her to take back her place at the podium.

"That's all we have time for today," she smiled at the reporters. "We'd like to thank you all for coming along and look forward to seeing you at the premiere when the movie is released."

"Right, let's go!" Tolan hissed.

"Don't forget to wave!" Alana added, doing exactly that, a motion that the rest of them copied as they made their way into the wings of the stage.

CHAPTER 2

"What the hell was that?"

The question was asked – yelled – almost before the door had even been opened. What followed the question was a stampede of military and politicians. As expected, General White was the first through the door. He stormed two feet into the room and stopped, his hands on his hips, his chest heaving, his eyes narrowed and glaring. Everyone else needed to make a quick detour to either side of him before spreading out in a line facing the seven teens.

"Well? I asked you a question!" General White demanded.

Vic glanced at Tolan, hoping that he'd take the lead. Thankfully, he did.

"If you mean the Press Conference, we did what was right."

"Right? Right! Do you have any idea what you've just done? How hard it's going to be to be taken seriously now? For the true facts to be believed?" General White asked, his face starting to go red.

"Actually, yes," Tolan replied simply.

A hand landing on the General's shoulder seemed to only push him further into his explosive rage. "*What?*"

Seeing the General blanche at the fact that he'd just snapped at the State Premier was almost funny and Vic had to stifle her laugh.

"Let's take a minute, shall we," the man said.

Seemingly reluctantly, General White gave the tiniest of nods.

"I don't think that I got a chance to meet all of you before but I'm guessing that you know who I am? David Narimono. I'm the Premier and, incidentally, the one who called the Press Conference in the first place," he said.

Tolan nodded at him. "Look, I'm sorry we crashed your Conference but we're not sorry we said what we did."

"How about you tell us *why* you told the world that the alien spaceship was a military aircraft designed as a movie prop instead of what it really is," Premier Narimono said.

Vic didn't need to be a mind-reader to understand Tolan's look at her.

"You know what we can do, right? What our powers are?" she began.

"I do," Premier Narimono replied.

"Good," Vic nodded. "Well, then you know about my premonition ability. Everything in me was screaming out that telling the world about what had been going on with the Hoppers, how they'd come to 'soften us up' by wiping out our tech and that an invasion force was on the way was bad. Very bad. End of the world bad."

"Okay, I think I can understand what you're saying," Premier Narimono nodded as he moved forward, pulled out one of the chairs of the conference table that stood between the two groups and took a seat. "But could you help me understand *why* it was such a bad thing to do?"

"Have you watched an end-of-the-world movie?" Matt asked rhetorically.

The Premier laughed. "More than a few. Love them, in fact."

"As a movie, yeah, it's fun to watch," Vic agreed. "But what about seeing it and living it in real life? What they show in movies, all that stealing and violence and everything, that would have happened. More than that, it would have meant the end of the world, the Hoppers would have had free rein to win everything."

"What do you know?" Colonel Jorgenen asked, his eyes narrowed suspiciously. "Do you have some intelligence that we don't?"

Tolan shook his head. "You know everything we know."

"Then how can you be sure?" Colonel Jorgensen insisted.

"I just told you, I *felt* it," Vic stated.

"You felt it!" General White repeated sarcastically. "That's nice but we need real intel."

"Don't you think the people have a right to know?" Premier Narimono asked, having held up a hand to stop the General's impending rant. "People can surprise you – that's definitely something that I've learnt in this job. And it's possible that someone out there might have information that we don't, information that could help us defeat what's coming."

"You don't even know *what's* coming, do you?" Colonel Jorgensen asked.

"The Swarm, that's what the Hopper said. A swarm of Hoppers," Kadee stated matter-of-factly.

"What does that actually mean? We don't even know if that translator works properly," General White replied dismissively.

"It's accurate," Vic stated. "I would have felt it if it wasn't. The translator said 'swarm', so that's what it'll be."

"We've seen one spaceship up there and we've destroyed it – but only because we had the *Scorpion* and the element of surprise. That missile that the US launched into space did nothing," Tolan added. "Now picture a dozen or fifty or a hundred or more of those Hopper spaceships in orbit, each one carrying hundreds of troops. What chance would we stand if we were already too busy destroying ourselves because people were panicking?"

"The lad does have a point," Premier Narimono nodded.

"Damn right he does," Paul muttered.

"Who's to say if you're right about what's coming? There's a chance that that alien was lying or giving us bad intel," General White insisted.

"That's true," Vic said, not that she believed it. "One way to find out: question it, test it."

"Not only that, we can get the Hopper to tell us more," Ray insisted, leaning forward, both fists on the desk. "How many ships and troops *are* coming. When the Swarm'll be here. If there are any weaknesses that we can exploit."

"I'm not willing to put all my chips on the word of an alien that we can't even be sure is telling the truth," Colonel Jorgensen stated.

"Neither am I," General White agreed. "And honestly, I believe that we need more resources than we have here. Other nations, civilians with extra skills, whatever it takes. Premier, you need to denounce that Press Conference, give the public the true facts."

"Are you going to call us liars? Throw us to the wolves?" Alana asked.

"You are liars!" General White shot back.

"You do that and we won't be able to do anything. We'll be hounded day and night and you'll lose your biggest asset in this fight: us!" Vic warned.

"Mister Premier?" General White asked, obviously expecting one answer.

Vic watched him. His fingers drummed on the table. His eyes shifted from General White and Colonel Jorgensen to the seven of them to the window and around again. For a full minute, not a sound was heard.

"I'm not willing to stake the future of the world on a spur of the moment decision," Premier Narimono said slowly. "To be honest, I'm not even the best man to do it. I'm simply the one that's here right now. Before we do anything, we need more information. We need to know how much time we have."

"We can interrogate the Hopper," Tolan volunteered. "We've done it before and got information out of it."

The Premier nodded. "It may come to that – assuming that the military can't make it talk first. But before that, I think we need confirmation from other sources, human sources. General, you were working with other bodies to detect that alien spaceship, weren't you?"

"Yes, the Pentagon and the National Astronomical Observatory of Japan in Mitaka primarily," he replied.

"Contact them again, see what they have and if they can detect this Swarm that's apparently coming," Premier Narimono ordered.

"What about the Press Conference?" Colonel Jorgensen insisted.

The Premier looked at the seven of them for a moment before replying. "For now, we'll leave it stand. As for you seven, I want you to come with me. We have a call to make.

Once again, they'd been rushed from one building to another. At the rate that they were going, Vic was sure that, given another day or two, they would have visited every part of the Army Base that there was.

"You can use this room," their escort Corporal stated, opening a door and stepping back.

The room wasn't large, although there was a screen that dominated one wall. A number of chairs were placed around the other three walls and a long table sat in front of the chairs at the back.

"Jasmine, please place the call," Premier Narimono asked his aide, pointing to a large pad set into the top of the desk.

"Who are we going to be talking to?" Matt asked.

"Prime Minister Donovan," the Premier replied. "He's not expecting this call, so it may take a little time before he answers. You might as well take a seat."

Vic's eyes bulged. The Prime Minister of Australia? Never in her wildest dreams had she ever imagined that she would talk to a politician, despite the fact that she was taking a seat beside one now.

"What are we supposed to say to him?" Paul whispered, leaning towards Tolan.

"Simply tell him the truth," Premier Narimono replied, obviously having heard. "He knows something of what's been happening but not everything. And he definitely does not know about what the alien said about the Swarm being on the way."

"This man we're going to talk to, is he important?" Kadee asked.

"It was Ged, wasn't it, the man in charge of the tunnels that you used to live in when you were younger?" Vic asked.

"Ged wasn't in charge, he just liked to act like he was. That was Robb," she replied.

Vic nodded. "Well, Premier Narimono here is like Robb, but on bigger scale. He's in charge of the state. The man we're going to talk to, Prime Minister Donovan is in charge of the entire country."

Kadee nodded slowly. "Very important, then."

"Sir, the Prime Minister is on the line," Jasmine stated.

Vic watched her press two buttons on the panel in front of her and replace the handset that Vic didn't even know she'd picked up. The big screen burst into life with the image of a man with dark brown hair going grey at the temples and an intense expression on his face. He was seated behind a rich-looking wood desk, a window behind him and an Australian flag on a stand behind his right shoulder.

"David, good to see you," Prime Minister Donovan said, nodding at the Premier. "I'm guessing this has something to do with *that* situation that's been happening up in your neck of the woods?"

"Yes, Sir, it does," Premier Narimono replied. "I'd like to introduce you to Victoria, Tolan, Alana, Paul, Matthew, Ray and Kadee."

"It's nice to meet you all," Prime Minister Donovan said, having nodded to each as they'd been introduced. "I've heard some special things about you seven. Especially you, Kadee. I'd be very interested in hearing your story about the world that won't come about now."

"Yeah, about that ..." Tolan said, before trailing off.

"There have been some developments, Sir," Vic added.

The Prime Minister's eyebrows rose even as his eyes flicked to Premier Narimono's.

"It's serious, Ken. I'll let these remarkable young people tell you."

Prime Minister Donovan leaned back in his chair and gestured to them.

"Please, tell me everything."

"If it's alright, perhaps it'd be easier to start with what you already know?" Vic suggested tentatively. "It'll save time and less doubling up."

"Very smart," he nodded. "Let me see. In a nutshell, my understanding is that six of you – minus Kadee – were caught in some sort of anomaly caused by the malfunction of some alien devices and sent to the future. There you met Kadee and, after some adventures, managed to travel back home again. There was also the added side effect of all of you gaining some rather extraordinary powers, which I have been briefed on as well as having seen a video of the demonstration that you gave.

"Since returning home, you were involved in discovering an alien 'cell' and capturing one of the aliens themselves. I believe that you went off on your own for a time as well," this last was said with something that sounded to Vic suspiciously like humour. "Then, if I'm not mistaken, you flew an alien spaceship into space and destroyed a much larger spaceship that was in orbit to set off a series of devices that would have rendered Earth's technology useless."

Vic nodded at him, impressed. Obviously, he'd been kept well informed on what had been going on.

"That's everything up to yesterday," Tolan nodded.

"Which tells me that something significant happened today," Prime Minister Donovan stated.

"Yes, Sir," Vic replied. "When we returned to Earth, we spoke to the Hopper again. It seems that destroying that spaceship to stop the EMP devices was only a stop-gap measure."

"There's a Swarm of Hoppers headed straight for Earth and when they get here ..." Matt summed up.

"A 'swarm'? What does that mean?" Prime Minister Donovan asked, once again leaning forward, a frown etched deep into his face.

Vic shrugged. "At the moment, we're not sure."

"I have tasked General White and his men with contacting the Pentagon and the National Astronomical Observatory of Japan in Mitaka to determine if we can detect this alien invasion force," Premier Narimono said. "His men will also conduct additional interrogations on the prisoner to ascertain whether it's lying or to gain a more accurate idea of what we're facing."

"Good," Prime Minister Donovan nodded. Then, "how likely is it that it's giving us false information?"

"Extremely unlikely," Tolan replied.

"If you know about our abilities, then please be sure that *I* would know if it was lying," Vic added.

"Very well. David, I was under the impression that you were going to hold a Press Conference earlier today about the threat that we'd faced and the fact that it'd been dealt with?" the Prime Minister said.

"Yes, well..." Premier Narimono began.

"We hijacked it," Matt stated. "Telling the public about the aliens and the Swarm that's on its way would have been a *very* bad idea."

"Yes, I can see that," the Prime Minister nodded, his frown etching even deeper into his face. "Can I ask what you *did* say?"

"We told them that the *Scorpion* was a modified aircraft for a movie and that General White was an extremely intense consultant," Alana replied.

The Prime Minister flinging himself backwards in his chair and laughing was *not* what Vic had expected. Judging by the expressions on her friends' faces, he'd surprised all of them as well.

"What do you need, David?" Prime Minister Donovan asked having recovered his composure.

"For now, your support when we find out more. Connections through your office to other governments and militaries if the threat is credible. Unfortunately, until we know more, this is more an FYI than anything else," he replied.

"You have it. I'll make sure that you're added to the list of people who can get straight through to me at any time, day or night. That goes for the seven of you as well," the Australian Prime Minister added. "You have already done this country and the entire world a service that we can never repay. Whatever you need, you'll have it."

"Thank you, Sir," Vic replied once she'd picked her jaw up off the floor.

"We're honoured, Sir," Tolan added, a sentiment echoed by all of them.

"David, keep me informed on any developments." Then, after a last nod to each of them, the screen went blank.

"Ray!"

"Alana!"

"Paul!"

"Victoria!"

Parents all-but running at them as they walked through the double doors into the rec centre where they'd first had their meeting with the military was not expected. Thus, when her mother, who reached her first, hit Vic, she was almost sent flying.

"Mum, let go!" Vic protested.

Her arms were pinned to her sides and she could hardly breathe let alone talk with her face smashed against her mother's shoulder. Her father joined in on the hug, enveloping her from her back, making her a Vic-sandwich. From what little she could see, most of her friends were receiving the same treatment.

"Kadee," she managed.

Thankfully, her mother got the message, for she instantly disentangled herself and made a beeline for the lone girl. As her father twisted her about and grabbed her hands and began looking her up and down, she saw that her mother had taken Kadee into a gentle hug as well.

"Are you okay?" her father asked, capturing her attention.

"Yeah, yeah, I'm fine. A little tired, I guess," she replied.

"Good," her father nodded. "In that case … what were you *thinking*? Taking a *spaceship* into space and getting into a battle with aliens? You could have been killed!"

"Dear," her mother admonished, joining them, her arm around Kadee and bringing her along.

"You know that you feel the same, Catherine," her father retorted.

"That may be but what's most important is that Vic and Kadee and all of their friends are perfectly fine," she replied. "And you know that you're jealous that they got to go space and you haven't."

"We have a spaceship, dad," Vic said quickly. "I could take you for a ride after this crisis is all over if you like?"

At first his eyes rounded before her words registered and they narrowed.

"Exactly what do you mean by that?" he asked.

Vic shared a glance and an exasperated sigh with Kadee. Exactly how many times did they need to tell this story?

The rec centre was a nice place to visit and an excellent place to demonstrate their abilities to sceptical adults but as a place to be confined to for hours on end, it left much to be desired.

Food had been brought for them and consumed. Questions had been asked, sometimes multiple times, by each of the parents. Groups had formed and reformed: families; teens; adults; a mixture of each; and some, including Vic herself, had sat apart for a time needing some time out. Sleep had been attempted, mostly to no avail.

Twice, an officer had strode in, located one or more of them and asked questions – once about the Hopper, the other about the *Scorpion* – before striding back out again, intent on their mission. The *Scorpion* questions had worried Vic. There was something there, something that her premonition ability was uneasy about, but she couldn't place exactly what it was.

Finally, after nearly six hours from when they'd first been led into the room, the doors slammed open.

Vic lifted her head from where it was resting on her scrunched-up jacket to see General White standing in the doorway, his hands on his hips. Recognising that whatever he was there for was going to be important, she sat up, swinging her legs down from the bench that she'd been lying on.

A look around the hall told her that she wasn't the only one to see him. Matt was slapping Paul's arm, causing him to look up and to nudge Alana whose head was lying in her boyfriend's lap.

Within moments all of them, as well as a number of their parents, were heading towards the General.

"General," Tolan greeted.

The man's eyes swept over the seven of them, ignoring the rest of the gathered crowd. Now that she was closer, she could see that there was something in his posture which she'd never seen before. What it was, though, she couldn't tell.

"Firstly, I've contacted the Pentagon and Mikata and a number of other observatories, the ones with the biggest and best telescopes in the world," General White began. "So far, they haven't found anything unusual and certainly no alien fleet headed towards us."

"That doesn't mean that it's not there," Tolan replied. "None of them saw the Hopper ship stationed in orbit and who knows *how* long it'd been sitting up there."

General White gave a single nod. "Agreed. Which is why all of them will continue watching. We also have the Hubble Telescope doing a sweep of space as well."

"That's not why you're here, is it, General?" Vic asked.

The smallest slump of his shoulders and his face going slack told her that she was right.

"No," he admitted. "I've had my best interrogators working on the captured Hopper for the past six hours, trying to get it to talk."

"I'm guessing that they've got nothing," Paul stated.

"You and your people don't know the Hoppers," Kadee said. "I do. I've lived with them my whole life."

"Is it time for us to take a crack at it, see what we can get out of it?" Matt asked, drawing one of his knives.

"Matthew!" his father admonished. "Put that away!"

"You are not going to go interrogating or torturing another person, even if it is an alien," Vic's mother stated flatly.

"Sorry, mum, but you don't understand. We need to do this," Vic told her.

"We're the only ones who can," Tolan added.

"As much as I hate to admit it, they're right," General White sighed.

"I don't like this," Alana's father stated.

"Believe me, Sir, neither do I. Interrogating prisoners is the job of professionals, *my* men," General White replied. "But these seven have proven that they can do a job that others can't. And when it comes right down to it, we *need* that intel. It could be the difference between the survival of the human race and mass extinction."

"Victoria? Are you sure about this?" her mother asked, using one hand to turn her around so that she could look into her eyes.

Vic could see the worry, the concern, the hope that Vic would refuse. But she couldn't refuse. Her gut feeling was that this was the right thing to do. And she knew much better than to ignore her feelings.

"We have to, mum. It has to be us," she replied before turning back to face the General. "When do we start?"

CHAPTER 3

The other side of the two-way mirror was pitch black, meaning that at that moment, it was acting like a true mirror. In lieu of staring at herself, Vic looked up at the monitor. The image was grainy and green, courtesy of the infrared filter attached to the camera. The Hopper was on its knees, its head pressed into the floor. Snaking out from under it were the thick, heavy chains that were attached to its four legs, its two arms, its neck, stomach and tail spike. And it was rocking backwards and forwards.

"Is there sound on that thing?" Alana asked.

Vic glanced at her to see her pointing to the monitor even as she stared straight ahead, her advanced vision obviously allowing her to see straight through the mirror and most likely lighting up the blackened room as though it was daylight for her.

A sergeant stepped forward, pressed a button and then retreated as a low keening sound filled the room. It undulated, momentarily gaining strength before once again sinking back into near inaudibility.

"Is that noise coming from the alien?" General White asked.

"Yes," Vic replied. "It's most likely terrified. Hoppers *hate* the dark. Not to mention it's probably a little upset with itself for giving us the intel that it already has."

"Who'd blame it?" Ray snorted. "Kadee's illusions seem more than real and we had it believing that it was going to be living at the bottom of deep hole in the ground for the rest of its life!"

"It deserves to! The damn thing is an advance guard for an army intent on taking over our planet!" General White growled.

"While true, we need it coherent enough to be able to answer some more questions. We need more out of it if we're going to have any chance of understanding what we're facing," Vic stated. "And to do that, we need it able to talk. Bring up the lights."

The lights in the room on the other side of the glass rose and Vic switched her focus away from the monitor. The Hopper didn't react, remaining in the same position with its face pressed against the floor, its body continuing to rock slightly as it wailed. If Vic had to guess – and with her premonition ability, she rarely had to take a true guess anymore – she'd say that it hadn't even noticed the lights coming on; most likely its eyes were screwed tightly closed.

A second before it opened, she switched her focus to the door in the other room. One by one, Tolan, Paul, Matt and Kadee strode in before taking up positions in a loose semi-circle around the Hopper.

Vic's mouth quirked into an ironic smile. Here they were, seven teenagers, deep in the middle of an Army Base and yet *they* were the ones leading the interrogation of the captured alien. Admittedly, *they* had been the ones to capture the Hopper in the first place and *they* had been the only ones to actually get any intel out of it so far. They had even been the ones to do something about that intel, to take an alien spaceship into space and blow up *another* alien spaceship to stop the immediate threat: the activation of the devices that would have caused EMPs to fire all over the world and destroy every piece of tech that humans had.

"I don't think the Hopper even knows that they're there," Ray commented.

"Paul, you want to get its attention?" Alana asked.

Vic saw him glance at the mirror where he knew they were, despite the fact that he wouldn't have been able to see them, and then to give a single nod.

When he turned back to the Hopper, it slowly floated upwards. Its legs and arms dropped away as its body rose, its head remaining limp and pointed towards the floor. Paul's telekinetic ability held it there for nearly half a minute with still no response from the Hopper.

"The thing's still alive, isn't it?" General White asked.

At that moment, it jerked violently from side to side – obviously Paul having grown frustrated and giving it a shake.

Instantly, the Hopper's eyes flew open, its head snapped up and it gave a piercing shriek. From this side of the glass it was loud; from the other side, it must have been a *lot* worse, for all four of her friends winced and slapped their hands over their ears. The Hopper dropped like a stone, landing in a heap on the floor where it remained unmoving.

"This isn't going to work. I think we broke it last time," Ray said.

Vic glanced up to where he was standing right behind her left shoulder to see the frown on his face. He was right. They'd tortured the Hopper with all of the illusions that they could in an effort to extract what information that they could already. And it'd worked. To a point. But what they needed now was everything that it knew on the threat that was coming: the Swarm.

"Guys, I think we need a new tactic," Vic said slowly, switching her gaze back to the room in front of her.

"What do you suggest?" Tolan asked, frustration in his voice.

"I think ... I think we try the *opposite* of what we've been doing," Vic said slowly. "Give it something to live for instead of something that it's terrified of."

"Okay. How?" Tolan asked.

"Kadee, can you change the room up so that it thinks its outside? Maybe on a grassy hill or something? Definitely add in a lot of blue sky," Vic said.

Kadee touched a finger to the comm in her ear before nodding. "I can do that."

And then, between one blink and the next, the other side of the mirror changed. Vic's jaw dropped. Even knowing what was coming, even having suggested it herself, Vic was astounded.

Gone were the concrete walls, floor and ceiling. Gone was the tiny, cramped space that the room was. Instead, the horizon stretched seemingly forever. The four humans and Hopper were now standing on the flat top of small hill. Long grass that was moving slightly in a non-existent breeze stretched as far as the eye could see, only broken up by the occasional tree. The sky was bright and blue and dotted with wispy clouds. There were even birds soaring high above them!

Vic tore her gaze from the wondrous sight to glance up at the monitor and blinked. It showed the room exactly as it had been, stark grey walls and hard concrete floor with her friends standing around the Hopper. *That* was something to file away – tech could see through Kadee's illusions.

Slowly, the Hopper's head came up, twisting from side to side. Its eyes were wide, its jaw dropped slightly. Suddenly, it shot to its feet even as there was movement from underneath the hard V-shaped shell on it back. It was trying to unfurl its wings, most likely in an effort to escape, Vic realised. Fortunately, those wings never emerged: the large metal ring that encircled it prevented them from extending.

Vic watched as the Hopper tested each of the chains that still held it captive, seemingly extending deep into the earth that it stood upon.

"What trickery is this?" the Hopper asked, the human words coming out flat from the translator around its neck in juxtaposition to its real alien voice.

"This is what we could give you if you cooperate," Tolan replied. "The outside world, open space and *maybe* a chance to stretch those wings of yours again."

"You lie!" it hissed. "You would never give me this! I'm a prisoner."

"Exactly how long have you been on Earth again?" Matt asked. "What makes you think you know what we'll do?"

"I've been here long enough and been on four other worlds not dissimilar to this one. Prisoners are always treated the same," it replied.

"I'm betting that the fact that you're still alive surprises you, that you expected us to have killed you already," Tolan said.

The Hopper glared at him, even as it flexed both arms again, drawing the chains tight.

"You still need me alive," it retorted.

"You're right, we do," Tolan nodded. "But even if we didn't, that doesn't mean that we'd kill you if we had no use for you. Humans aren't like that."

"You have use of me," the Hopper repeated, its eyes narrowed. "What do you want?"

"You're right, we do. What we want is to know more about this Swarm of yours. When it's coming, how many ships and people, what to expect when it gets here," Tolan stated.

The Hopper glared at him, its head then shifting to each of the others before it simply shuffled around, turning its back on them.

"This conversation's not over," Paul said even as the Hopper lifted off the ground, was spun about and placed once more so that it was facing them.

"I will tell you nothing!"

"Believe me, you'll tell us exactly what we want to know!" Matt stated, taking half a step forward even as he drew a pair of knives from his belt.

A hissing, spitting sound filled the room and Vic realised that the Hopper was laughing.

"See? You are no different! You don't get what you want and you threaten to take it by force!" it sneered.

Tolan's hand came out low to his side and Matt stopped.

"We have no interest in torturing you or hurting you," Tolan replied. "Simply tell us what we want to know."

"Even if you don't kill me, my own people will when they arrive. They'll kill me for helping you to destroy our ship and stopping the advance attack."

"Will they?" Tolan asked. "Are you sure about that?"

The Hopper snorted. "It is what will happen."

"Well, they'll have to get through us to get to you," Matt stated, flipping his knives up and catching them again.

"A simple task," the Hopper sneered. "They are the Swarm! They outnumber any army that you try to bring against them."

"Any army? I'm betting not the combined armies of Earth," Tolan said.

"It will not matter; the Swarm will prevail!"

"Maybe, maybe not," Tolan replied. "Either way, they're not here yet which means we have time to prepare. We won't be caught unaware."

"Plus we still have all of our technology in play," Paul added. "I'm betting we can give as good as we get."

"Time? You think you have time? Your pitiful excuse for spaceships are nothing!" the Hopper laughed.

"We humans are pretty resourceful, give us a year and who knows what we'll accomplish," Tolan replied.

"A year?" the Hopper laughed. "You think your species has so long to live?"

"I'm betting we'll surprise you, no matter how long we have," Paul replied.

"No planet, no species, has ever posed a threat to the Swarm," the Hopper stated. "No matter how much or how little time they had to mount a defence. They all perished at our hands."

"Hey! We stopped your EMP attack, so maybe we have a little more going for us than you think!" Paul retorted.

"I have told you before. That method of softening our prey is not how we have always subjugated worlds," the Hopper replied. "Even without it, the Swarm will kill you all."

"You seem pretty certain of that," Tolan said.

"It is fact!"

"Is it? Is there no way for us to win? Or simply for us to convince your people to leave us alone and to go somewhere else?" Tolan asked.

"None."

Tolan looked to Paul, to Matt, to Kadee, shrugged and dropped his head.

"You said that you've been a part of attacking how many worlds now? Was it four?" Tolan asked.

"Four myself. The Swarm has subjugated eight worlds and completely destroyed three others," the Hopper confirmed.

"You're right, we don't have a fleet of spaceships waiting up there to defend us. Not yet at least." Tolan sighed. "And you're sure that we don't have even a year to prepare?"

The Hopper laughed. "No."

"How long do we have left then?" Tolan asked. "Only, there's a few things that I'd like to do before I die. Hang-gliding and scuba diving. Maybe go on an African safari. You know, live a little. I'm sure that you can appreciate that, getting to enjoy what the world has to offer."

He finished with a sweeping gesture at the illusion world that they were standing in.

The Hopper stood there, staring at him before tilting its head back and staring up at the sky.

"Fifteen days," it said.

"Sorry?" Tolan asked.

Its head lowered so that it was looking at Tolan once more. "Fifteen days. That's how long you have until the Swarm arrives. That is how long you and your planet have left to live."

"Fifteen?" Paul breathed.

"Two weeks," Matt added.

"I was hoping for more," General White stated from behind Vic.

“It’s better than twelve. Or tomorrow. Or today,” Vic replied.

CHAPTER 4

The steam rising from the cup hit her nose and Vic inhaled deeply. Her eyes closed as she savoured the aroma. Manna from the gods, that's what this was. The Elixir of Life. Coffee. It was what she needed, what she'd been craving for far too long.

The fact that said liquid gold was in a Styrofoam cup and had come out of a machine that had obviously seen better days was ignored. It was coffee. That was enough.

Lifting the cup, she blew gently and took her first sip. Once again, her eyes closed. Yes, it was exactly what she needed. Well, sleep probably would have been better, but that was something that wasn't on the horizon anytime soon. In its place was the next best thing. Or the only thing that could trump sleep.

Pouring a second cup, she added some milk and, on afterthought, a teaspoon of sugar. Then, with both cups in hand, she made her way across to where Kadee was sitting.

"You look dead on your feet," Vic said, holding out the second cup. "Here, this'll help."

Kadee took it and looked at it, a frown on her face. "What is it?"

"Coffee," Vic replied simply. "Drink."

She watched intently as the girl from the future who'd never even heard of coffee before, let alone seen it, took her first sip. The scrunched-up nose was not expected and a definite insult to the delicious brew.

"That's really bitter," Kadee stated. "You like this?"

"Gods, yes," Vic breathed, taking another sip, feeling it beginning to work its magic to revitalise her body. "Drink. You'll get used to it and believe me, you'll come to like it as much as I do."

Kadee gave her a disbelieving look but drank nonetheless.

"Is that coffee?" Alana asked, materialising beside them.

"Yep."

"Where?" Alana asked.

"There's a small room through that door," Vic pointed. She paused, debating with herself but ultimately decided that it was only right. "It's old; looks like it's been brewing since sometime last week."

"I don't care," Alana tossed back over her shoulder.

Vic nodded. That was the right attitude. Even old coffee was better than none. Especially when you were so low on energy.

The warmth of the cup in her hand, combined with the soothing taste of the coffee allowed her body to lose some of its tension and she allowed her head to rest back on the wall behind her. By the time that she was ready to face whatever was to come next, her cup was three-quarters gone.

"Vic? We may have a problem," Paul said quietly.

She started, not having heard him join herself, Alana and Kadee. Her eyes snapped open and she jerked – thankfully not enough to slosh any of the precious coffee over the rim of her cup.

"What?" she asked.

He was standing directly in front of her and shifting slightly from side to side.

"There's a Sergeant here that's demanding that we give him access to the *Scorpion*," Paul stated. "Tolan and Matt are trying to convince him that that's not going to happen but I don't think that they're going to have much luck."

Vic leant to the side, almost ending up laying on Alana to see around Paul and frowned at what she saw. There wasn't just a single soldier. No, the Lieutenant who appeared to be doing the talking was backed up by half a dozen others.

"We can't let them have the Hopper ship," Kadee said.

"I'm not sure that we have much choice," Vic countered. "Come on."

With a snap of her wrist, she drained the last of the coffee, doing it no justice at all and placed the now empty cup on the seat as she stood. Then, with Alana and Kadee to either side of her and Paul towering over her from behind, she made her way across the hall.

"You will hand over the device now!" the lieutenant in charge ordered.

"Not going to happen!" Tolan snapped back, his hands folded across his chest.

"This is not up for discussion; it's an order!" the Lieutenant countered.

"In case you haven't noticed, we're not in your army," Matt replied flippantly.

Ray's eyes met hers as she approached, and she could see the plea in his eyes asking what they were supposed to do.

"Guys, relax," Vic said, stepping between Tolan and Matt, a hand on each of their shoulders.

It took a second and neither budged an inch, but she felt that they were willing to let her decide how to proceed.

"Now, Lieutenant ... Daniels," she said, taking a second to read the name on his shirt. "What seems to be the problem?"

"I have been ordered to board the alien spaceship and examine it for anything that may prove useful," Lieutenant Daniels replied. "My understanding is that you have a device that opens the ship. I'm here to collect it."

For a second Vic considered the idea of resisting, of having her friends use their abilities to make the lieutenant and his men regret the idea of demanding anything from them. But that didn't feel right. No, this wasn't the time for that sort of action.

"One condition," she said instead. "We go with you."

She could feel her friends staring at her, a feeling she ignored in favour of staring at the Sergeant.

"I don't have the authority to allow that," he said tentatively.

"I'll make this easy for you," Vic replied. "You allow us to go with you. Anyone asks, you tell them that you were using us as guides considering that we've been on the ship before so we could tell you what was best to leave alone."

"I don't know," Lieutenant Daniels replied, obviously wavering.

"We *could* just make a phone call. Perhaps Prime Minister Donovan's word might change your mind?" Tolan suggested.

"You don't ..." Lieutenant Daniels began doubtfully.

"Actually, we do. Want to test us?" Tolan pushed.

"Very well," Lieutenant Daniels relented. "I would appreciate the seven of you accompanying me onto the alien spaceship to inform me of any potential dangers and to give us a tour of the ship. Once done, you will be expected to hand over the device that controls the ship."

"Agreed," Vic replied quickly, ignoring the indignation that she could feel coming from her friends.

"We're not really going to hand over the device, are we?" Matt asked Vic sotto voce as they approached the *Scorpion*.

Vic simply gave him a Look and raised her eyebrow. "I said that we would."

"Vic ..." Ray began, stopped and tried again. "What's the *real* plan? Get on board, overpower the soldiers and fly away?"

"No," Vic replied. "No plan. We tour the ship and hand over the cylinder. That's it. It's the right thing to do."

She hated being questioned like this. Especially when even *she* didn't understand why it was the right thing to do. It'd be so easy...

"If you would?" Lieutenant Daniels asked, gesturing to the rear of the *Scorpion* where the ramp was located.

A quick *thump* of the cylinder against her thigh turned it on before her finger automatically stabbed the right button. Obediently, the ramp *clunked* and began lowering. As soon as it touched the ground, Tolan and Matt led the way on board.

Just like the first time, lights activated as they walked in. At the first cross-corridor, they stopped.

"Engine bays are in the rear doors down each corridor," Tolan informed the soldiers. "I *strongly* suggest that *no one* – and I mean absolutely *no one* – opens the other door down there."

"Why?" Lieutenant Daniels asked suspiciously.

"Because that's the Hopper's latrine. And believe me, you do *not* want to smell that," Tolan replied. "There are crew quarters down there and also down the next set of corridors."

"What about the other rooms?" Sergeant Daniels asked.

"Mess, medical and food storage," Tolan shrugged. "I'm assuming that you want to see the flight deck?"

Without waiting for a response, he walked on.

"Ray?" Vic asked, noticing that, instead of following everyone else, he'd turned down one of the corridors.

"I'll catch up," he replied.

Her curiosity was piqued but the smile that he shot her reassured that he'd be okay. With a nod, she turned and hurried off after everyone else. Lieutenant Daniels, she saw when she stepped out onto the flight deck, wasn't the only soldier now with a computer tablet in their hand.

"Please tell us everything that you've worked out about how the ship works," Lieutenant Daniels requested. "And we'll start with the flight controls."

That being her cue, Vic stepped forward, squeezed between the crowd and settled into the pilot's chair. When next she looked up, it was to see that she was surrounded by soldiers, all intently watching her and waiting for her to begin.

With a grimace, Vic turned away. For the first time since she'd found it laying on the desk in the 'abandoned' building, the metal cylinder that controlled the *Scorpion* was no longer in her possession. She wasn't sure how to feel about that. Needing something else to focus on, she eyed the bag that Ray was carrying. There was one definite thing about it: it was obviously heavier than when he'd carried it onto the *Scorpion.*

"Gonna tell us what's in the bag?" Paul asked.

"When we're alone," Ray replied, his eyes darting about.

"Like that's likely to happen anytime soon," Matt snorted.

It was a statement that all of them could agree upon. Soldiers watched their every move; there were even guards assigned to be in any room that they'd been assigned ever since they'd gotten back from space. If that wasn't enough, unless they were specifically doing something for the military, their parents didn't let them out of their sight.

"Perhaps I can help with that?" Kadee suggested.

Vic shook her head. "Won't work. Your illusions cover sight, not sound. You could hide us or make it so that we appear to be somewhere else, but we'd still have to be close enough for that to work and if we're close, then we're going to be heard."

"They could cut us some slack," Matt groused. "We've been to fricken space! Even gave the planet a fighting chance. Surely that should be worth something?"

"The problem, my man, is that we're still teenagers," Paul stated, clapping his best friend on the back.

"Vic, got any ideas?" Tolan asked.

Really, she should have expected that. Her premonition ability gave them an edge. Most of the time. What it didn't do was tell her what they should be doing. Tolan and the others knew that. Didn't stop them from asking her to decide what they should do, though.

"Don't look at me!" she snapped.

"New plan," Alana stated forcefully, her eyes lingering on each of the boys one by one before she continued. "We're all tired. None of us has really slept since *way* before we went to space. Whatever's in Ray's bag can wait..."

"We only have fifteen days..." Tolan began before promptly slamming his mouth shut in response to her glare.

"I don't care how long we have," Alana continued. "It. Doesn't. Matter. Not if we're too tired to think properly and start snapping at each other and fighting amongst ourselves."

"Sorry," Vic said quietly.

"It's okay, Sweety, we're all tired," Alana smiled. "So, sleep first. Then we can plan or Ray can tell us about his bag or whatever new thing pops up to demand our attention. Everyone agree?"

The only sound was the slight rustling of clothes as heads were rapidly nodded.

"Right. You!" Alana said, focussing in on a Corporal standing nearby. The soldier startled, obviously not expecting to be singled out. "You're going to take us to the nearest barracks or room with beds or whatever you've got around here. Then you're going to stand *on the outside of the door* and not let anyone in until we wake up and come out. I don't care if it's General White, the Prime Minister or even the Queen of England. You let anyone in and you will not like it."

The Corporal gulped, darted his eyes about and then did something which Vic considered incredibly stupid.

"I don't take orders from you," he said.

"No, you don't," Alana replied sweetly. "And *I* can't make you do anything. But just out of curiosity, did you know that my wonderful boyfriend here can move things with his mind? It's called telekinesis. He even proved how strong he is by moving that great big alien ship out there all the way up into space *with just the power of his mind.* Now. Are you *sure* you don't want to do what I've asked?"

"There's a set of barracks not being used this way, Ma'am," the Corporal stated quickly.

CHAPTER 5

The room was ablaze with light when she opened her eyes causing her to groan, roll over and pull the cover over her head. Surely another hour or two couldn't hurt and she sure felt like she needed it.

"If you're awake, Vic, it's time to get up."

Tolan's voice was soundly ignored.

"Just leave her, Tol," Matt said. "If she wants to sleep and miss out on finding out what's in Ray's bag, that's her problem."

Once again, her eyes opened, this time into darkness. Ray's bag. Her sleep-fogged mind fumbled about, trying to remember what was so important about that. And then it came to her. The *Scorpion* and Ray going off by himself. He'd refused to tell them what he had in his bag after they'd left the ship.

"Damn boys," she grumbled as she flung back the covers, letting the light flood her eyes once again. "You'd think they'd know not to use a girl's curiosity against them."

"Are we alone, Alana?" Tolan asked.

As Vic pulled on her shoes, she saw Alana twisting about to look all around her.

"The only person anywhere near this building are the two guards standing on the other side of the door," she replied.

"I'd say that that's about as good as we're going to get," Paul stated.

"Agreed," Tolan nodded. "Alright, Ray, the floor's yours. What've you got in there?"

Thankfully, Ray was kind enough to wait until Vic had stumbled across to sit on the bunk beside him that he was sitting on with Kadee. Directly across from them, seated on the opposite bunk were Tolan, Paul and Alana. All that could be seen of Matt was his head which was currently dangling down from the top bunk, looking on intently.

The bag in question was pulled from under the bunk between Ray's feet and spun so that he could grab the zip. One tug later and the bag was pulled wide.

"I grabbed a heap of those Hopper fruit things," Ray explained. "There's a bunch of the fruit, a few tubs of seeds and four of the smallest plants."

Vic could see the strange baseball-sized fruit in the centre of the bag. Yes, she'd seen them before – she'd even *eaten* one. That didn't mean that their weird maroon and orange skin wasn't still a very strange sight.

"Okay," Paul said slowly. "Why?"

"Why what?" Ray asked.

"Why'd you take some? And why not tell us earlier?" Paul elaborated.

"I wasn't sure how the soldiers would react," Ray shrugged. "They seemed pretty insistent that everything on the *Scorpion* was something that they were going to be examining in pretty close detail."

"You're not wrong there," Matt said. "But that doesn't answer Paul's other question. Why'd you take some of them in the first place?"

"Well, you can't argue that they taste really good," Ray replied.

Vic narrowed her eyes at him. The hairs on her arm had just stood on end, even as a chill washed over her body.

"That's not the real reason, though, is it?" she asked.

Ray dropped his head to look at the alien fruit in the bag at his feet. She could feel his reluctance to say whatever it was that he was thinking. It didn't help that he started to fade out.

"Ray," she said gently, placing a hand on his knee. "Talk to us. We're a team now. We can work together to solve this."

His head came up and for a brief moment, his eyes connected with hers. She felt the tension in him lessen slightly.

"I think that *this* is the answer," he said.

"Answer? To what?" Kadee asked.

"To our problem with the Hoppers," Ray replied. "You were all there, you heard the Hopper. Their whole reason for invading and taking over other planets is because they don't have enough space on their own planet for their people to live nor enough space to grow their own crops. Kadee, you said that you've only ever seen Hoppers eat these melon-things, right?"

She nodded. "It's all anyone has ever seen them eat. At least in my time."

"This is your time now," Alana reminded her, reaching across to squeeze her hand.

"So, if these things are so important, then it only stands to reason that they can also be the answer," Ray stated.

Vic tilted her head as she considered what he was saying. She thought she knew, but for the life of her, she couldn't see how it would work.

"What do you mean, Ray?" she asked. "How can these melons solve our

Hopper problem?"

"Don't you see?" Ray exclaimed. "If we can grow enough of these things, maybe set up some sort of trade or agreement or something, then the Hoppers wouldn't have any reason to take over the planet!"

"A diplomatic solution," Paul nodded.

They'd discussed the idea once before, trying to find a way to coexist with the Hoppers. But that discussion had gotten sidelined by events running too fast for them to stop and consider it properly.

"Just one problem, Ray," Tolan said. "Well, one big one. If we're going to have any sort of leverage to suggest a diplomatic solution, then we're going to need to prove that we can grow those melons. Without it, I can't see the Hoppers even bothering listening to us."

"It's worth a try," Ray insisted.

"Dude, we only have fourteen days until the Hopper Swarm arrives in orbit and they begin their invasion," Matt pointed out. "Time is against you. There's no way that you can plant and grow a crop of alien melons in that time!"

"Ray, he's right," Vic said gently. "If we had more time, I'd be in; but the simple fact is, we don't. Only having two weeks left is just too big a thing to get around. If, by some miracle, we *do* manage to find a way to stop the invasion then I promise you that we'll find a way to plant those melons and grow field after field of them."

"Be a nice little money spinner, even if the Hoppers never come back," Paul added. "We'd be the only ones growing them. We'd make a fortune!"

"What would you call them?" Alana asked.

Ray shrugged but Vic could tell that he already had a name in mind. "Ray?"

Ray's eyes flittered about before dropping to rest on the rusty-orange and deep mauve melons.

"Sunset melons," he murmured.

"Not bad," Vic nodded. "I could see it catching on.

"Time," Tolan muttered.

"What?" Matt asked, leaning further to peer at Tolan sitting on the bunk under him.

Tolan looked up, a fierce, angry look on his face. "Time. I *thought* we'd bought ourselves enough. We travelled to the future and got a good look at what was coming. We brought that knowledge back, even did the right thing and told the authorities. We worked our asses off, even killing aliens and stealing an alien ship to use it to blow up another ship in space! We did everything right to make sure the timeline changed! And where'd it get us? Right back to where we started! Fourteen days and the Swarm arrives and then the timeline will veer right back on course again!"

"No. No, I don't believe that!" Vic retorted.

"Premonition?" Tolan asked, his face carefully bland.

As much as she hated to, Vic had no choice but to shake her head. "No."

"Then, believe what you want," Tolan spat. "Nothing that we do will stop what's coming."

"There's still time!" Matt pointed out. "Fourteen days of it. And we've got our powers."

"Against a thousand, a million alien grasshoppers? We don't stand a chance!" Tolan declared.

"If only we had more time," Alana moaned.

Vic's head snapped to her. There. There was something there. She was sure of it. She could almost *taste* it.

"Fourteen days is still a lot. Anything could happen," Matt was saying, but she barely heard it.

"There's time to get people to safety," Kadee added. "Hoppers don't like the dark. We could tell people to hide in dark places, help them prepare."

Time. There it was again. Her gut was clenching and unclenching. Waves of hot and cold were washing over her.

"Our parents!" Alana said. "We could find some caves or tunnels. Get them to buy lots of food and camping gear..."

Alana's voice, all of their voices continued but Vic ignored them, letting the sounds wash over her.

Tunnel. Alana had said it. Tunnel. There was something there.

Time. Tunnel.

Tunnel. Time.

They needed more time.

Before, they had extra time, extra foreknowledge of what was to come because they'd been shifted in time, moved forward a hundred or so years to Kadee's time. There they'd found the evidence to tell them what was to come so that once they got home, they could do something about it.

Tunnel. Time. Foreknowledge.

The idea was *right there*!

"What's the bet that the Hoppers would have some kind of device or scanner that could find people hidden underground?" Matt asked.

Device! That was it! She was sure of it. The last piece. Now all she had to do was put it all together so that it made sense.

Tunnel. Time. Foreknowledge. Device.

“We need more time,” Vic blurted.

“We know, Vic!” Tolan snapped.

Her eyes blinked rapidly back into focus. “What?”

“You said that we need more time,” Alana told her.

“What? I did?” Vic asked. She hadn’t even realised that she’d spoken out loud.

Shaking her head, she dismissed it. But it was there. They *did* need more time. The last time they’d gained time, they’d walked into that tunnel right when those Hopper devices misfired.

Vic bolted to her feet.

“That’s it!” she exclaimed.

“What is?” Ray asked, looking up at her.

“We need more time!” she replied.

“Yeah, we know. Not something that we can arrange,” Matt replied sarcastically. “Can’t stop an alien armada in the middle of space, can we?”

Vic frowned up at him. “Not what I meant. Well, I don’t think so.”

“Sweety, perhaps if you actually explained what you’re thinking, then we might understand too?” Alana suggested.

She considered sitting back down; instead, she moved out into the aisle between the two rows of bunks and began pacing.

"We need more time," she began, knowing that she was repeating herself but not caring. Her brain was still putting the pieces together and she was happy to let it get there at its own pace. "The last time we needed more time, we didn't even know it until we'd jumped forward in time. We even found the answers we needed there."

"That was a fluke, definitely not planned," Tolan pointed out.

Vic waved his interruption aside. "We know what caused us to shift in time. The multicoloured lightning storm and *that* was caused by those two Hopper devices malfunctioning and feeding off each other."

"Are you suggesting that we cause a pair of those devices to do that again and for us to go forward in time again?" Paul asked.

"No. Yes. I don't know!" Vic replied desperately, throwing her hands up. "What I do know is that my premonition abilities are going haywire right now and it's got something to do with those devices and us shifting through time."

"Those devices are still a threat, you know," Matt pointed out.

That stopped Vic dead in her tracks and she spun to stare at him.

"All of those devices are still hidden all over the world," Matt continued, everyone's eyes firmly fixed on him. "Yes, we destroyed that one Hopper ship that would have sent the signal to detonate them but there's a whole *swarm* of Hopper ships on the way and I'm betting that any one of them has the code to send the signal to set those devices off too."

"Rendering all tech on Earth useless and sending us back into the Dark Ages," Tolan moaned.

"How many were there again? Five hundred?" Ray asked.

"Five hundred and ten," Alana corrected.

Paul let out a low whistle. "That's a lot."

"We need to find them and take them out of the equation," Tolan stated.

"Vic, was that what your premonition was telling you?" Kadee asked.

Vic stopped and considered what she was feeling from her own body. The hairs on her arms had settled and the hot and cold flashes were gone. As for the pain in her stomach, it was ... still there, just muted?

"I don't think so, not totally, although it's sort of on the right track?" she replied, knowing that she was doing a lousy job at explaining.

"What does that mean?" Ray asked.

Vic shrugged. "I think it means that we run with that thought and the rest will come together later."

"Better than sitting here doing nothing but waiting for the end of the world to come," Tolan shrugged. "Let's go."

The Corporal at the desk in the front office hadn't wanted them to go in. He'd been most insistent, in fact. Of course, that meant that they'd had to insist right back. Kadee had simply distracted him with a swarm of flies and, while he was busy waving his arms every which way and spitting the non-existent insects away from his mouth, they'd walked right by him.

Knocking had been considered and discarded.

"What?" General White snapped at the sound of his door opening, quickly followed by, "you!" when they'd trooped in.

"Sorry to disturb you, General, we just have a quick request," Tolan said in an overly cheery voice.

The General's eyes narrowed. "I'm listening, but it had better be good."

"We need the *Scorpion*," Tolan stated matter-of-factly.

"Really, it's less of a request, more of a 'we're just letting you know' kind of thing," Matt added.

"Before I answer, how about you tell me why you want it," General White said sitting back in his chair.

"You're aware that there are over five hundred pairs of devices scattered all over the world that were designed to emit an electro-magnetic pulse strong enough to destroy the world's technology," Tolan began.

"Which you stopped from being an issue by destroying that alien spaceship. By yourselves, without backup or military expertise or permission," General White pointed out.

Somehow, Vic prevented her eyes from rolling.

"Those devices are still out there," Tolan continued. "And as soon as that Hopper Swarm gets here, *one* of those ships is going to activate those devices."

"Which will destroy our tech," General White finished. "Shit!"

"We want the *Scorpion* to go find those devices and eliminate that threat," Paul summed up.

"You couldn't have brought his to me last night?" General White asked rhetorically.

A cold shiver swept down Vic's back. "What have you done?"

The General's eyes dropped to his desk momentarily causing Vic's feeling of dread to intensify.

"That alien ship – which isn't yours, by the way, no matter how much you seem to act like it is – was moved last night to a secure facility," General White stated.

"Then bring it back!" Matt stated forcefully. "Or take us to it."

"It's out of my hands. I can't get it back," General White replied.

"Crap!" Tolan swore. "Right, there goes *that* idea. We've got two weeks; I say we try to find a place where we can hole up when the Hoppers get here."

"Now, hold up a minute," General White said. "Getting those devices diffused is incredibly important. I'm guessing you know how to do it?"

"I worked out how to fly an alien spaceship; I think that I could work it out pretty quickly," Vic shrugged.

"And you know where they all are?" General White continued.

"We know where *one* set is. Out of over five hundred," Paul replied. "We were hoping to use some tech on the *Scorpion* to find the rest."

"Is there any Hopper technology still here?" Paul asked hopefully.

"Nothing except that translation collar around our prisoner's neck," General White replied.

"Then we're screwed," Tolan said, slumping forward with his head down and his hands on the back of the chair in front of the general's desk.

"What about in the tunnel with the devices that sent you to my time?" Kadee asked. "Would there be anything there?"

Vic stared at her, considering the suggestion. She wasn't getting a feeling one way or the other.

"Only one way to find out," she said.

CHAPTER 6

Having an Army escort was a novel experience. Especially knowing that they *were* simply an 'escort'. The seven teens weren't under guard, they didn't need to take orders from the sergeant, pair of corporals or the private. It was strange. They hadn't been specifically told that they were in charge but the way that the four soldiers reacted, it was clear that they were. They were being 'escorted', plain and simple.

They'd asked to be brought there, the soldiers had requestioned a truck and within twenty minutes they were on their way. Having arrived at the park, the soldiers had simply spread out, giving them room to do their thing while also keeping civilians out of the way.

"Now what?" Matt asked as the seven of them stood in the tunnel where it'd all started staring at a concrete wall pockmarked with black splotches. "We don't have the cylinder any more which might have been able to open the secret door for us."

"Who needs a device to open a door?" Paul grinned.

Paul stepped forward, rubbing his hands together. Vic caught Alana's eye and they grinned while simultaneously rolling their eyes, which progressed to head shakes when Paul planted his feet and thrust both hands out, fingers splayed.

"What are you doing?" Tolan asked.

"Opening the door," Paul replied, hamming it up even more by jerking his arms backwards as though he was pulling a great weight.

A great ear-piercing *screech* echoed throughout the tunnel before suddenly cutting off as a massive slab of concrete pulled free of the rest of the side of the tunnel. A flick of Paul's finger had the slab drifting sidewards before settling down to stand out of the way.

"You're an idiot," Matt told his best friend.

"Hey, I can't make it look too easy, can I? Gotta impress my girl here," Paul said, slipping his arm around Alana's waist and drawing her in close enough to kiss the top of her head.

"I'm already impressed, Babe. You don't need the theatrics," Alana told him.

"Let's get to work," Tolan cut in. "And remember to be careful with those two devices – we don't want them accidentally misfiring again and sending us god knows when."

The secret room that had been built into the tunnel was tiny, barely large enough for the two Hopper devices. Thankfully, due to the Hopper's intense dislike for the dark, it was well lit – a pair of bright lights having been automatically activated the instant that the door was opened.

"Anyone see anything?" Tolan asked.

"There are three small devices down here," Kadee said from where she squatted on the ground. "I've seen Hoppers use this one quite a lot."

"Which one?" Tolan asked, then after Kadee had picked it up, "any guesses what they used it for?"

"They used it to track us when we were above ground," Kadee said.

Now that Vic got a better look at it, she vaguely recognised it. Back in the future when they were hiding from the Hoppers, not long after they'd first met Kadee and before they'd discovered their abilities, the seven of them had been hiding in a shop. Vic remembered peeking out at the Hopper patrol on the street and seeing one of the Hoppers holding something that looked a lot like the device that Kadee was holding.

It had a longish handle that was attached to a simple black box about the size of half a shoebox. Most of the lower half of it was taken up by a screen; the upper half by half a dozen buttons and a pair of dials.

"Could we use that to find the Hopper EMP devices?" Ray asked.

"Depends what it's calibrated for," Tolan shrugged.

"What sort of range does it have?" Matt asked.

"I'm not sure. Not large. I could usually outrun it or out-smart the Hoppers using it," Kadee replied.

"It has possibilities," Vic said, to which Tolan gave her a firm nod.

"What about the other two things down there?" Paul asked.

Unexpectedly, both of them lifted from the ground and floated up and into the middle of the group. One had the same long handle with an oval top. There was no screen on this one, simply a collection of buttons, dials and switches. The other was the largest of the three. The main section of it was, once again, box-shaped, about twice as big as the other. The centre of it contained a large screen with the left side having two smaller screens, one on top of the other. To the right of the larger screen were rows of buttons and dials. Twin handles running parallel to the sides of the box made carrying it easy.

"I've never seen anything like them before," Kadee replied.

"Then, I guess there's only one way to work out what they do," Matt stated, reaching for the smaller of the two.

Instantly, Vic's body was bathed in intense cold, a feeling of dread filling her.

"NO!" she screamed.

Thankfully, Matt's hand instantly whipped backwards, his eyes wide.

"Bad?" he asked, somewhat shakily.

"Very," she nodded frantically.

"What would it have done if he'd turned it on?" Tolan asked.

Vic shook her head. "I don't know, but we did not want to find out."

"Right. That one stays here," Ray said, reaching out carefully with two fingers to pluck the smaller device out of the air and return it to its place on the ground inside the secret room.

"What about the other one?" Tolan asked.

Instead of intense cold, Vic felt something like a warm breeze sweep across her.

"That one's okay," she said. "Possibly even useful?"

She hated that the ability was so imprecise. One day she hoped that she'd understand it better.

This time it was Tolan who stepped forward and took the largest device from where it floated. With both hands around the handle, he looked up, checking with her and Vic gave a smiling nod. He was right to continue.

"I guess we take it from the top," he muttered.

Collective breaths were held as he reached out and pressed the first button in the top row on the left. The fact that nothing happened, no lights appearing, no screen flickering on was rather anticlimactic.

There were five buttons across the top and Vic's eyes kept straying to the one on the end at the right, not that she said anything. Instead, she watched as Tolan pushed each of the middle three buttons, each eliciting no response from the alien device. Finally, his finger reached for the last button, and she felt herself lean forward slightly in anticipation.

As she expected, the instant that Tolan's finger pressed the button, the entire thing lit up. Bright orange lights raced over every button in a wave; the main screen burst with green light, the smaller two flashed white before setting into a light grey.

"Woah! Right, that's the on switch," Tolan exclaimed. "Now what?"

"How would we know?" Paul asked.

"Does that kind of look like a map to you?" Ray asked, leaning over Vic's shoulder to touch the main screen. "I mean, this line here could be the river?"

Vic only had a fraction of a second to focus on it before the screen shifted. The dark blue line that had wiggled through the middle of the screen shifted and leapt forward until a great blue swathe filled a good quarter of the screen, from top to bottom.

"What'd you do?" Tolan asked, his voice higher than usual.

"Nothing!" Ray protested. "Just touched it, that's all!"

"I think it zoomed in?" Alana suggested. "I mean, if it is a map like Ray said, then maybe Ray made it zoom in on one particular section."

"That makes sense," Paul agreed. "So, that blue is the river? Then what's this green section on this side or the grey section on the other side mean?"

Vic laughed. "Look at the black lines that criss-cross the grey. Streets. That side is the city. The green's the parkland that runs beside the river."

"So where are we?" Matt asked.

Tolan shook his head. "I can't tell. Ray, can you make it zoom back out again?"

"I don't know what I did to make it zoom in in the first place," Ray replied with a shake of his head.

"Give it here, Tol," Matt said, reaching forward and all-but snatching the device out of Tolan's hands. "If this thing can zoom in and out it's probably not much different than human tech."

Vic watched as he placed two fingers close together in the centre of the map before quickly spreading them apart. Expectedly, the map zoomed back out again, leaving a mostly grey centre with patches of green dotted about, more green on the fringes and a wavy blue line bisecting it all.

"There. Zoomed out. Simple," Matt beamed.

"That still doesn't answer where we are," Tolan stated.

"Actually, it does," Vic corrected excitedly. "Look!"

Being careful not to touch the screen, she pointed at a spot very near the middle of the map where she could see a miniscule, blinking purple light. She watched as Matt placed two spread fingers on either side of it and slowly inched his fingers together. Obediently, the map shrunk, even as the purple light grew.

"Is that where we are?" Alana asked.

"Looks about right," Ray replied, his head cocked to the side. "See the curve of the river? And the purple light is in the green section of the parkland."

"Makes sense," Paul nodded.

"Then what's that light mean?" Kadee asked, her finger pointing to a light near the bottom left-hand corner of the map.

The blinking light was surrounded by grey with a number of black lines – roads – surrounding it.

"No, it couldn't be that simple, could it?" Vic breathed, realisation dawning.

"Vic? What is it?" Tolan asked.

"Assuming that this thing detects anything Hopper..."

"That's a *huge* assumption," Paul interrupted, a sentiment that Vic ignored in favour of continuing with her thought.

"... and we're here because that's where those two EMP devices are, then I can only think of only one other thing in the city that's Hopper-made."

"The *Scorpion*?" Ray asked.

"Makes sense," Tolan agreed with Vic's nod. "But as Paul pointed out, there's a lot of assumptions in that thought. This thing might not be detecting Hopper tech at all, it could be something else."

"Like what?" Matt challenged. "You can see the map for yourself! It's blinking right where we're standing."

"Which could mean that it's just detecting itself," Tolan stated.

"One way to find out," Ray said, interrupting them. "Anyone interested in a field trip?"

Corporal Knox glanced around and back to where Matt was sitting in the rear passenger seat behind Sergeant Reid.

"You want me to keep going straight or turn?" Corporal Knox asked.

Vic could see that the Corporal was struggling with following the directions that Matt was giving, unsurprising, really. Twice already, the Corporal had had to find places to turn the transport truck around to get them back on track after Matt had read the map wrong and given the wrong directions. Vic thanked her lucky stars that she'd somehow made it into the seat beside him – only four could sit in the cab, driver, front passenger and two rear passengers; everyone else had to sit in the rear of the truck and sitting back there would *not* have been fun when they'd done those U-turns.

"Turn left," Matt instructed.

"Are we close?" Vic asked sotto voce as Corporal Knox took the turn.

"Yeah, should be right up ahead," Matt replied, lifting his head to look out the front windscreen.

The road ran straight as far as they could see. What made this particular road unusual was the fact that there were no buildings to either side. No shops, no businesses or warehouses. Not even any houses.

Unexpectedly, the truck began to slow.

"Why are we stopping?" Matt asked.

Sergeant Reid's face appeared, blocking their view as he turned in his seat to look back at the pair of them.

"Are you certain that this is where you want to go?" he asked.

Matt glanced down at the device in his hands and then back up. "Yep."

"Well, you might want to rethink that," Sergeant Reid stated flatly.

"Why?" Vic asked suspiciously.

"Because we won't be going in there. It's a government-run research facility and we'd need special clearance to even get through the gate. Clearance which none of us have," Sergeant Reid replied.

Vic and Matt shared a pointed look. A government-run facility that needed special clearance? That answered that question. There was no doubt that the *Scorpion* was in there somewhere. And that the device was mapping where Hopper-made tech was located.

"We could...?" Matt suggested and Vic was already shaking her head before he finished the thought.

"Not a good idea," she replied. "We know where it is if we need it later."

Matt sighed, frowning, clearly not happy with the decision even though he probably expected it. "Fine."

"Sergeant, Corporal, can you please take us back to Base now?" Vic asked, her mind whirling with thoughts as she tried to work out what their next, best move should be.

CHAPTER 7

The truck had barely rolled to a stop before a face appeared at the driver's window. The soldier peered in, looked across at Sergeant Reid in the passenger seat and then twisted his head to take in Matt and Vic. A quick sidestep was preceded by a knock on Vic's window. Obediently, she rolled it down.

"You and your friends are requested in General White's office ASAP," he said.

"Okay?" Vic replied and shared a glance at Matt.

It was rare that the General asked to see them. Sure, they'd been in his office a number of times, but each of those instances had been them crashing his office. By the time she looked back, it was to find that the soldier had disappeared. No escort?

"I'll get the others," Matt said as he opened his door.

Within a couple of minutes, all seven of them had gathered and started walking towards the right building.

"Mind if I tag along?"

Vic looked to her right to find Sergeant Reid striding along beside them.

So, they did have an escort, did they? she mused.

"Suit yourself," Tolan shrugged in reply.

This time when they reached General White's outer office, the secretary was not only already standing but also waiting by the door to open it for them. Vic's senses heightened. Whatever this was, it was important and most likely urgent.

"You're here," General White stated and Vic could hear the unspoken addition: 'about time!'.

There weren't enough chairs for all of them, so they simply spread out in a line, keeping the two chairs and desk between the General and themselves. A quick glance told her that Sergeant Reid had taken up a position near the door. What was strange, though, was his posture; he didn't look as though he was guarding them, simply standing in the room as well.

"I understand that you found what you were looking for?" General White half-asked, half-stated.

"The two Hopper devices and this Hopper Padd-thing which we can use to track other Hopper-made tech," Tolan replied.

"What's happening with those two devices?" Ray asked.

"They've been moved here to the Base," General White replied.

"Not together?" Vic blurted urgently.

"They're in separate warehouses. We do know what we're doing," General White replied dryly. Without looking, his hand reached out and he stabbed a button on his phone. "Send Captain Fuller in."

Vic turned to see a tall man with salt and pepper hair stride into the room. His slate grey eyes darted to each of them, taking them in and Vic was sure that he was evaluating them. Two feet into the room he stopped, came to attention and snapped off a crisp salute.

"Captain Fuller reporting as ordered."

"At ease, Captain," General White nodded before his focus shifted back to the seven of them. "The last time you were here, you had the start of a plan to find all of those alien devices and ensure that, when the aliens get here, that they couldn't use them against us to eliminate our tech capabilities. Then, you didn't have the equipment to execute the plan..."

"Because you wouldn't give us back the *Scorpion*," Matt muttered. The fact that no one reacted, led Vic to assume that either she was the only one to hear him or, the more likely option, that everyone had decided to simply ignore him.

"... do you have what you need now?" General White concluded.

Tolan glanced to either side at them before shrugging. "We can probably find them using the Hopper Padd and our abilities, sure. But they're scattered all over the world."

"Captain Fuller can help with that," General White stated, nodding at the man.

"Sir?" Captain Fuller asked.

"Captain, I'm giving you a new assignment. You and your crew will be at the disposal of these seven. You'll be travelling wherever in the world they tell you to go. Don't worry about clearance entering countries, that'll be taken care of at the very top."

"I'm guessing that Captain Fuller flies a plane?" Paul asked.

"He does but what he normally flies won't be big enough for this mission," General White replied. "With the seven of you and Sergeant Reid and his team, not to mention all of those devices that you're going to find and collect ..."

"You want us to *collect* them?" Ray blurted.

"I don't think it's a good idea to leave them where they are, do you?" General White asked rhetorically.

Vic, though, was focussing on the burst of warmth that unexpectedly filled her. It was akin to being engulfed in the best hug that she'd ever had.

"Yes!" she exclaimed, reaching out and grabbing Ray's hand in her excitement. "This is *good*. Very good! It's exactly the right thing to do!"

"Premonition?" Tolan asked, looking at her with wide eyes.

"Yes," she nodded enthusiastically.

"If I may, Sir, what will I be piloting?" Captain Fuller asked, interrupting any other questions from her friends.

"I've got us a loan of a Boeing C-17," General White replied with an unaccustomed smile.

"A Globemaster?" Captain Fuller replied and Vic could hear the wide smile in his voice.

"I believe it will do the job," General White nodded. "It's big and fast. It'll get you where you need to go faster than anything else we've got and it'll carry every single one of those damned devices. Sergeant, gather your team, requisition anything that you think you'll need; no limits. Captain Fuller, you'll find your new plane at Amberley. Get yourself and your crew there ASAP and get her prepped for launch. I want all of you airborne within four hours."

"Yes, Sir," the Captain and Sergeant replied, snapping to attention as one and performing precision salutes.

"Whatever you people need as well, tell us and we'll get it for you," General White stated. "Keeping the world's military operational when that invasion force gets here is our top priority at the moment and, loathe as I am to admit it, the seven of you are best equipped to handle this mission."

"We won't let you down," Tolan assured him.

Alana had veered off nearly five metres before any of them realised.

"Babe?" Paul called after her, drawing Vic's attention.

The girl in question spun about but continued walking, only backwards. "If we're about to go on a whirlwind round-the-world trip that might not get us back in time before the Swarm gets here, then I'm going to see my mum and dad before we go!"

Between one step and the next, Vic changed direction to follow. She wasn't the only one, even Kadee went with them.

They found their parents in the mess hall. The instant they entered, meals were abandoned and seats were knocked backwards in the rush to get to them.

"Where've you been?" Vic's mother asked, intently looking her over, most likely to make sure that she was alright.

"We had to go find some Hopper tech and get it somewhere safe," Vic replied, instantly pushing the thought that they were about to go find the alien devices from all over the world and bring them back *to where their parents were* firmly from her mind.

"So, you're back now? No more 'missions' or traipsing off to 'save the world'? You're going to let the Army do their job now?" her father asked intently.

Vic couldn't help herself, she laughed. "Funny you should ask that."

"YOU'RE WHAT?"

Vic winced; Alana, it seemed, had already told her parents what they were about to do.

"Vic? Is there something we should know?" her father asked flatly, drawing her attention back on to him.

This was *not* how she intended on telling her parents. Still, needs must. Especially when she didn't have much choice in the matter.

"Mum, Dad," she began and instantly started talking faster and slightly louder before her father could begin getting up a full head of steam. "What we did today, it worked. We found what we were looking for."

"And?" her father prompted.

"And, with what we found, we're going to have to go off again," she sighed. "If Earth is going to have a fighting chance when that Hopper Swarm arrives, then there are things that we need to do."

"What things, Victoria?" her mother asked. "And why you? Why not let the Army do it?"

"Because we're us," she replied simply. "You know what we can do."

"That didn't tell us exactly what you'll be doing," her father frowned.

"Nothing dangerous," Vic replied quickly, fervently hoping that that was true. "All we'll be doing is collecting some Hopper technology to make sure that they can't use it against us."

"Where is this 'Hopper technology'?" her father asked suspiciously.

Vic's eyes darted away even as she sighed. He wasn't going to like this answer. "The devices are hidden all over the world."

"All over the world?" her mother repeated, her voice rising, though thankfully not as high or as loud as Alana's mother's had been.

"Do we get any say in this?" her father asked, his voice hard. "You're still underage, remember?"

A tingle in her shoulder had Vic jerk so forcefully, that she was left half-turned away. And left staring at her father's hand where it was still outstretched.

"Dad! What do you think you're doing?" she asked, shocked that he'd try to grab her arm like that.

"I just told you. You're our daughter and, abilities or not, we still get a say in this," he snapped.

"I'm sorry, Dad, Mum but no, you don't. Not anymore. Not with the fate of the entire world hanging in the balance like this," she replied, hating that she had to say it, despite the fact that it was true. "Besides, we're not going alone. There's a bunch of Army guys going with us."

To illustrate her point, she looked around to find one of them. Unfortunately, the only green uniformed soldier that she could see was sidling along the wall near the door. Even as she watched, he turned sidewards and disappeared through it.

Well, that's helpful! she thought sarcastically.

"Look, Dad! This is important!"

Ray's raised voice caught her attention and her eyes darted that way. The bag that he was holding up in front of his father had her blinking until she realised what it was. And what it meant.

Subconsciously, Vic found herself drawn to him, even taking a few steps in his general direction. Not that she was the only one; all around her, her friends were pulled in the same direction and with them, their parents.

"A bag? What do I care about a bag?" Ray's father asked, pushing the thing away. "You just said that you're going away again, and if I'm understanding correctly, there's a chance that you might not make it back!"

"Exactly! That's why you need to listen!" Ray insisted. "And *this* is incredibly important! It might be the key to everything!"

"Ray..." Tolan began.

Ray, though, wasn't listening, his entire focus on his father. "Just look and you'll understand!"

He dropped to one knee, placed the bag between himself and his father and unzipped it, pulling the sides wide.

"What the hell is that? That's not from Earth is it?" his father exclaimed.

"Ray..." Tolan tried again.

"No. It's not," Ray replied to his father, looking up at him, one hand now holding one of the Hopper fruit. "*This* is what the Hoppers eat. It's some sort of melon – sunset melons, I've been calling them."

"They're striking!" Paul's mother commented, her eyes, like everyone's there fixed on the melon with the dusty orange top that merged into and changed into the deep mauve bottom half. What made it even more amazing was the lilac-coloured leaf attached to the stalk.

If Ray heard her, she was ignored, his focus never leaving his father.

"I've got a heap of them in here, as well as a few buckets of seeds and even a couple plants," Ray stated. "You need to find a way to grow them! Do that and there might be a way to negotiate some kind of diplomatic solution for peace with the Hoppers."

"I don't..." Matt's father began only to have Ray talk right over the top of him.

"These things are delicious; we've all eaten them. Sweet and juicy and filling," Ray said. "*This* is a big part of why the Hoppers take over planets, to grow more food for their people. But if we can grow it *for* them, then maybe they'll be open to some sort of trade deal?"

"Makes sense," Ray's father replied slowly.

"No, it doesn't," Tolan stated, shaking his head.

"Fourteen days," Matt agreed, not that Ray was listening to either of them.

"I don't have the time to get the farming of these melons going. But you do, dad!" he insisted.

Slowly, Ray's father reached out and took the sunset melon that Ray was still holding out.

"How do I grow them? What sort of soil? How much water and sun?" he asked.

"I don't know," Ray admitted shaking his head. "You'll have to find that out yourself. But I know that you can do this!"

Vic stared at father and son. Something passed between them, some silent agreement that was sealed with a single nod from Ray's father. In response, Ray firmly zipped the bag back up, stood and handed it to his dad.

Tolan's glance in her direction had Vic looking at him. His raised eyebrow was answered by a shrug.

"I'm guessing that I'm not wrong in thinking that everyone here knows what's coming and what we have to do," Tolan said, drawing all eyes to him.

"Aliens are coming and for some idiotic reason you lot seem to think that *you're* the only ones who can do something about it," Matt's father stated.

Tolan shrugged. "Yeah, that's about it, I guess. But it's not idiotic. We have to do this."

"Why?" Vic's mother asked, desperation clear in her voice.

"Because we can," Vic replied. "Because if we don't, then things will be a *lot* worse."

"You're still kids," Paul's mother argued.

"Can normal kids do this?" Paul asked, eliciting a high-pitched squeal when his mother instantly floated a couple of metres into the air.

"Paul! Put me down!" she screeched.

Obediently, the telekinetic lowered his mother back to the solid ground.

"Okay, you've made your point," Paul's father stated bitterly.

"If you want to help us, then get somewhere safe," Tolan said, looking around at the gathered parents. "We'll be able to concentrate on what we're doing better and get it done faster if we're not worrying about what's happening back here."

"Exactly what does that mean? 'Somewhere safe'?" Matt's mother asked.

"Hoppers hate the dark, so find somewhere underground. Tunnels, a cave, a basement, something like that," Kadee replied.

"You've got two weeks until that Hopper Swarm arrives. Use it," Vic added. "Get camping gear, food, weapons, anything and everything that you think you'll need. "Round up family and friends if you've got the space and can convince them to go with you."

"And let us know where to find you," Tolan said. "No matter what, we'll make it to that location as soon as we're done neutralising all of the Hopper tech that's hidden around the world."

"Somewhere in the city?" Vic's father asked in the sudden silence.

"Maybe," Vic shrugged. "Or out in the countryside. There are bound to be caves somewhere in the mountains. The more remote the better. Don't make it easy for the Hoppers to find you."

"Are we really going to do this?" Alana's mother asked. "Just let our children go off while we run away?"

Her husband stepped closer, pulling her in for a hug with his arm around her shoulders. "I don't think we have much choice."

The sound of the door opening followed by a set of measured steps had the group turning.

"It's time to go," Sergeant Reid stated. "The Globemaster will be fuelled and ready for take off in less than an hour."

Vic could feel that her parents were about to protest once again, so she did the only thing that she could think of: she flung herself at them, one arm around each of their necks, pulling them into a group hug.

"I'll be alright," she told them firmly. "You just make sure that you, Damien and Selina are as well!"

"We will," her father replied over the muffled sniffling from her mother.

"Time to go," Tolan announced a minute or so later.

Disentangling herself wasn't easy, a fact that it seemed most of her friends were finding as well. Still, within a minute or so, final goodbyes had been said and the seven were clustered together. At the door, Vic took one last look back. Each set of parents were standing there, holding their partner, most with tears running freely down their faces. Only Ray's dad had no one. In lieu of a person, he was cuddling the precious bag that Ray had given him as though it was a lifeline keeping him upright.

Swallowing the lump in her throat, Vic's eyes fixed on her parents one last time.

“I love you,” she mouthed to them before forcing herself to turn and walk through the door.

CHAPTER 8

The Globemaster was impressive. There was simply no other word for it. Huge. Gigantic. Enormous. All of those would have fit just as well. But impressive seemed a much better word in Vic's mind.

Wingtip to wingtip was easily fifty metres, with a pair of engines mounted on each wing. And it was tall. Vic needed to seriously crane her neck upwards to see the upper portions of it when she was standing on the tarmac.

"This way," Captain Fuller commanded.

Like the *Scorpion*, the Globemaster was fitted with a rear ramp. Unlike the Hopper vessel, this ramp was big enough to drive a tank on. Or three. And its opening was like a great maw, opened wide, ready to swallow anything. The sound of a helicopter's rotors beginning to spin caught her attention and Vic looked across at it. Her eyes narrowed and switched back to the Globemaster. She could be mistaken, but she was *sure* that the great plane could swallow that helicopter whole without blinking!

"What's the range on this thing?" Paul asked.

"Upwards of ten thousand kilometres," Captain Fuller replied proudly, eliciting low whistles from the boys.

"Let's just hope that there are runways long enough to let us land close to wherever the EMP devices are," Alana said.

Captain Fuller laughed. "That won't be a problem. Most commercial runways are about the right length, giving us a great deal of flexibility."

"This is a lot of empty space," Ray commented as they reached the top of the ramp.

"My understanding was that we're going to need it," Captain Fuller replied. "Five hundred pairs of alien devices, right?"

"Five hundred and ten," Alana replied.

"Five hundred and nine," Vic corrected. "We've already got the first set."

"Right. One down, many to go," Matt nodded.

"What's our first destination?" Captain Fuller asked.

"We think there should be eight here in Australia alone," Tolan replied. "Matt?"

Matt had already been pulling his backpack around to him; from it, he took out the handheld Hopper device. Looking about, he found a seat against the side of the Globemaster. Pulling it down from where it rested in its 'up' position, he sat and touched the button to turn the Padd on. As the map flared into life, everyone crowded around to see.

"I've got no idea how far out we can zoom the map," Matt said. "Nor how easy it's going to be to see the purple lights showing us where the devices are."

"Only one way to find out," Paul told him.

Vic's eyes were glued to the screen as Matt's pinched fingers were laid in the centre of the screen before they quickly spread out. Obediently, the map zoomed out, showing more and more of the city and then the country with each repeat. It took nearly a dozen movements before the entirety of Australia was shown on the screen.

"I was worried about that," Matt sighed.

There were greens and blues and browns on the screen, but no blinking purple lights, nothing to indicate where any Hopper devices were located.

"Vic? Think you could weave your magic?" Tolan asked.

She rolled her eyes but took the offered device from Matt.

All that they'd really been working with was the big touch screen in the middle of the thing. There were still rows of buttons and dials on one side which they hadn't touched, as well as the two smaller screens – still showing nothing – on the other. The reasoning was clear: they had the map working, no one wanted to accidently change a setting and lose such a precious resource.

Unfortunately, she got to be the one to chance that.

Her eyes searched the Padd, looking for any sort of clue as to how to make the purple lights show up. There was nothing, not even any Hopper writing – not that she could read that anyway.

The dials. Her eyes kept drifting back to the dials. Getting a firmer grip on the Padd with one hand, she moved her other hand towards the row of dials. Strangely, though, a cold feeling engulfed her fingers no matter which dial she tried. The dials were right, she was sure of that. But they were also wrong, which didn't make sense.

Once again, she allowed her eyes to search the Padd. Unfortunately, nothing was jumping out at her as feeling the right course of action. With an internal shrug, she decided to try Matt's approach of starting from the top buttons and pressing each one in turn, with one difference: she was starting with the button beside the power-on button.

The instant that her finger pressed it, she felt a warm tingle travel up her finger into her hand. She smiled as the two smaller screens blinked to life, the top with a series of Hopper characters that they had no way of translating, the bottom with a multi-lined graph of some kind.

"What do they do?" Captain Fuller asked.

"No idea," Vic replied simply, her eyes now fixed back on the dials.

The first dial didn't feel right but the second... Eagerly, her fingers grasped the dial and twisted it. At first, there was no response on the main screen. The smaller screens were a different matter. The lines of Hopper text on the top screen changed instantly, scrolling from right to left and bottom to top, all completely indecipherable and the graph on the bottom screen undulated with hidden meaning.

"Vic? You're sure twisting that is the right thing to do?" Tolan asked.

"You asked me to try, remember?" she shot back, even as she continued twisting the dial.

And then specks of purple appeared. At first, they were miniscule but the more that she kept twisting, the brighter they became and easier to see. What was even better was the fact that there were nine of them – the exact number that they'd predicted would be needed for the number of devices to blanket the entire country with EMP bursts, plus one for the *Scorpion*.

"Is that them? The things we're looking for?" Captain Fuller asked.

"That's my guess," Matt replied.

"Let's have a look at it," Captain Fuller said, taking the Padd out of Vic's hands. "If I'm reading this right, I'm guessing Brisbane, Canberra, Hobart, Adelaide, Perth, Alice Springs, Darwin and Cairns. Makes sense, most of the major cities and giving the maximum amount of coverage."

"What? No Sydney? Bet they're going to be upset," Paul joked.

Captain Fuller didn't even look up when he replied. "There was no need to put one there. Sydney's too close to Brisbane and would have meant overlap. By placing one in Canberra, it covers both Sydney and Melbourne. Smart actually."

"What's the plan, Captain?" Tolan asked.

"Anti-clockwise," he declared. "Start with Cairns, end in Canberra, that'll make it easy to duck across the ditch to New Zealand before we hit the Americas. I've mapped out a basic route of the most likely trajectory that we'd need; that fits in nicely."

The rumble of a truck hitting the ramp and driving up into the Globemaster caught their attention and halted conversation. A second truck was quickly followed by a jeep and half a dozen motorbikes. Each was parked before soldiers rushed about securing tyres with specially designed straps.

"Captain, what's the likelihood that we'll find all of the devices before the Swarm arrives?" Alana asked.

"In fourteen days?" Captain Fuller replied, his face grim. "Let's just hope that it takes those aliens a while to remember that they have those devices that they can detonate."

The flight to Cairns was relatively short – just under two hours, with a good portion of that being ascending to cruising altitude and then coming back down again.

They'd all been assigned a seat in the large cargo section of the Globemaster and given headphones to enable them to hear and talk with each other. It was rough, not designed for comfort at all and definitely not conducive to getting much rest, not that Vic felt that she could have slept even if she'd wanted to. She was too hyped up.

On the other hand, at least she'd coped with air travel a lot better than some of the others. Ray's eyes had been wide all the way up and only went back to normal once the Captain had announced that they'd levelled off. Kadee, understandably, had been terrified the entire trip. This had been her first conscious air flight – her last one being as a Hopper captive in the future that hopefully now would never be and discounting their trip into space which had felt very different. Alana and Vic had held her hands most of the way and it'd taken everything in her not to react to the tight hold that Kadee had had. Finally, nearly an hour in, she'd relaxed. Slightly. But that was still nothing compared to Matt. They'd all found out the hard way that he got airsick. Not counting the mess that he'd made on the floor, he'd filled three bags during the flight and left the rest of them feeling nauseated with the smell.

They hit the ground with a solid *thump*, bounced, hit again, stuttered then kept on rolling. A stern look and hand held out in a universal 'stop' gesture prevented her from unbuckling.

"Wait until we've come to a stop," Sergeant Reid instructed. *"It's a safety thing. We don't want anyone getting hurt unnecessarily."*

She nodded to show her understanding

"Matt, are you up to finding out where we need to go to find the EMP devices?" Tolan asked.

His thankfully less-green face nodded and Vic watched as he leant over to get his bag. He was back upright a second later, minus the bag and with his eyes screwed tightly shut, his chest working overtime.

"Matt?" Paul asked worriedly.

"Just give me a sec," he replied.

Finally, he reached back down, his head remaining tilted up, his eyes closed. He fumbled about, grabbed his bag and hefted it up onto his lap where he wrapped his arms around it and seemed to be simply concentrating on breathing.

Eventually, his eyes opened and he undid his bag to pull out the Padd. They waited, watching as he did his thing.

"It is now safe for you to remove your headsets, unbuckle and move around the craft," Captain Fuller stated over the comms.

Vic quickly unbuckled before removing her headset and twisting about to hang it on the hook behind her. She stood and stretched, lifting her arms over her head as she did so and smiled at Ray who was looking at her.

"Okay, got it," Matt announced. "I'm not sure if I'm reading this right, though. It looks as though it's in water?"

"May I?" Private Dillon asked, holding out her hand.

She was young for a soldier Vic thought, only being a few years older than they were themselves. She also seemed the friendliest and was always ready with a smile or a look of annoyance when a lock of her fringe came loose and hung over her eyes.

"That's the marina," Private Dillon stated.

"You're sure, Jo?" Sergeant Reid asked.

"I used to live up here as a kid – not in Cairns itself, an hour down the road. But I've been here enough times to know," she replied.

"If it's at the marina and looks like it's in the water, what's the bet that it's on a boat?" Paul asked.

"We'll use the big truck," Sergeant Reid stated. "Corporals Browning and Knox, get those straps loose. The rest of you, grab what you need."

The pause at the airport gate was brief – either they'd already been cleared ahead of time or their being in the back of an Army truck meant that they were given right of way. Either way, Vic was glad; the less time they spent dealing with Red Tape, the more time they had to find all of the devices.

Once again, they were bounced around the back of the truck as they drove through the streets, despite how much they were hanging on. Or, in Vic's case, doing her best to hang on to Paul and Ray to either side of her. This was one of those times where being the smallest was not a good thing. She had no doubt that by the end of this mad-dash race around the world, she'd be covered in bruises from head to toe.

Finally, after what seemed ages but was probably less than half an hour, they jerked to a stop. A double *bang* on the side of the truck told them that it was time to disembark.

The view when Vic jumped down and had a chance to look out was beautiful. Blue water stretched out past a line of boats bobbing at anchor. Palm trees were dotted along the edge of the marina, their large leaves swaying in the breeze. She took a deep breath and sighed at the salty smell that she remembered from all her holidays to the beach with her family.

"Which way?" Captain Reid asked, drawing her attention and shattering her chance to relax.

"That way!" Matt replied, his arm outstretched.

The group had barely gone fifty metres when they encountered their first problem: the Marina clubhouse. Finding their way around it proved frustrating due to the fences that stretched across the walkways and all the way down to the harbour on one side and out and around the facility on the other. When they did finally find an access gate, it was only to discover that it was locked and needed a card and pin code to open it.

"Now what?" a frustrated-sounding Tolan asked.

"I could levitate everyone over?" Paul suggested.

"Let's leave that sort of thing as a last resort, yes?" Sergeant Reid half-suggested, half-ordered.

Paul shot the others a nonplussed look. None of them were happy about the delay. They were only about two hundred metres from another pair of devices, devices that they needed to find, collect and remove if this entire section of the country wanted to retain their technological dependency and yet they were being told to wait?

"Sir!" Corporal Knox said, nodding off to the right.

"Wait here," Sergeant Reid ordered before striding off along the fence line.

They were forced to watch and wait as the Sergeant firstly captured the attention of the groundsman riding the mower – a feat harder than it seemed, as the man was wearing noise-cancelling earmuffs. From what Vic could tell, it was only the combination of Sergeant Reid's uniform and credentials held up in his hand that convinced the groundsman to climb off his mower and approach the fence. One short conversation later and the two men were walking back towards them.

"I thought you said this was Army business?" the groundsman asked suspiciously, his eyes roving over the seven teens.

"It is," Sergeant Reid stated flatly. "These people are accompanying us."

The uncertain *humph* from the groundskeeper wasn't enough to stop him from opening the gate, though.

"Matt?" Tolan asked the second the man had turned back towards his mower.

"That way," Matt nodded. "Third ... no *fourth* pier along."

The few people that they passed as they strode towards the correct pier only glanced at them curiously or offered polite nods; none challenged their right to be there, a situation that Vic was immensely grateful for.

The boats that lined the pier, each in their own small dock, looked expensive and *big*. Most were catamarans with an enclosed section in the middle, many with a second, higher deck. A few were smaller sailboats with masts that stretched high into the sky.

Halfway along, Matt stopped with the Padd held out in front of him. His eyes glued to it, he slowly pivoted about in a circle. Finally, after turning back slightly, he looked up.

"That one!" he declared.

Instantly, the four soldiers had their guns up, trained on the big yacht. They separated, spacing themselves up and down the pier. Vic simply rolled her eyes at them.

"Alana?" she asked.

"It's empty. No one aboard," she replied.

"You can't know that," Sergeant Reid snapped. "Until we've checked every cabin on that ship, you seven are to stay right where you are."

"Alana *can* know that!" Tolan snapped right back. "We have abilities. Remember? It's why we're here. And Alana's is that she can *see through things*!"

"Sarge?" Corporal Dillan asked.

Sergeant Reid sighed and lowered his gun. "Private Dillon, Corporal Browning remain on the pier, keep everyone away."

That was obviously enough for Tolan for he instantly jumped the small stretch of water between the yacht and the pier and headed for the door.

"Locked," he reported, rattling the door.

"Babe?" Paul said, stepping aboard and holding his hand out to Alana.

“I see it,” she replied. “Simple tumblers, you’ve done ones like this dozens of times before.”

Seeing Sergeant Reid’s confused expression, Vic explained for him. “They use their powers to work together. Alana looks inside the lock, Paul moves it about telekinetically, unlocking the door.”

The *click* of the lock highlighted her point.

“Vic?” Tolan asked.

Closing her eyes, Vic concentrated on her feelings. Nothing stood out other than a vague sense of wariness, but that, she decided, could simply be a response to the fact that there was alien tech on board.

“We’re clear. No booby traps,” she replied.

“Matt, be ready for anything,” Tolan instructed.

With a nod, Matt handed the Padd off to Kadee and pulled his knives. Then, with Tolan in front in case his shield was needed, they entered the main cabin.

It looked to be a lounge more than anything. An oval table was surrounded on three sides by cushioned bench seating with large windows, currently with their curtains drawn spanning the entire side towards the front of the ship. A ladder on one wall led up; twin staircases, both extremely narrow led down on either side.

“The left,” Vic stated.

“You’re sure?” Tolan asked.

“I think so. Why?” she replied.

“You don’t normally frown like that when you’re directing us,” he stated.

It was only because he pointed it out that she realised that something was wrong. The two Hopper devices were down the left-hand staircase, she was sure of that. But there was something ... not ... quite ... right down the right set of stairs.

"The devices are to the left," she stated.

That was enough for Tolan, for, with a glance at both Matt and Paul, they clattered down the steps, quickly followed by Sergeant Reid.

"Vic?" Ray asked quietly.

Tearing her eyes from the other set of stairs, she looked into his eyes, surprised to see concern for her shining out of them. A tingle in the back of her mind had her starting to look deeper. There was something else there...

"Vic? Is there something down there?" Alana asked, interrupting her thoughts.

"Something, yes," she replied. "But don't ask me what."

"I'll go take a look," Corporal Knox stated as he moved towards the stairs.

Vic followed, curious as to what had caused the strange, conflicted feeling in her ability; she wasn't surprised to hear Alana, Ray and Kadee following her.

The stairs curled around and came out facing a corridor that stretched out to either side. At either end, she could see doors; two other doors were also set into the corridor partway along. And all of them were closed.

Her feet moved towards the front of the yacht and she followed. Her nose twitched. There was something in the air. Taking a deeper breath, she gagged. Whatever it was was *foul*!

"Wait!" she called.

Unfortunately, she was a fraction of a second too late. Corporal Knox had already opened the door before her call registered. Instantly, a wave of putrid air filled the corridor. Vic retched, one hand on the wall, the other firmly clasped over her mouth. She retched again, this time tasting bile in her mouth.

"Out! Out! Out!" Corporal Knox ordered.

A slam of the door was only partly registered, the hand on her side, forcefully turning her about got her moving. Vic stumbled forward, doing her utmost to hold her breath. The stairs tripped her up and she fell hard, banging her knee. A cry of pain escaped her and with it, an intake of toxic air that had her gagging once again.

She felt herself hauled upright and half-dragged, half-pushed up the stairs. The hand didn't let up until she was propelled through the cabin and out onto the main deck. The smell of fresh air hit her lungs and she dragged lungful after lungful of it into her system, trying desperately to clear out the noxious smell from down below.

"What was that?" Alana asked.

"Someone had died down there, hadn't they?" Kadee asked.

Vic stared at her. Someone was there? She'd been smelling a dead body?

"It's not the first I've found," Kadee sighed. "It doesn't get any better."

Encountering that smell once was bad enough. But to have smelt it more than that? Vic knew that the future that Kadee came from was rough, but that was simply unthinkable, unimaginable. Three small steps was enough for her to throw her arms around Kadee and hold her as tightly as she could. A second later, Alana had joined the hug and the three stood there for some time, consoling each other and regaining their equilibrium.

The clatter of multiple footsteps had Vic looking up and stepping back.

"Sergeant," Corporal Knox said, the instant that his superior officer was in sight.

At the Corporal's gesture, the two stepped to the side. Vic could imagine the conversation. It didn't help that both soldiers kept glancing back at the teens. That, of course, led her to thinking about the *subject* of that discussion and her imagination went into overdrive. Hoppers appearing with their devices. A man, the owner of the yacht, seeing them. The Hoppers killing him. Most likely by using that nasty tail spike of theirs, the Hopper rearing up on his hind legs and impaling the man. It'd be quieter, than using a gun or a blaster. Probably. The Hoppers then stashing the body in a cabin even as they were setting the EMP devices for what was to come.

Bile rose in her throat once again and she forcefully swallowed it down. She took a deep breath. Another. A third. When she thought she could speak again without throwing up, she approached the boys.

"Were the devices there?" she asked.

"Yep," Matt replied happily. "Exactly where the Padd said they'd be."

"The plan is for Paul to move them from here back to the truck," Tolan stated. "Kadee can cover us by hiding them from anyone who's looking."

Vic nodded in agreement, not fully trusting her voice.

"Alright, Corporal Knox, Paul, get back down there and get those alien devices up here," Sergeant Reid ordered as the two soldiers re-joined them.

Honestly, Vic didn't want to know. Really, she didn't. But she asked anyway. The only deference she made to the others was to wait until she could draw Sergeant Reid a little apart from everyone else.

"What's going to happen to ...?" she asked, nodding down towards the lower deck.

“I’ll make an anonymous phone call to the police after we’ve left,” Sergeant Reid replied quietly. “It’s not how it should be done but if we did it by the book, we’d get caught up in the investigation and it could be days before we got away.”

Vic nodded. That made sense. The most important thing, at least as far as she could see, was that, whoever he or she was down there, whoever their family or friends were, those people could get closure from being told what had happened.

CHAPTER 9

The very air was charged. From the window, the tops of a mountain could be seen, all green and white. In a very few minutes, they'd be landing. Landing in a different country!

"I've never been to another country before," Alana said.

"We know," Vic replied with a laugh, "you've only told us a dozen or more times since we left Australia."

"Tolan's the only one of us who has," Paul told his girlfriend.

"And before all of this, Kadee had never even seen all of Brisbane, let alone gone anywhere else," Ray said. "This is new to all of us."

Alana, though, seemed to have latched on to the one difference amongst them. "Where've you been?"

Tolan glanced at her before resuming staring out the window. "Israel. My father's from there so there are heaps of aunts and uncles and cousins, not to mention my grandparents."

"What's it like? Is Israel on our list of places we need to go?" Alana asked eagerly.

"We haven't looked much further than here," Sergeant Reid interjected.

"After here, our next stop will be South America but we have yet to look at the map in that Padd of Matt's to determine our exact flight path and schedule."

Alana nodded but her eyes never left Tolan. "What's Israel like?"

"I don't remember a lot. I was four when we went there. From what little I do remember, it was hot, dry and loud – although that last might just have been because normally it's just me and my mum and dad and we were crammed into a small house with nine other people."

"Welcome to New Zealand," Captain Fuller said over the loudspeaker. *"We're just pulling into our parking spot now; you'll be clear to lower the ramp in two minutes."*

His announcement wasn't unexpected; they were getting used to the procedure already, which was why they'd already unbuckled and taken off their headsets as soon as they'd touched down and slowed to a more sane speed. Thankfully, Matt's airsickness was even almost cured with all of the quick flights that they'd already had. Mostly, at least.

"Alright, Matt, let's take a look and see where we're going," Sergeant Reid said.

They all crowded around him and watched as he powered the Padd on and then used the buttons and dials to zoom in.

Wellington, the capital of New Zealand, was ideally placed to hide a set of Hopper EMP devices – the country was split into two islands with the capital located at the bottom of the north island. A device set off from there would easily cover both islands.

"Got it," Matt said a minute later.

"That looks close. Real close," Ray commented.

The map showed the entirety of the city; the purple dot showing the location of Hopper tech wasn't far away from the centre of the map, which was always centred on the Padd's location.

"Can you zoom in, please?" Sergeant Reid asked.

Matt did so, pinching his fingers and moving them outwards. For a second, the purple dot disappeared but a simple move back in had reshowed it.

"Is that some sort of park?" Tolan asked.

"No!" Alana exclaimed, holding up her phone and waving it around making it hard to see the map of Wellington that she had on it. "It's the zoo!"

Thunk

The sound of the ramp hitting the ground behind them had then turning. The light streamed in and Vic was forced to squint to see outside. A new country. Admittedly, it was just the tarmac of the airport, but still. The first of many new countries. Shadows appeared and she frowned, trying to determine what they were until they coalesced into a group of four people.

"Let's go, people. Time to meet our hosts," Sergeant Reid said, stepping out and striding away, leaving them to quickly fall into line behind him.

Three of the four waiting for them at the bottom of the ramp wore military uniforms.

"Welcome to New Zealand," the last of the four said, greeting them. "It's an honour to meet you. My name is Kaia Paewai and I'm from the New Zealand government, assigned to be your escort for your mission here."

"You know who we are?" Paul blurted.

She smiled at him, "I do. Your government has spoken to ours – after all, New Zealand and Australia are the closest allies that we each have. I have been briefed on all of you."

"It's good to meet you," Sergeant Reid said, stepping forward to shake her hand. "Your assistance in this is greatly appreciated; time is of the essence in our mission."

Kaia bypassed his hand, instead placing her hands on his shoulders and pulling him slightly forward, even as she also leant forward. She touched his forehead with her own before stepping back from him.

She smiled as she stepped to the side so that she was in front of Tolan and repeated the gesture – hands on shoulders, lean in until their foreheads were touching and straighten. She repeated the gesture with each of them; it was only when it was Vic's turn that she realised that she quietly added a phrase as well, firstly in what she assumed was Māori, then in English, 'welcome to our land'.

It was the strangest embrace that Vic had ever received but it left her feeling warm all over and immensely pleased that this was the first country that they came to after leaving Australia.

Finally, Kaia stepped back so that she was beside the three New Zealand military officers once again.

"Can I ask if you have any idea where you need to go here in New Zealand?" Kaia asked.

"We have a device that allows us to find the alien devices that could transmit the electromagnetic pulse. Matt?" Sergeant Reid prompted.

"There is only one in New Zealand, actually here in Wellington," Matt said.

"That makes things easier," Kaia nodded. "Do you have a more precise location?"

"We were just looking at that when you arrived," Matt replied.

"It's at the zoo!" Alana blurted.

"That's not far, we can have you there in ten minutes," Kaia said. "We have arranged a series of cars and a truck that you can use to transport the devices back here."

"Thank you," Sergeant Reid said. "That'll definitely make things much easier."

"If you're ready?" the New Zealand Captain asked. "Sergeant, if you'd like to ride with me?"

"You get the impression that that guy just dismissed us completely?" Ray whispered to Vic, turning slightly so that his mouth was close to her ear.

"Yeah," she replied unimpressed. "But as long as he helps us get to the devices and doesn't get in the way, then I don't really care how he treats us."

Kaia gestured towards the two remaining soldiers, "If you'll follow these officers, they'll escort you to the vehicles."

Within a very few minutes, they'd piled into the cars and were driving through the airport gates and towards Wellington city proper.

A tug on her sleeve had Vic turning to find Kadee looking at her with pleading eyes. Vic cocked her head at her, unsure what was wrong, after all, they'd just arrived at the zoo and had gotten out of the car. Kadee flicked her head, her eyes darting away from the others. Taking the hint, Vic followed her.

"Kadee? Are you alright?" Vic asked once they were alone.

"What is this place?" Kadee asked quickly, her eyes flicking to the entrance building with the enormous pictures of the tiger and tamarin bracketing the 'Wellington Zoo' name.

"Wellington Zoo," Vic replied, confused.

"Yes, you keep saying that, especially Alana," Kadee replied clearly frustrated. "But what's a zoo?"

Vic felt her jaw drop. Kadee didn't know what a zoo was? But when she thought about it, it made sense! Zoos were something special and there were countless zoos all around the world, not that people tended to go to them all that often. But in the future, in a world ruled by alien grasshoppers where humans had to fight just to survive hidden deep underground, a zoo would definitely not exist. Even the very concept of one would be even more alien than real aliens were.

"A zoo is a place where special animals, usually ones that aren't native to the country that the zoo is in, are kept so that people can see them and learn about them," Vic explained, trying to keep it simple for Kadee to understand.

"So, not animals that one would eat?" Kadee asked uncertainly.

Vic laughed. "No, that's a farm. We definitely do not eat animals in a zoo."

"What sorts of animals are here?" Kadee asked.

"Vic! Kadee! Let's go!" Tolan called, interrupting them.

"You'll probably get to see some of the animals as we're finding the Hopper devices," Vic said, leading Kadee back towards the others. "We won't have time today to look at them all but I promise that, after all this is over and we've driven the Hoppers away, we'll go to a zoo together so you can see them all properly."

"Thank you, Vic, I'd really like that," Kadee replied as they joined the clump of bodies all facing inwards.

"The tiger exhibit," Matt said, looking between the Padd in his hand and a map of the zoo that Alana held beside it. "It's got to be there."

"How the hell did the Hoppers hide their devices in a tiger enclosure?" Paul asked.

"The better question would be how are we going to get them *out* of the tiger enclosure?" Ray asked.

"Tigers are dangerous?" Kadee asked sotto voce.

"Very," Vic replied.

"Everyone!" Kaia called, getting their attention. "This is Gerald Ferguson, he's one of the Head Zookeepers here. He'll help us with whatever we need."

"Excellent!" Tolan exclaimed. "We need access to the tiger enclosure."

The ginger-haired man with the big, bushy beard visibly blanched before he managed to rein it in.

"Which one?" he asked. "We have two Sumatran Tigers, Senja and Bashii. They live in habitats beside each other."

Matt glanced down at his Padd, across at the map, looked up and shrugged. "No idea yet. We'll know when we get there."

The walk through the zoo, from the entrance to the tiger enclosure was surreal in a way for Vic. She'd been to a couple of zoos in her life and had loved them. The Wellington Zoo wasn't all that different and felt familiar in a lot of ways. But this time felt very much like the first time all over again. She held Kadee's hand to keep the girl moving instead of stopping to stare at every new thing.

The otters had been the first distraction. Kadee had slowed to nearly a crawl as she stared wide-eyed at the playful creatures cavorting about in the small man-made lake. But it was the monkeys that stopped her dead in her tracks. The marmoset and cotton-top tamarins seemed to especially be her favourites; Vic was sure that Kadee would have stayed there for the rest of the day if she hadn't tugged her along. It didn't help that the spider monkeys – while too far away to be seen, out on their own island down a different track – were in prime voice, singing and calling away, their voices echoing over the zoo. At first, Kadee had shied away from them, looking as though she was trying to find somewhere to hide. It was only after Vic had explained what they were that she seemed calmer.

Their arrival at the tiger enclosure didn't end the new and wonderous things for Kadee to experience either. For a start, she'd never seen a cat so big before – and it was being very cat-like, lazing as it was on a large rock, one paw dangling down, its muzzle resting on its other paw. But right next door were the sun bears and Kadee didn't seem to know which one to look at; her head kept swivelling from one to the other.

"It's definitely here," Matt said, drawing Vic's attention.

"Any guesses where?" Tolan asked.

Matt consulted the Padd, his head flicking up and down from it to the enclosure even as his fingers kept minutely adjusting the zoom on the screen.

"Um, would you believe the rock that the tiger's sleeping on?" he said.

"Of course it is," Ray muttered.

"Alana?" Vic asked.

"Yep, I can see them."

"Mister Ferguson, we're going to need to get into this enclosure," Sergeant Reid told the zookeeper. "How quickly can you have the tiger removed?"

"Are you certain that this needs to happen?" the man asked.

"I'm sorry, but yes," Kaia said, backing the request up.

"It'll take some time but I'll make it happen," the zookeeper sighed before striding off back down the path.

"Is there any other way we can do this?" Tolan asked. "This is going to take too long."

"Not safely," Vic replied.

"What about Paul just moving the tiger himself?" Matt suggested.

"Do you remember what it's like being lifted telekinetically without warning?" Ray asked. "Now, imagine what a hundred and fifty kilo enraged tiger would be like. Not something that I want to be around, even if it *is* on the other side of the bars to me. Or worse, suspended in the air above us as we work."

"Besides, we'll probably need Paul's ability to get inside the rock to find the devices," Alana pointed out.

"The Hoppers don't seem to be all that creative, do they?" Vic asked rhetorically. "Just like the ones in the tunnel back home. There'll probably be a secret, hollowed out space and a secret door."

"What about Kadee's illusions? Could that help? Could we use them to get us in so we can do our thing without the tiger realising that we're there?" Paul asked.

"No," Kadee replied flatly. "I make people see what I want them to see. They don't mask sound or smell. And we've never tested to see if they even work on animals."

"I guess there's nothing for it but to wait," Tolan sighed.

The wait felt like it took forever. To pass the time, the closest animals were visited and admired, but never for long; any excursion would always end with them back in front of the tiger enclosure within a few minutes.

Finally, Mister Ferguson and two other keepers entered the enclosure. They watched as they attempted to cajole the tiger down from his rock and back into the cage at the back of the enclosure. Of course, the great cat was enjoying the sun and wasn't happy about the idea. His paw flashed out a number of times, as if to bat them away. Interestingly enough, Vic noted that not once did she see any of the tiger's famous, razor-sharp claws. Maybe the tiger was simply putting up a token resistance?

Unfortunately, they weren't the only ones watching the unscheduled close encounter of the tiger kind. A largish crowd materialised, standing in groups to watch what was happening. Once the tiger had been safely caged away, the crowd started to disperse.

"Now what?" Matt asked. "There's a great big fence in between us and the rock."

"Paul, can you do your thing from here or do you need to be closer?" Tolan asked.

"I think I can get it from here, but I'll need Alana to guide me," he replied.

"Shouldn't we have someone in there checking the devices before we remove them?" Vic asked and instantly regretted it when an unexpected feeling like that of a bucket of cold water enveloped her.

"Good idea," Sergeant Reid nodded. "Paul, can you levitate Vic in there? Your ability to know what might happen will be useful and the more up close and personal you are, the better chance we'll have of not accidentally setting the things off ourselves. Kadee, we'll need you to cover us so no one notices what's going on."

"I can do that," Kadee replied.

A small *squeak* escaped Vic as she felt herself lifting from the ground. "A little warning next time, yes?" she called down.

"Quiet! I don't do sounds," Kadee reminded her.

On impulse, Vic spread her arms, imagining what it'd be like to fly and enjoying the sensation of the wind in her hair and rippling her clothes. All too soon, she was over the fence and down. Obeying Kadee, she kept her mouth shut, instead simply pointing directly at the middle of the rock.

"A little to your left," Alana called and Vic shifted her arm slightly. "That's it."

"Paul, you got it?" she heard Tolan asked.

"Yep. Vic, you'll want to stand back and out of the way!" Paul replied.

Instantly, Vic retreated around to the side of the big rock. Her nose twitched and wrinkled. She hadn't noticed it from the other side of the fence but in here, it *reeked* of cat. Tigers definitely had an odour to them.

Shrieeeek! Craaack!

The sound of the hidden door being forced open was *loud* and Vic winced – it was sure to bring people running to see what it was. The fact that her friends were also looking up and down the path told her that they thought it was quite likely as well.

"Don't waste time!" Sergeant Reid snapped.

That was her cue, Vic realised and she rushed back around the rock. The 'door' was laying on the ground just to the side of a roughly-hewn cave that had been carved out of the inside of the rock. It wasn't big or deep, simply large enough to stuff the two devices inside and to shut the rock door that had been reinforced with metal back into place.

The two devices – one a short, squat, cube-shape; the other a taller cylinder that ended in a dome on its top with a number of rods sticking out of the top of it – simply sat there benignly. She couldn't feel anything from them, no danger or sense that they had anything to worry about. To make sure, she thrust her arm inside and waved it around, being careful not to touch anything but her senses all remained the same.

"Okay, it's safe. Get me out of here," she called in a low voice.

Once again, she found herself flying, a sensation that lasted for far too short a time.

"It's safe to remove them," she reported.

"Paul, do your thing," Sergeant Reid said.

"What about the hole in the rock?" Alana asked. "Aren't people going to notice?"

"Not to mention the tigers?" Ray added.

"Nothing we can do about it," Tolan said with a shake of his head. "Besides, you know cats, they love exploring things, maybe they'll like their new cave."

CHAPTER 10

The water cascading down her body felt divine. Taking half a step forward and tilting her head back, she allowed it to flow over her face and through her hair. Sure, she'd already washed it, *three* times at that, but another wouldn't hurt. Yes, she finally felt clean, all of the dirt and sweat and grime finally washed away, but she could still be cleaner, she was sure of it.

It'd been days since she'd last had a proper shower; they'd been moving around far too often and far too quickly for any of them to take the time for proper showering. Deadlines were a bitch, she decided. Still, what was the point of saving humanity if one ended up not feeling human? Thus, showering *needed* to become more of a priority.

Bang bang bang.

"Vic, hurry up already, you've been in there for ages and some of us are still waiting our turn!" Alana's muffled voice came through the door.

For an instant, she was tempted to ignore it – maybe her head was under the water and she didn't hear? But that wasn't in her. Being selfless, putting others first, was too ingrained, too much a part of her.

With a sigh, she shut off the taps. The last of the water ran in rivulets down her back, stomach and legs and she watched it circling the drain.

Finally, she pulled the curtain across and stepped out, feeling a blast of cool air hit her and raising goosebumps all over her body. Quickly she snatched a clean towel from the pile and wrapped it around herself.

If it wasn't for knowing that Alana was probably standing on the other side of the door waiting for her, she'd take her time drying off and getting dressed. For that matter, if it wasn't for Alana, she'd still be *in* the shower, enjoying that nice, hot water some more. Grabbing up her clothes, Vic stepped across to the door that led to the hallway. A knock to let Alana know that the shower was free and she'd duck out the second door into the room on the other side.

But as she raised her fist, a thought struck her. Alana could *see through walls*. What's the bet that her best friend *already* knew that she was out of the shower? Had she been watching her shower? Possible, likely even. Alana *had* admitted, just once at least, that she'd taken a look at Paul using her advanced vision. Somehow, Vic suspected that she'd done it a *lot* more and not just with her boyfriend, either.

Deciding to test her theory, Vic neither knocked nor called out, instead simply leaving the bathroom through the other door.

She guessed that it had once been a bedroom, not any longer. Racks of shelving, piles of boxes, trolleys, coils of both rope and cord and drums piled high to the ceiling met her gaze. The storeroom wasn't the nicest or the cleanest place to be straight after showering but it was what it was.

The sound of water turning on in the bathroom confirmed her theory – Alana *had* been watching her shower and knew that she'd left the room. Well, Vic hoped that she'd enjoyed the show!

Dumping her clothes, she unwrapped the towel and began drying herself.

She was bent over, hair still damp, one leg extended as she towelled it dry, when the door unexpectedly burst open.

"Let me help you with that..." she heard Ray say.

Her head shot up to find him standing in the doorway, one hand still on the door handle, his jaw dropped. His big, rounded eyes met hers, for a moment at least, before they slid downwards.

"Ray!" she exclaimed, shooting upright and fumbling the towel into place to cover her exposed body.

"Sorry," he gulped.

Before she could say or do anything else, he backed away, closing the door behind him, although his eyes never once looked away.

"Great! That makes *two* people who've gotten a good eyeful today!" she muttered.

Really, there was no doubt in her mind that Ray hadn't seen nearly everything. Boobs definitely, possibly more. Before a third person could get a look, she quickly dressed, ignoring the damp parts of her body.

Vic came out into the corridor and looked right and left. Nothing. Completely empty. Not that she expected otherwise. Seeing it empty caused her to pause.

Was it worth it? she wondered. After all, confronting him about him walking in like that, what he saw, it could, no *would*, be an incredibly uncomfortable conversation to have. He'd seen her completely naked! Oh, sure, she'd been holding a towel. Around her leg!

Heat shot in flames from her chest, up her neck and across her cheeks. But this wasn't any sort of premonition flare. No, that was plain, unadulterated *embarrassment!*

But if just the thought of looking him in the eye was enough to have her blushing, then what would it be like to actually talk to him. Or work with him. She and Ray, along with everyone else, were on a mission. A very important mission with the fate of the world hanging in the balance. There was no room for error. No time for awkwardness. Or for *things* to develop. Not that she'd thought of him like that. No, definitely not. And especially not in the middle of the night.

Desperately, Vic pushed those thoughts aside, just as she had every other time that they'd tried to worm their way into her consciousness. There was a job to do.

Was it worth it? she asked herself again. *Yes, most definitely.* She and Ray had to put this thing behind them so that they could work together. Yes, it was going to be an embarrassing and awkward conversation, but it had to happen.

Decided, Vic turned and stalked up the corridor after her prey.

At the first door, she paused. Should she? A grin exploded on her face. Definitely. Payback was a bitch and if Alana wanted to go around looking through walls at people, people in showers, then she needed to learn what it was like to be looked at.

Without knocking or announcing her presence in any way, Vic slammed open the door to the bathroom.

"Ahhh! Vic! What the hell?" Alana screamed.

"Don't take too long," Vic grinned. "There are still others who haven't had their shower yet."

"Get! Out!" Alana screeched at her, her movements behind the frosted glass shower door alluding to the fact that she was desperately trying to cover bits that Vic couldn't actually see.

Laughing, Vic pulled the door closed behind her and resumed her search for Ray.

The corridor opened up into an enormous warehouse. Or what was now a warehouse. From what Sergeant Reid had said, this used to be something different, back when it had first been built but when the Bolivian – at least, that's where Vic *thought* they were – government had acquired the place, it'd been repurposed.

A simple glace around confirmed that Ray was nowhere in sight. He wasn't anywhere near the tables and chairs that had been set up near the kitchen area, nor could he be seen around the dozens of pallets of boxes and barrels that filled nearly a third of the place.

She'd thought that he might have been resting on one of the cots at the very back of the building but, on closer inspection, none of the three people lying there were any of her friends, just Captain Fuller and two of his co-pilots.

Movement on the opposite side of the warehouse caught her attention and, seeing Matt and Paul, she made a beeline for them.

"Hey, have either of you two seen Ray?" she called as she approached.

Of course, it being the two of them, she had to wait for an answer. They were deep into the middle of whatever game it was that they were playing, not that Vic could work it out.

They were standing on opposite sides of a great, circular table and pushing a small puck towards the centre where a dozen or so red and blue balls were grouped inside a circle drawn on the felt. Even though Vic had no idea of the rules, the fact that there were a lot less blue balls than red balls told her exactly who was winning.

She watched as Matt flicked his wrist, sending his puck skimming across the felt where it slammed into the opposite side, bounced back and hit a blue, ricocheted into a red which rebounded perfectly to knock the remaining blue balls out of the drawn circle.

"Guys?" she asked.

"Just a sec," Matt said, holding up a hand towards her. "Right, you know the rules."

Paul looked doubtfully at her, the floor, the roof then back at Matt. "Couldn't I just pay you when we get back to Australia?"

"Nup. I'm not waiting that long. And, since there aren't any here, you just have to do this instead!" Matt declared.

Vic watched, confused, as Paul sighed and shuffled back away from the table. Then, after looking doubtfully at her, he took a little run up and threw himself to the side. He landed on one hand even as both legs kicked off the ground. If they were supposed to swing up and over his body, then it was a miserable failure. She stared. Felt it coming and stuffed her hand over her mouth. That was supposed to be a ...? It was the worst one that she'd ever seen! She'd been able to do better when she was *four*!

"I told you, man, I can't do a cartwheel!" Paul complained from the crumpled heap that he'd fallen into.

"Have either of you two seen Ray?" Vic blurted, needing to get an answer and get away before she couldn't hold her laughter in any longer.

"That ... was ... gold!" Matt wheezed through his laughter, bent over as he was, both arms wrapped around his stomach. "Totally worth it!"

Paul refused to look up. He did, however, answer.

"I think I saw him heading towards the trucks."

"Thanks," she replied and hastily beat a retreat.

Four trucks and three jeeps were parked just inside the doors to the great warehouse. At first glance, she couldn't see Ray and she wondered whether he was, in fact, still there. A slight tingle on her left arm told her which way to go. Following her ability led her to the truck parked right up against the wall.

Her first guess, the back of the truck, was wrong – the bed being devoid of life. Her initial thought was the same with the cab. Something, though, made her pause.

"Ray," she said.

There was no response, nothing to say that she wasn't just talking to thin air. Her mind flitted back to that time weeks before when they were in the old, half-caved in shopping centre in the future when they were first discovering their powers. He'd been an expert at hide and seek then, too. And, unbeknownst to her at the time, she'd always found him, even when he was camouflaged. The difference now was that she knew what his power was. And hers.

"Come on, Ray," she tried again. "We need to talk."

Again, she waited, this time not so long.

"I'm not mad," she added.

She had barely blinked when Ray shimmered into being sitting in the driver's seat, his head down and staring at the wheel.

"Ray," she greeted, aware that her face and neck had instantly flared bright red with how hot they were feeling.

"I'm sorry," he said quietly, his eyes remaining fixed firmly on the steering wheel, his head lowered.

"It's okay," she replied, more automatically than really meaning it, although now that she thought about it, she did mean it. Mostly.

"I didn't realise that we were using it as a bedroom," Ray mumbled, racing through his words, making it hard for her to hear and understand. "Corporal Knox had asked me to help Private Dillan move some boxes. I had the wrong room."

She could see the tips of his ears were now a brilliant shade of red, just like the side of his face that she could see and his neck. It comforted her to know that she wasn't the only one embarrassed by his getting to see ... everything.

Vic sighed. An honest mistake. Not that she'd thought otherwise. Ray wasn't that type of guy. She *knew* that type of guy and actively tried to avoid them. No, Ray was sweet and kind and a lot more intelligent than anyone – including him – gave himself credit for. Ray's biggest flaw was simply how shy and introverted he was.

Impulsively, she pulled open the door to the truck, grinning at the 'yelp' he let out at the unexpectedness of it

"Shove over," she ordered.

She waited a moment for him to slide across the bench seat before she climbed in and shut the door behind her. At least this way they'd have some privacy. Once she was seated beside him, the feeling of awkwardness shot through the roof. She kept her head straight, barely even allowing herself to look at him out of the corner of her eye. From what she could tell, he was doing the same.

"Look," she sighed. "I know it was an accident."

"I'm *sorry*!"

The anguish in his voice nearly broke her and she realised that he was beating himself up over it. Vic felt her embarrassment fade somewhat and forced herself to shift on the seat so that she was partly facing him.

"Ray," she said.

"I'm so sorry. I didn't mean to walk in on you. I didn't mean to see ... you ... like that!"

"I know," she replied.

Still, he wouldn't look at her, which, while understandable was becoming frustrating. The whole point of her seeking him out and talking about this was so that they could get over it and be able to continue the mission.

"Ray. Ray! Look at me!" she said firmly.

He started and partly turned before turning back away. Vic frowned. Maybe it was time to shock the guy. Well, shock him again. Just in a different way.

"Ray! You've seen me starkers, I think you can look at me while I'm clothed," she told him. "Or am I that hideous to look at?"

"What? No!" he exclaimed, his head shooting up and around. "You've incredibly beautiful! Perfect."

And there was his blush back full force, combined with her own – not that she was going to think about that.

"Thank you," she replied. "Now, isn't it better that we be able to look at each other?"

His shrug was accompanied by his eyes dropping.

"Ray, we need to deal with this," she told him. "Yes, it happened. Yes, you saw what you did. But it was an accident. And there are a lot more important things going on right now."

"The Hoppers," he nodded.

"Exactly. Them. And what we're doing," she replied.

"What should we do about ..." he asked, his hand waving vaguely backwards and forwards between the two of them.

Vic cocked her head slightly, wondering what he meant. Was it simply what he'd seen or was it ... more than that? Well, they didn't exactly have time for the second, not with everything going on, especially being in such close quarters with everyone else and, honestly, she wasn't entirely sure what she wanted there, even if she was interested. Instead, she chose to interpret his meaning as simply the first option.

"We pretend that it never happened," she stated firmly.

"You want me to pretend that I never walked in on you and saw ...?" he asked.

"Exactly!" she said quickly, speaking over the top of his sentence. "It's for the best, Ray. We need to concentrate on the mission, on finding all of those devices. We can't let anything distract us. It's too important."

His shoulders slumped, his head dropped and she wondered ...

But before she could complete her thought, his head came up and firmly met hers. There was something there, something that she couldn't make out, as though he was trying to block something off from her. Whatever it was, she was willing to pretend that he'd succeeded.

"We can do that," he said. "For the mission. For the world."

"For Earth," she agreed.

Impulsively, she thrust her hand out towards him and he took it, shaking it firmly, just as firmly as Vic ignored the warm tingle in her palm.

CHAPTER 11

The hand shaking her shoulder barely registered. Nevertheless, she lifted a hand to swat it away.

"'Nother five minutes," she mumbled.

"Time to wake up, Vic. We're here."

The words were there but in her sleep-addled brain, they were easy to ignore.

"There's no use frowning, Victoria. It's time to wake up. We've got work to do."

That, or more precisely, that most hated of names, was enough to get her eyes to open. Exactly who'd used *that* name and who'd woken her had already moved away from her. Wise on their part. She looked to either side of her but no one was in their seat against the side of the Globemaster, in fact, everyone was up and moving about, gathering their gear.

They'd landed? Vic blinked. When did that happen? She didn't remember the thump and jerk of the wheels hitting the tarmac. And now that she was thinking about it, the feel of the great engines had also disappeared. Not only had they landed, but they'd already rolled to their parking spot and there'd been time for the engines to be shut down.

"We're here?" she asked, fumbling with her belt.

"I just told you that," Tolan shot over his shoulder.

Her eyes narrowed at his back. So, *he* was the one who'd dared to use *that* name! Retribution was in store for him. Later. Once she'd properly woken up.

"Where are we?" she asked.

"Boston," Sergeant Reid replied.

Vic frowned, searching her memory. "I thought that we were headed for New York?"

"We altered course," Matt replied. "I zoomed the Padd for a closer look and realised that we were wrong."

"Actually, Boston makes much more sense," Corporal Knox stated. "From here, the EMP would cover all the way to New York and beyond as well as cripple the three biggest cities in Canada: Ottawa, Montreal and Quebec City."

"Fair enough," Vic replied, not that she overly cared.

She knew that she should care more but, after days of hopping from city to city, they'd all started to blur together. It didn't help that they never got more than the briefest glimpse of each of them. Thinking back, the longest time that they'd spent on the ground had been seven hours and most of that had been at night. No, their entire focus had been on finding and recovering the devices, not what city they were in or what the range of them would be.

"Any clues as to exactly where we're going here?" Paul asked.

"Matt?" Tolan asked.

Obediently, Matt pulled the Padd out, switched it on and began manipulating both the map and the dials. He'd become the closest thing to an expert at it, unsurprising really, considering that Vic couldn't remember a time since they'd left that he'd let it out of his sight.

"Um, guys?" he said, looking up, his tone of voice stopping everyone in place and drawing all eyes onto him. "There are *two* readings in the city."

"You're sure?" Sergeant Reid asked.

"I'm sure," Matt replied, spinning the Padd around and holding it up so that everyone could see.

Sure enough, there were *two* pulsing purple dots on the map of the city.

"That doesn't make sense," Tolan stated. "Why would the Hoppers place two sets of EMP devices here? Does having multiple extend the range? Make it more effective?"

"An EMP would destroy any technology within its blast radius," Corporal Browning replied. "A second one wouldn't make it any more effective."

"What about range? Would two sets of devices going off at the same time double the range?" Ray asked.

"It's possible but I don't think it would make that much of a difference to matter," Corporal Browning shrugged.

"That doesn't explain why there are two readings," Paul said.

"Why there are two is irrelevant. There are two so we go after both," Sergeant Reid stated.

A cold shiver swept up Vic's spine before washing straight back down her body. Caution. Danger. She was sure of it.

"Tolan!" she said, grabbing his arm as he started to walk past. "Something's not right here. it's bad."

His eyes searched hers. Whatever he was looking for, he obviously found.

"I'll tell the others," he assured her. "Any guesses which one of the two?"

"No," she replied. "Not yet at least."

He gave a single nod, understanding that the moment that she had a better reading on the situation, that she'd let them all know.

Vic had one hand up, hanging onto the strap above her head where she was sitting and swaying in the back of the truck. Her eyes were closed as she tried to get a better understanding of what her premonition ability was telling her. Unfortunately, she wasn't getting much. The same sense of unease with an added side of caution and danger.

There'd been some debate about whether to split into two teams and tackle each 'target' simultaneously. Thankfully, before she could give voice to the stabbing pain in her stomach at the idea, Sergeant Reid had vetoed it and declared that they'd stick together and deal with the two spots one at a time.

With one of the purple dots being relatively close to the airport – just over the river and on the edge of the harbour – it was deemed the perfect first target. The other, located a suburb or two further in towards the centre of the city, would be tackled second.

Unfortunately, Vic's premonition ability wasn't giving her much in the way of whether that was the correct course of action.

"Vic? Anything?" Tolan asked.

"No," she replied, frustrated, looking at him sitting directly across from her.

And then they were there. The truck ground to a halt, swaying them forward in their seat. The engine shut off and, as they'd done countless times before, they were swinging into action, flowing from the back of the truck to the ground.

The area that they were in had obviously been abandoned years ago. Long tufts of grass and weed shot up amongst the broken concrete. The fences that remained standing were rusted and lopsided, parts of the chainmail either cut away or having been torn away from their support posts.

As for the building that they were standing in front of, it was dilapidated. Barely a single window remained intact. Graffiti covered nearly every inch of the walls, at least as high as people could reach. Looking up, Vic could see sheets of iron dangling over the side of the roof three stories up that looked ready to come down in the next storm.

"This is the place?" Sergeant Reid asked.

"Definitely," Matt confirmed.

"Alright, we don't know what we're going to encounter. Everyone be ready," Sergeant Reid stated, pulling his sidearm.

"Vic?" Tolan asked.

"I don't know," she replied. "There's something here though."

She wasn't sure what caused her to say that last part – there had been no escalation in her feelings or ability that she could pinpoint. Still, it was enough for Tolan to act. At his nod, Matt handed off the Padd to Kadee even as a bow and quiver appeared over his shoulder.

"Where the hell did that come from?" Corporal Knox exclaimed.

"Abilities, remember?" was Matt's grinning reply as he settled the bow into his hand and pulled an arrow.

"Alana?" Tolan asked.

"It looks clear," she replied. "I'm not seeing the EMP devices yet, though."

"They could be hidden in a basement or behind some material that Alana can't see through," Paul suggested.

A frown appeared on Sergeant Reid's face, a not uncommon sight when the seven of them took over the running of an operation using their abilities, subsequently ignoring the soldiers.

Private Dillan was the first to the door, rattling it as she tried to open it. "It's locked."

"Paul?" Tolan asked.

The piercing *screech* of metal tearing away from metal had Vic wincing. When next she looked up, it was to find that a panel beside the door had been twisted away, leaving a gap that they could easily walk through.

"You didn't want to just unlock the door?" Matt asked.

"Nah, where'd be the fun in that?" Paul grinned back.

One by one, with Tolan in the lead closely followed by Sergeant Reid, the group stepped through the hole that Paul had made. The inside wasn't much better than the outside. It was huge, not unlike a school auditorium. Most of the interior walls, what few of them there once were, had been pulled down and lay in crumped piles, the timber posts that once held them up scattered all around.

"Wait!" Vic called in response to the tingling in her left arm.

Her friends froze instantly; the soldiers taking another couple of steps before stopping.

There was something... Vic's eyes darted about, trying to find what it was. On her left, it had to be, but what? With all of the dirt and bits of rubbish, broken wood and metal and pieces of glass that littered the ground, it was impossible to make anything out.

Impulsively, she reached her hand out towards the left. Then, with eyes closed, she moved it about, higher, then lower, to one side then the other. As she did so, she concentrated on her feelings. The tingling remained the same, assuring her that there was something. A burst of cold, needle-like prickles over the palm of her hand had her freezing in place.

Her eyes snapped open. Her hand was positioned just a little lower than head height and very close to the doorframe. Keeping her eyes on that spot, she shuffled closer but frowned in the dim light. Using her other hand, she dug into her back pocket for her phone, fumbling her finger into place to open it. Then, as quickly as she could, she turned the torch on.

The bright white light lit up the flecks of dust in the air before hitting the dark wood. It was extremely tempting to reach out and brush the stray bits of wood and bugs away in an effort to find what had set the warning off in her premonition abilities but she knew how stupid an idea that would be.

A cockroach scuttling away from the light caught her eyes for a moment and she scrunched her nose at it. How many bugs and cockroaches and creepy crawlies were there in this place? Probably rats and mice, too. As long as there were no snakes, then she was sure that she could cope. Or, at least, fake it.

It was only after the cockroach had disappeared that Vic realised that not all of the bugs had run from the light. One had remained.

Her eyes widened. She'd seen something very like this before.

"Here!" she exclaimed, pointing exactly at it.

"That bug?" Paul asked.

"That's not a bug," Ray stated, "Vic and I've seen them before. *That's* a Hopper sensor. There'll probably be another five of them all around this door. If we'd opened it, we would have tripped the net."

"Good catch," Sergeant Reid nodded.

"See? Now aren't you glad that I didn't unpick the lock?" Paul asked smugly.

"What worries me is the fact that the door has a sensor net over it in the first place," Tolan stated, ignoring him. "None of the other places we've found the devices in have had them."

"The only time that we've encountered them ..." Matt said before whipping his bow up, swinging it around and pointing it at a random point every other second.

"When?" Sergeant Reid prompted.

"Twice before. Once in the future – that time was as part of a much larger sensor net surrounding a Hopper Camp. The other back home in the building where we found the *Scorpion*," Tolan replied.

"There are Hoppers here somewhere," Kadee stated, the certainty in her voice unmistakeable.

"Here?" Private Dillon asked nervously.

"No," Vic replied slowly. "Not here."

"Premonition?" Tolan asked.

"Only in that it's not going haywire with danger signals," she shrugged.

"Then I think we know what's at the other location on the Padd," Alana stated.

"Right, let's get our job done here and then decide the best course of action," Sergeant Reid declared, moving ahead once more.

"Wait!" Tolan called. "I think it'd be best if Vic was in the lead. She'll be able to warn us if we're about to trip any other sensors."

Sergeant Reid obviously didn't like the idea of letting a sixteen-year-old girl lead a dangerous mission, but that didn't stop him from allowing it.

Most of them were coughing and all of them had tears streaming from their eyes by the time that the last of the bricks had clattered to the concrete. Dust filled the air making visibility near-impossible.

"Can you do something about the dust?" Matt gasped.

"Dunno," Paul replied.

A breeze swirling around her legs startled Vic. They were not only inside the basement of an abandoned building but a dozen or so metres from the only entrance – it should have been impossible for any sort of wind to reach down there. Hand raised, she squinted out between her fingers. What she saw would have had her blinking, if the dust in the air hadn't already had that effect.

Instead of a massive cloud of white dust hanging over everything, the dust was twisting and swirling about itself in the air between them and the room beyond. She watched as it condensed into a loose ball about the size of a beachball before whipping past her, down the corridor and up the rickety staircase.

"Much better. Thanks," Matt said.

"I didn't know you could do that," Tolan commented, wiping his eyes.

"Me either," Paul admitted. "I just figured that, since I could move stuff with my mind and dust is stuff, even if it is really, really small, then I figured that I should be able to move it too."

Not all of the dust had been whisked away in Paul's ball, but the vast majority had, allowing a better look at the hole in the wall that he'd created. Where once there had been a brick wall, there was now almost nothing left. A few bricks here and there at the top and bottom and raggedy brick edges outlining the new 'door'.

"The Hoppers really didn't want anyone getting here without anyone knowing about it," Ray said, in reference to the additional two sensor nets that Vic had discovered on their trek through the building to find the EMP devices.

"Didn't help them much," Tolan replied.

"Only because we're us," Alana stated. "The devices are good, no damage done when Paul brought the wall down."

"Right, let's get them topside and loaded," Sergeant Reid stated.

A heavy ball settled in her stomach as Vic looked at him. "And then?" she asked.

"And then we go find these Hoppers," Sergeant Reid replied grimly. "They're too dangerous to leave here. There's no telling what they might do if they come and find that their tech has been stolen."

Vic swallowed hard. She was afraid he was going to say that.

CHAPTER 12

"I don't get it," Corporal Browning muttered.

"What don't you understand, Corporal?" Sergeant Reid asked, without shifting the binoculars in front of his eyes or looking away from the high rise building that they were currently staking out.

"These aliens, these Hoppers," Corporal Browning replied. "They're supposed to hate the dark, right. And the fact that we think they're in the penthouse of that great, big, glassed building would support that. So, then, why hide their devices in dark places? We've found them in basements, hidden rooms, tunnels and even inside caves!"

"That's because that, to Hoppers, dark places and places underground are places to avoid at all costs," Kadee explained. "If they had to force themselves to go there to hide the devices, then it makes sense in their minds that no one else would ever go there either, not unless they really had to or had no choice."

"But we're humans, not giant grasshopper aliens!" Private Dillan protested.

"We gave up trying to work out how Hopper minds work a long time ago," Matt replied.

"What's the plan?" Tolan asked, cutting into the conversation.

"I still haven't confirmed that there are even any Hoppers up there," Sergeant Reid groused.

Vic looked out again from the alleyway where they were hiding. Instantly, goosebumps formed on her arms and the hairs on the back of her neck rose.

"They're there," she stated.

"I need more than that!" Sergeant Reid snapped.

"Which you're not going to get!" Tolan insisted right back. "The Hoppers aren't going to just come out and say 'hi'! If Vic says that they're there, then believe it. You know what we can all do, it's time that you started trusting that we might know a thing or two and have some experience."

Vic watched as the binoculars that Sergeant Reid was using shifted fractionally. His head was fixed as though he was using them, but clearly wasn't; obviously he was deep in thought, making some tough decisions in his mind.

"You're right," Sergeant Reid finally admitted. "You seven have abilities that are incredibly useful. But using them to retrieve objects in abandoned, out of the way places is one thing. Seven teens going up again God knows how many aliens is a very different matter. But I'm willing to listen. What do *you* think we should do?"

The way Tolan took a half-step backwards almost had Vic laughing. For all his pushing that they were up to the job, being put on the spot and asked to form a plan had him backpedalling.

Or so she thought.

Tolan surprised more than just her when he took a deep breath and stepped forward again.

"Right," he said, running a hand through his hair. "Right. Thanks to Vic, we know that the Hoppers are in that building. It stands to reason that they're on the top floor, in the penthouse. It has the most windows, light and access to a terrace that they can fly from."

His eyes darted about, landing on each of them one by one before flicking back to certain individuals.

"Okay, here's the plan..." he began.

"We're in position," Matt announced, his voice sounding loud in Vic's ear.

"What's the view like from up there?" Tolan asked.

Automatically, Vic looked up, not that she could see the top of the building from the alley that most of the group was still loitering in.

"I've got a perfect view," Alana replied. *"I count five Hoppers from here, all in the penthouse, just like we thought."*

"Corporal Browning, do you have a shot?" Sergeant Reid asked.

"Negative. No clean shot from this position," the Corporal accompanying Matt and Alana replied.

"Matt?" Tolan asked.

"Not from here," he replied. *"They're all too deep in the house and there aren't any windows or doors open."*

"Okay, that was a long shot anyway," Tolan replied. "Keep an eye on things from up there. The rest of us, we're on!"

In ones and twos, the remaining team slipped out of the alley and sauntered up or down the street before finding a place to safely cross the unending stream of cars. As one would expect from a multi-storey building, the entrance was security locked. The only way in was with a key, unless you had someone buzz you in after you first contacted them through the intercom connected to each room. That wasn't a problem for them. The handle on the inside of the door simply turned, seemingly by itself.

The second that it clicked open, Sergeant Reid pulled the door wide and rushed through.

"You want to take the stairs?" Tolan asked incredulously, seeing the three soldiers making a beeline for the appropriately labelled door.

Sergeant Reid spun about, an eyebrow raised. "I don't particularly relish the idea of arriving at the penthouse in the elevator. The advantage would be completely with them."

"Yeah, I've seen enough movies and played enough computer games to know that," Tolan replied. "That's why we'll get out of the elevator two floors down and use the stairs from there."

"Unless you *prefer* to walk up sixteen flights of stairs and meet us there?" Paul asked.

It was a squeeze getting eight people into the elevator; somehow they managed it. Thankfully the ride up was uninterrupted and they were able to tumble out in short order.

"The stairs are over there," Private Dillan pointed out.

"Vic first," Tolan said quickly before any of the soldiers could take the lead.

She'd known it was coming, didn't mean that she had to like it. Yes, her premonition ability was going to come in extremely handy but that didn't mean that she was their *only* advance warning system.

"Alana, you got us?" she asked at the first turn once she was sure that everyone was in the stairwell.

"I see you," she confirmed. *"The Hoppers haven't moved. You're clear to proceed."*

Vic nodded, safe in the knowledge that Alana would see it, even from the roof of the building across the road.

"Matt, make sure you're ready," Tolan instructed. "If this all goes to hell, then you and that bow of yours might be our best bet of containing them."

"I'm ready," he confirmed.

After taking a deep breath, Vic allowed her sense of self to become more prevalent – her hands, arms, stomach, back, even the very hairs on the back of her neck. Finally, when she felt completely centred, she began the climb.

Each step was taken slowly and carefully. At the landing for the next level up, she paused, tested again and pushed on. At the next turn, she felt it. A sharp stabbing pain in her gut, her feet unexpectedly feeling cold and goosebumps running up and down her arms.

Caution! Danger! Her senses were screaming at her.

She looked up. The door to the penthouse level was right there, only six steps away. Sweat broke out on her forehead. Regardless, she took a single step up. The sense of danger intensified, exactly as she predicted.

Really? she thought, shaking her head.

She pulled her phone from her pocket and activated the torch. From this distance, the beam of light didn't do a lot but it did enough. Her eyes narrowed and she took another step forward.

A black speck near the door handle. Another directly above but just above the level of the top of the door. That was all she needed. The other four would be exactly where she expected them to be.

Turning, she waved her arms and shooed everyone back down. Once they were all safely one level down, she glanced back up to satisfy herself that they hadn't been seen or detected.

"Sensor net," she stated succinctly. "Covers the door."

"There's no way to pass that without tripping it," Ray stated.

"Anything I do will be *loud,*" Paul said. "They'll hear and come running."

"Then we'll need to do this the hard way," Sergeant Reid stated. "We're going to have to go in hard and fast. *We* go first, got it? If you *really* have to follow, make sure that you stay low and find some cover as quickly as you can."

He stared each of them in the eyes, only moving on to the next when he'd received an answering nod.

"Corporal Browning, Matt, be ready in case any of them try to escape by air," Sergeant Reid ordered.

"We're watching," Alana replied.

"Are there any explosives or something we should know about connected to the door or is it simply an alert system?" Sergeant Reid asked.

Vic hesitated for a fraction of a second to be sure of her answer. "No explosives, it just tells the Hoppers if someone comes through the door."

The three soldiers heading up the stairs, their guns raised, their faces set, caused Vic to flatten herself against the wall. Paul and Tolan went next, quickly followed by Ray.

"You remember what to do?" Vic asked Kadee as she stepped up to her level.

Her determined nod was answered in kind and the two ghosted up the steps as far as they could, crowding behind Ray and Tolan.

Sergeant Reid held up a fist; they froze, watching silently, ready.

Three fingers appeared.

Two.

One.

Vic glanced at Kadee the instant that the door handle was thrust down and the door pushed open. Kadee's eyes were closed – she was doing her part.

Cold shivers raced up and down Vic's arms; a sweat had broken out on her forehead.

"The Hoppers are moving towards you!" Alana announced in her ear, unnecessarily.

Finally, it was her turn to exit the stairwell.

Vic's head swivelled backwards and forwards. A short corridor, no cover at all. She darted left, away from the elevator and towards the opposite wall, as far from the door to the penthouse as possible, right behind Paul and Tolan.

Sergeant Reid and Corporal Knox had flattened themselves on either side of the door. Private Dillon, she saw, was hunkered down in the meagre cover the elevator doorframe offered. The only one missing was Ray, but that was expected.

Suddenly, the penthouse door was pulled open and Vic held her breath.

A Hopper. All seven-foot of it, grey-green skin with orange highlights on its shoulders and knees, stood there. One of its hands was grasping the doorframe as it cautiously stepped forward, its head swinging from side to side.

Feeling her panic rising, Vic thrust a hand over her mouth.

It took another step forward, a low scraping sound indicating where the larger two of its four antennae brushed the ceiling. One of its four legs appeared. Another. And between them, the shiny tip of that powerful, razor-sharp tail spike.

From beyond it, Vic saw Sergeant Reid raise his gun, its muzzle disappearing from sight behind the Hopper's head.

Boom!

The gunshot jerked the Hopper's head towards her and Vic felt something slimy and wet hit her cheek. Almost in slow motion, the Hopper crumpled, falling into the doorframe and crashing to the ground.

Almost automatically, Vic felt her hand rise and her fingers touch her cheek. Somehow, she managed to tear her eyes away from the dead alien to look at her fingers. They were covered in a sickly yellow-green ichor, and it took her mind a few moments to process what it was: Hopper blood.

A high-pitched *scritching* brought her mind back into focus. The Hoppers! There were four more still in that penthouse and they'd probably just witnessed one of their friends being killed.

"They're coming!" Alana screamed over the comms, causing almost everyone to wince.

For a second, Ray shimmered back into being.

Vrrt-boom!

The explosion rocked Vic backwards and she stumbled into Kadee standing behind her.

A flare of blue marked where Tolan was, pieces of what was left of the wall bouncing off his shield.

Multiple gunshots deafened her, echoing about the small corridor.

Vrrt-boom! Vrrt-boom! Vrrt-boom!

Vic hit the floor, her hands wrapping around her head as the wall that she'd been standing against only moments before exploded, showering her with detritus.

A scream rent the air. She prayed that it wasn't one of her friends.

More gunshots rang out, interspersed with indecipherable words and the sounds of the Hoppers *scritching*-talk and the much louder blasts from the Hopper weapons.

"Two down!" the voice was female but not Kadee. Private Dillan, Vic decided.

"Give me some cover, dammit!"

That had to be Sergeant Reid.

Pulling her arms away from her head, Vic looked up and around.

Massive holes littered the penthouse wall, their edges dark and smouldering. Pieces of plaster lay everywhere, including on her and ... the bodies lying in front of her.

"Tolan! Paul!" she screamed.

Please, please, please! she silently screamed in her mind. *Please don't be dead!*

"I'm ok," Tolan coughed. "It'd take a lot more than that to get through my shield."

"Then let's use it!" Paul yelled, telling Vic that he, too, was still alive.

"What? How?" Tolan asked.

"Sorry, man, but this is the only way. I need to see what I'm aiming at!" Paul said.

She watched him jump into a crouch and scuttle towards the closest hole in the wall. Unexpectedly, Tolan levitated half a metre off the ground; a yelp escaping him as he did so. Vic watched wide-eyed as Tolan's body drifted to fill the space where one of the holes was.

Vrrt-boom!

"Ahhh!" Tolan screamed even as his shield flared brighter than Vic had ever seen it and he shot backwards to slam into the wall behind him.

Paul, it seemed, had used the distraction to take a quick look through a different hole. He grinned as he spun back around, his back against the wall. Dozens of pieces of plaster and wood lifted, spun about and shot through the hole.

Hopper cries of pain were like music to Vic's ears. Hoppers were getting hurt and that gave her time to evaluate where she was and what was around her. And where she was was in the middle of a bloody warzone! How the hell she ended up there, she had no idea. Especially defenceless and weaponless.

A tattoo of gunshots *ripped* through the air and she looked around to see Sergeant Reid and Private Dillan, bodies low, ducking in through the door and disappearing.

An intense wave of fear gripped her. Her body screamed at her, hot and cold and spikes of pain shooting all through her back. Vic's eyes widened in terror.

Somehow, she got her feet under her and, slipping and sliding on the bits of plaster, lunged forward.

Vrrt-boom!

Vic collided with something that went "oof" and she bore them both to the ground, even as a beam of intense heat seared her back.

Booom!

The wall opposite exploded, showering her in shrapnel and sending a plume of white into the air.

She coughed and wiped her eyes enough to open them again.

“Ray?” she asked,

“Yeah,” he grunted. “Thanks. I was standing right in its path. If you hadn’t ...”

“I’m just glad you’re okay,” she replied.

“You can get off me now if you want,” he grinned at her.

“Ah, yeah, sorry,” Vic replied.

As she crawled off him – no way was she standing back up and potentially giving the Hoppers another chance to shoot her – she registered the sound of gunshots going off from inside the penthouse.

Something green laying on the ground, half buried by a large chunk of wall caught her eye and she froze.

“No. No no no no no,” she muttered.

She stared, trying to see if whoever it was was still alive. The slightest shift of plaster near their chest had her sighing in relief. Instantly, she was up on her hands and knees and moving towards them.

A feeling had her jerk backwards just as a *Vrrt-boom!* went off, a flash of intense poisonous green flashed before her eyes and the wall on the opposite side of the corridor exploded. The sound of gunfire intensifying signalled to her that it was safe to keep moving.

Reaching the downed soldier, Vic skidded around to the far side.

"Corporal Knox. Hold on, I'll get you out of here," she assured him.

His eyes were wide and it took him a lot of blinking before he could focus on her.

"Thanks," he gasped. "My arm, I think it's trapped. It's hurting like hell and my fingers are tingling."

"Okay," she replied, already pushing at the wood and plaster that he was buried in.

His legs were fairly easy to uncover but the piece on his chest was huge and heavy. Where was Paul when she needed him? She shook her head. That piece would have to wait. But he'd said his arm, hadn't he? His right, the one on the other side of him, she could see sticking out from under a piece of plaster and it looked like he was moving it okay, so she guessed that it must be his left that was trapped.

Quickly, she began digging at the detritus that was burying him closest to her. A flash of red caught her eye and she paused. Blood?

"Are you hurt?" she asked him.

"Chest is a little sore but otherwise I think I'm alright. Apart from my arm, of course," he replied, his words slurring together somewhat.

Maybe this wasn't such a good idea, moving this stuff? If he was hurt, then she could potentially make things worse. But that was more for a spine injury. At least she thought it was and she was leaving the big bit on his chest alone. No, all she was trying to do was to free his arm. At worst, if it was bleeding, she could make some kind of bandage or something to help?

Decided, she kept digging.

Shoving a piece of wood aside, she found his arm. Quickly, she moved another piece off his hand. That just left his shoulder.

"How are you going? I can't feel you doing anything," he asked.

Vic stared at him and then back at his hand. He couldn't feel her moving the stuff off him?

"Can you feel this?" she asked, clasping his hand.

"Feel what?" he slurred.

"Your hand," she replied.

"All I feel is it tingling. Feels like it's got pins and needles or something," he told her.

He couldn't feel that? That wasn't good. Panicking, Vic put her hands against the big piece of plasterboard and pushed with all of her strength. Her feet moved backwards and she was forced to scrabble about, trying to get better purchase. Suddenly, it gave, sliding straight across Corporal Knox's body and off onto the floor.

"Ahhh!" the soldier screamed, causing Vic to apologise over and over.

"I'm sorry, I'm sorry, I'm s..."

Her eyes widened and her throat contracted. Hurriedly, she spun about and threw up. What she'd just seen popped back into her mind and she threw up a second time and then a third. Finally, when her stomach had settled enough, she wiped her sleeve across her mouth, steeled herself and turned back around.

Corporal Knox lay there, still partly covered by wood and plaster, his uniform a muted green from the dust that had settled everywhere. He was still breathing, his chest rising and falling, even if it sounded a little ragged. There were a few cuts and scrapes on his legs and face. But it was his arm ...

Vic couldn't help it, she looked again.

Just below his left shoulder, his sleeve was black dotted with red. It was obvious that he'd taken a direct hit from one of the Hopper's weapons, for, beyond that blackened sleeve, was a gap showing only floor before the rest of his arm, sleeve and hand kept going.

The man's arm had been completely blown off!

Once again, Vic felt bile rise and she spun back around. Even as her stomach heaved, she couldn't help hearing him complaining about the pain in his arm and the tingles in his hand. Phantom pain, her brain supplied, whether helpfully or not was up for debate.

When next she turned around, it was to see Corporal Knox's eyes on her. He looked confused and worried.

"Just stay still, I'm going to get you some help," she reassured him.

She looked up and around and only then realised that the noise had stopped. No gunshots. No alien blasters firing. No Hopper *scritching*-talk. No voices at all.

"Guys?" she asked anxiously, getting to her feet and taking a step forwards.

"We're here," Ray said, appearing at the doorway to the penthouse.

"Is everyone okay?" she asked before viciously shaking her head. "Get someone! One of the soldiers! Call an ambulance! Something! Corporal Knox ..."

"Is he ...?" Ray asked, his eyes wide.

"He's alive," she replied grimly. "But Ray, please, just ... just get some help!"

She saw him dash off. That was good enough. Swallowing hard, ignoring the disgusting taste in her mouth, she turned back around. As bad as it was, as horrible, she couldn't leave him. She wouldn't. No one should be alone, not when...

Slowly, focussing on his face, she sunk to her knees.

“It’s okay,” she told him, forcing a smile. “Help’s on the way.”

CHAPTER 13

How long it took for the paramedics to arrive, Vic had no clue. All she was focused on was Corporal Knox, John, laying there on the floor, broken pieces of wall all around him and on him.

She kept talking to him the whole time. If anyone had asked her what she'd been saying, what they'd talked about, she doubted that she'd be able to answer. Mostly, she was constantly reassuring him that he was okay and that help was on the way.

At one point, she'd shifted a large piece of plaster and lay it back over John's arm and blackened shoulder. Surprisingly, there was very little blood; Vic assumed that the intense heat of the blast had almost instantly cauterized the wound. Still, it wasn't something that she wanted to keep looking at and she sure as hell didn't want John to see it and start panicking and hurt himself more or something.

When the elevator *dinged* and the doors opened to reveal the paramedics, she looked up in time to see them baulk. Their eyes were huge as they stared around at what was left of the corridor and the penthouse wall. Their training, though, kicked in quickly and they made a beeline for her and John.

"See, help's here, I told you it would be," she said. "Now, just hold on a second, I need to tell them about the pins and needles in your hand."

She didn't think a little, white lie would hurt; the fact that he attempted a smile for her told her that she'd done the right thing.

"My name's Laura, this is Tim. We're here to help. Are you hurt?" the female paramedic asked, her eyes raking Vic up and down.

"No, I'm fine," she replied dismissively. "But John ..."

"Don't worry, we'll take care of him," she was assured.

Vic frowned and deliberately stepped in front of the stretcher, halting it in its tracks. "There's something that you should know. About his injury."

That stopped them and had both of them focusing on her.

"Yes? Where is he hurt?" Tim asked.

"I don't know what you've been told about what happened here...?" she began, fishing for details.

"Only that there were reports of gunshots and explosions," Laura replied with a frown.

Internally, Vic shrugged. That was close enough to the truth as it didn't make any difference. It helped that, between the time of the end of the battle and now, Paul had moved the bodies of the Hoppers. Where to, she had no idea, nor did she care right at that moment.

"John was caught in one of the explosions," she said. "He had most of a wall on him when I got to him. I think his chest is hurt and his breathing isn't quite right."

"Is that the extent of his injuries?" Tim asked.

Vic took a deep breath. *Here goes nothing.*

"No. His arm. His left. It was blown off."

Both paramedics blanched and made to push past her but Vic held her place.

"He's not too bad," which *really* felt like the weirdest thing to say, all things considered. "He didn't lose much blood. The wound was cauterized in the blast. I put that piece of plaster over the top of it so that he wouldn't panic if he saw it. He doesn't realise what happed. He just keeps saying that his arm hurts and that his hand tingles."

"Not much blood?" Tim repeated incredulously.

"The wound was cauterized?" Laura repeated doubtfully.

Vic knew that they wouldn't believe her until they saw for themselves so she simply stepped aside and gestured for them to continue. Which they quickly did. She could hear their murmuring voices as they spoke with John and to each other but decided to leave them to it; she'd only be in the way if she followed.

"Vic? Are you there?"

She blinked and raised her hand to the earpiece; she'd forgotten that she even still had it.

"Alana?"

"Yeah," her best friend replied and Vic sighed, at hearing her voice, she hadn't realised how much she needed it. *"Looks like everything there is under control at the moment. Can you go into the penthouse? Tolan and Sergeant Reid need you."*

"Sure thing," she replied. "I'm on my way."

Getting into the penthouse required a lot of careful stepping. There was detritus from the battle everywhere and more than once she nearly slipped on something. The inside of the penthouse wasn't much better. A dining table was on its side, a pair of holes blown through it. A lounge chair was completely blackened. Pieces of glass and wood were all that remained of a picture that had once hung on the wall. Bullet holes littered walls, chairs, bookcases and the television.

She lifted her foot to walk inside and paused at the tingling feeling in her foot. Frowning, she looked down. A splatter of greenish ichor covered the ground right where she'd been about to step. Stretching her foot, she hopped over it. Now that she looked, she could see three other patches of the same grey-green Hopper blood scattered about the floor.

"Vic. Good. You're here. This way," Private Dillan said, appearing in a doorway further into the room. Then, "how's John?"

"Alive," Vic replied simply. "The paramedics are with him now."

"Good," Private Dillan nodded. "What happened to him … I just … I can't imagine it, what he's feeling."

"He doesn't know yet. About his arm," Vic said. "I thought it best to keep it from him."

Vic followed her down a corridor to a set of double doors, one of which Private Dillan opened for her. Vic paused in the doorway.

"I need to wait here," Private Dillan stated. "We're bound to have company any minute now and Sergeant Reid isn't fond of surprises."

Vic gave a single nod, stepped inside and closed the door behind her. She took one look at what once had been the master bedroom and blanched. If her stomach hadn't already been emptied so recently, she was sure that she'd be throwing up at the sight before her.

The giant, king-sized bed set in the very centre of the room was occupied. *By a pair of dead Hoppers!* Both were on their sides, one with its head towards her, dangling over the end of the bed; the other the right way up, three of its legs and an arm dragging on the floor.

What was even worse were the two others piled on top of each other off against the far wall. The head of the top Hopper was half-missing, one eye completely gone, its mandible hanging by a piece of tendon and copious amounts of grey-green ichor coating its head, antennae, shoulders and chest.

"That is ... that is," Vic managed, swallowing hard.

"Yeah. Gross," Paul agreed. "Try being the one who had to move them all in here."

"No thanks," Vic replied quickly. Then, "hang on! Isn't there supposed to be *five* Hoppers?"

"It's down there," Kadee said, pointing out the window and down towards the ground. "One tried to escape by flying off the terrace. Matt shot it. Made quite a big mess to the car that it landed on."

Vic's eyes bulged. There was a Hopper on the ground? Where everyone could see it?

"Don't worry," Kadee said, obviously reading her expression. "I've got it hidden."

"That's a problem for later," Sergeant Reid interrupted. "We've got bigger ones to deal with right now."

Vic shot him an incredulous look. If Kadee was using her illusion ability to mask a crushed car sporting a Hopper on its roof from this height and distance, then the strain on her would be enormous! Vic doubted that she could hold it for very long.

"Paul, take Kadee and get her down there," she ordered. "And get that Hopper somewhere hidden away."

“Excuse me ...” Sergeant Reid began, an intense frown on his face.

“Vic’s right,” Tolan agreed, speaking right over him. “Use the window. The elevator and stairwell are probably choked with people.”

Paul nodded, looked around and snatched up a blanket that was draped over a chair. A snap of his arms had the blanket laid out on the floor. A few seconds later, both he and Kadee were seated in the middle of it and it was lifting gently off the carpet, headed for the window.

Vic couldn’t help but share an amused grin with Tolan at the way Sergeant Reid’s jaw had dropped.

“The paramedics are with John now,” Vic said, regaining his attention. “He’s still alive. I think he’ll be alright.”

“Thank you for staying with him,” Sergeant Reid said quietly. “Knowing that you were with him made it easier for us take care of the clean-up.”

Vic nodded. “Alana said that you wanted me?”

“Yes,” Sergeant Reid replied. At his gesture, she followed him towards the door on one side of the room. “What do you make of this? Anything that we can use?”

Inside the room – what was once the walk-in robe, although where all the clothes were was currently a mystery – were four large machines. Three of them stood taller than she was, screens, buttons, switches and dials covering the face of the top third of them. The other was squatter, only half her height, with only a series of buttons and dials on the top of it.

“If you’re asking if I know what all of that is, then I don’t have a clue,” she replied.

“I was more thinking about your premonition ability,” Tolan interrupted. “What sort of ‘vibes’ you get from them.”

Vic nodded slowly as she considered it. What he said made sense. Her ability had drawn her to the cylinder that controlled the door to the *Scorpion* and it'd helped them work the scanner that they were using to find the EMP devices, even if it *was* in a very limited fashion.

"Guys, I'm seeing police making their way into the building," Alana said over the comms.

Vic glanced briefly at Tolan. If the cops were coming, then they had a very limited window of opportunity. She gave him a nod of understanding and turned back to the four machines.

The three big ones were against one wall, the other directly across from them. She decided to start with the big ones. Ever so slowly, she began side shuffling into the room, facing them. As she did so, she closed her eyes and held her hands out, close to but not touching the machines. Every sense that she had was focused inwards. Temperature, pain factors, if goosebumps formed, what the hairs on her arm and back of her neck were doing.

She jolted when her shoulder hit the far wall and her eyes snapped open.

Nothing?

She'd just walked past all three machines and felt absolutely nothing? In disbelief, she reversed, going back past the three big machines again. This time, though, she kept her eyes open and moved her hands about, making sure that they hovered over every switch, dial and button.

Vic shook her head when she got to the end. Once again, there'd been nothing. Whatever those three machines were or did, they neither posed a threat nor were useful in any way. They could have been three great, big lumps of rock for all that her senses picked up from them.

"I'm getting nothing from those three," she said as she spun about to give the smaller Hopper machine the once over.

This one, though, was *very* different. The second that she was facing it, even before she'd raised her hands to 'test' the buttons and dials, her entire arms and hands registered an intense cold. Goosebumps exploded all over her skin. The cold seeped into her stomach and chest, causing her to shiver uncontrollably. She stumbled, inadvertently edging even nearer to it. She gasped as what felt like red-hot knives stabbed into her hands, stomach and thighs.

"Vic!"

It was Ray's voice, laced with concern and horror. Hands grabbed her shoulders and yanked her backwards and away. Instantly, the cold evaporated and the knives vanished.

"What the hell is that thing?" she gasped.

"What happened?" Sergeant Reid demanded.

She shook her head, not sure how to describe it.

"I've never seen you react like that," Ray said and she realised that one of her hands was between his hands as he rubbed life back into her. "Your skin went blue and you were icy cold to the touch."

"It looked like you were in pain," Tolan added.

"I was," she replied. "Thank you."

"What is that thing?" Sergeant Reid demanded, repeating his question.

"I don't know," Vic replied, shaking her head. "But whatever it is, it's dangerous. Very, very dangerous. Destroy it! Don't let anyone near it or touch it!"

"We will," Tolan promised. "I know just what to do."

He lifted a finger to his ear. "Paul, as soon as you're done down there, we need you back up here."

"Understood," Paul replied.

A series of loud voices caught Vic's attention and she realised that she'd been hearing them for a couple of minutes. She looked at Ray with a frown and a cock of her head.

"Sir! We have a situation out here that requires your presence!" Private Dillan's voice shouted through the bedroom door.

"Damn. I'd hoped we'd have more time," Sergeant Reid muttered before focusing on the three of them. "Contact Captain Fuller, tell him to hurry that assist up. And make sure that *that* gets dealt with at all costs. If it's as dangerous as you say, then it needs to be taken care of ASAP."

"Sir!" Private Dillan's voice was starting to sound panicky.

Before any of them could respond, he was striding for the door and pulling it open. In the brief second that it was open before Sergeant Reid slammed it shut behind himself, Vic caught sight of four police officers crowding in the small hallway, Private Dillan stubbornly standing in their way.

"Either of you two know what assist Captain Fuller is supposed to send?" Ray asked.

Tolan shook his head. "Not a clue."

"Well, I don't have a phone, at least, not one that works in this country," Vic replied. "Not that I know what his number is anyway."

"Corporal Browning," Tolan said, touching the comm in his ear. "Are you able to contact Captain Fuller at all?"

"That's an affirmative. What do you need?"

"We have a message from Sergeant Reid," Tolan replied. "Tell him to 'hurry that assist up'. That's a direct quote."

"Acknowledged. Will pass the message on," the Corporal replied.

"Right, that's one thing taken care of; now the other," Tolan said, grimly turning back towards the walk-in robe.

"What's your plan for destroying that thing?" Vic asked.

"It looks pretty heavy but the three of us might be able to get it over to the window and drop it out. An eighteen-storey fall would definitely work," Ray suggested doubtfully.

"And crush how many people standing down there?" Vic asked incredulously.

"Hey, I didn't say it was a good plan, just that it would work," Ray defended himself.

"We're not dropping anything out the window," Tolan stated. "All we need is Paul. You there, buddy?"

"We're on our way back up," the guy in question replied.

Less than a minute later, during which time a lot of angry, raised voices could be heard being shouted back and forth from the other side of the bedroom door, Paul and Kadee floated back in the room on the blanket.

"What'd you need?" Paul asked as he got to his feet, the blanket now resting on the carpet.

"What'd you do with the Hopper down there?" Vic asked, cutting Tolan's response off.

"I kept it hidden so no one could see it until Paul could put it in a dumpster," Kadee replied.

Vic felt her jaw go slack and her eyes widen. "You put a seven-foot grasshopper alien in a dumpster?"

"Seemed appropriate," Paul shrugged. "You know, taking out the trash?"

Ray's laughter was both unexpected and contagious. "Good one!"

"That's one way to clean up the planet," Tolan agreed with a chuckle.

"Glad you approve," Paul grinned. "Now, what did you need me for up here?"

Tolan instantly sobered. "Vic did her thing with those machines in there. Most of them are harmless but there is one."

"It's bad, Paul," Vic supplied. "And I mean *bad*. Needs to be destroyed for the good of everyone bad."

"You want me to drop it out the window?" Paul asked

"See! It wasn't such a bad idea!" Ray exclaimed.

"No," Tolan replied to Paul, completely ignoring Ray. "I want you to crush it."

"Crush it?" Paul repeated, sounding as confused as Vic was.

"Yes. Force its sides inwards. Do it hard enough and whatever tech is inside the thing will be destroyed, useless."

"That's a good idea," Vic nodded, impressed.

"Sure, should be easy enough," Paul nodded. "Which one?"

"The smallest one by itself on the left," Vic stated.

Paul stepped up to the door to the walk-in robe and simply stared. A great, ear-piercing *shriek* of metal rent the air. The sides buckled inwards. A *pop* was followed by an intense crackling.

Boom!

Vic slammed her hands over her ears, the sound echoing through the room. Her nose crinkled at the acid smell even as smoke billowed out the doorway. Cautiously, she peered in. The squat machine was no more; instead a crumpled ball of slightly smoking metal sat where it once had been, the tiniest flickers of flame peeking out of the cracks at the top before dying down even as she watched.

"That'll do it," Tolan remarked flatly.

"Freeze! Nobody move!"

Vic spun. Two police officers were standing in the bedroom doorway, their weapons up, aimed straight at them. Directly behind them, she could see Sergeant Reid and Private Dillan holding guns to the officer's heads, while behind *them*, another two cops were in the process of pulling their guns to point at the Australian soldiers.

"Shit!" Paul summed up for everyone.

CHAPTER 14

"I said, freeze!"

The police officer – sergeant, Vic corrected, seeing the triple stripes on his sleeve – shifted his gun so that it was pointing directly at her. She froze, despite the fact that her pose, somewhere between the crouch that the imploding Hopper machine had forced her into and standing which she was in the process of doing, wasn't exactly comfortable. Freezing seemed the best decision; she didn't think that even her predictive abilities would be enough to evade a bullet fired from that small distance.

"Paul," Tolan said out of the corner of his mouth.

"No!" Vic countered, seeing the edge of the blanket begin to drift upwards.

Wrapping the two police officers in a blanket would not end well, every sense that she had screamed it.

"Freeze means no talking!" the police sergeant snapped. "Now, what the hell is going on here?"

"And what the hell are those things!" his partner demanded in a terrified-sounding, high-pitched voice.

“Damn,” Ray murmured and only because Vic was standing right beside him was she able to hear it.

“I think everyone needs to take a breath and calm down,” Sergeant Reid stated firmly.

“You do not give the orders here!” the police sergeant shot back. “You have no jurisdiction here. You’d know that if you’d been listening to anything that I’ve been saying for the past five minutes.”

Sergeant Reid’s eyes flicked to the five of them. “Was that sound what I thought it was?”

“It’s done,” Tolan replied, his words so fast they almost slurred together.

“Next person who talks when I haven’t asked them to, gets a bullet in their leg!” the police sergeant stated.

Clearly, he was out of patience and wanting answers. Which made complete sense. He and his partners had obviously responded to the sounds of gunfire and explosions coming from the penthouse. They would have arrived to see complete carnage, walls with massive holes in them, bits of wood and plaster and other detritus strewn about. The penthouse looked like a warzone, a fact only emphasised by John lying half buried with *his arm blown off*. And then, to make matters worse, the officers had been blocked by firstly, a lowly private from a foreign – albeit allied – nation, then by a stubborn Australian Army sergeant.

And all that had been before *another* explosion had gone off and he and his partner had burst into this room to find a bunch of teens standing beside four clearly dead aliens that looked like overgrown grasshoppers.

“Now. Let’s try this again,” the police sergeant said, his gun remaining unwaveringly pointed directly at Vic and her friends. “What the hell has been going on here? We’ll start easy. What the hell are *those*?

His gun flicked to the Hoppers on the bed before quickly reacquiring its original target.

The sound of an electric guitar playing, its volume getting louder each half second froze everyone. Every eye was drawn to Sergeant Reid, or more specifically, his pocket.

"What is that?" the police sergeant asked exasperatedly.

"That would be my phone," Sergeant Reid replied.

"Is that ...*Thunderstruck?"* Paul asked excitedly.

"Nice, Accadacca!" Tolan agreed.

"I have no idea what you just said," the junior-ranked police officer stated.

"Foreigner," Matt snorted derisively over the comms.

Vic rolled her eyes. *They* were the foreigners. And she'd seen enough YouTube videos to know that Americans had no clue when it came to simple Aussie slang.

"I'm going to holster my weapon," Sergeant Reid said as *Thunderstuck* continued playing from his pants' pocket. "We both are. And then I'm going to answer my phone."

The police sergeant spun about, his gun now focused on Sergeant Reid. "Don't move!"

Sergeant Reid, though, ignored him. Slowly, he took one hand off his gun while cocking his gun with his other hand and raising the gun's barrel so that it was pointed at the ceiling. Then, still in slow motion, he holstered his weapon with one hand while, with the other, he fished his phone out of his pocket. Behind him, Vic could see Private Dillan mirroring his actions, minus the phone part.

"Yes?" Sergeant Reid said, answering the phone and shutting off the music.

He listened for a moment, his eyes never once leaving the police sergeant's.

"Sir, the situation here has gone FUBAR. I have a police sergeant here, would you like to speak to him?" Sergeant Reid said into the phone. Then, "he'd like to talk to you."

"FUBAR?" Vic mouthed to Ray who simply grinned at her, his eyes twinkling with amusement and mouthed back that he'd explain later.

Meanwhile, the police sergeant, seemingly against his better judgement, took the phone and held it to his ear.

"This is Sergeant Michael Williams of the Boston Police Department."

Whoever or whatever he heard on the other end of the line had the sergeant's eyes widening more comically than anything that Vic had ever seen before. What made it even more bizarre was the way that he suddenly snapped to attention.

"Yes, Sir. Yes, Sir. Of course, Sir. Yes, Sir," were the only words that he said.

Finally, he handed the phone back to Sergeant Reid and took a deep breath. His eyes closed, opened and looked around, as though seeing the room and everyone in it for the first time. It was only then that he realised that he was still holding his gun pointed at a group of teenagers. Once again, his eyes widened and his arm dropped.

"It's alright, holster your weapons," he ordered his men.

"Sarge?" the officer in the room with him asked. "What was that?"

"That, Andrews, was the Pentagon," Sergeant Williams replied. "Seems that whatever this is, is so far above our paygrade that we shouldn't even be breathing the same air as these people."

The police officer, Andrews, looked incredulously at his partner then at the bodies of the four dead Hoppers, his eyebrows so high that they'd almost disappeared into his fringe.

"If you say so, Sarge," he said doubtfully.

"What do you need from us?" Sergeant Williams asked.

"Secure the entire floor," Sergeant Reid replied. "No one comes in without our permission. We'll get the sensitive objects cleared up and be out of your hair as quickly as possible."

Sergeant Williams nodded once, then with a gesture, he gathered his partner and the other two officers still in the corridor and strode from the room.

"The Pentagon?" Tolan asked once they were out of earshot.

"Yes, a General McKenzie. I believe that you 'met' him once when all this started?" Sergeant Daniels replied.

An image of an older man with grey hair, his mouth moving as though he was chewing a cigar popped into Vic's mind. He'd been the one to authorise the missile that was sent into space in the failed attempt to blow up the Hopper spaceship. They'd only seen him via a screen, but they knew who he was.

"Yeah, we did," Tolan replied. "I didn't know that he knew what we were doing here."

"He was a 'call only in the case of an emergency'," Sergeant Reid replied.

"Captain Fuller! That's who you ordered him to call!" Ray exclaimed, snapping his fingers and received an answering nod.

"Okay, we need to get this place cleaned up..." Sergeant Reid began before being interrupted by the sound of approaching footsteps.

His annoyed frown was perfectly understandable, especially after finally getting rid of the police and, assumedly, ensuring that no one was to enter the penthouse at all. After glancing at the Hopper bodies, he quick-stepped out into the hall to intercept whoever it was.

Quickly, Vic crossed the room and partially closed the door, hiding the room from view but still allowing them to hear who it was.

“Sergeant? My name is Tim Walters, I’m one of the paramedics that’s been working on your officer.”

“How is he?” Sergeant Reid asked quickly.

“We have him stabilized,” Tim replied. “We’re taking him to Massachusetts General Hospital. He’s going to need immediate surgery. Do you have someone who could accompany him?”

“Private!” Sergeant Reid bellowed but she was already running through the door.

“I heard, Sir,” she replied. “I’m going.”

“Thank you,” Sergeant Reid replied. “And Jo, look after him.”

“Goes without saying, Sir,” she replied.

Seconds later, the sound of footsteps retreated and Sergeant Reid re-entered the room.

“Now, as I was saying, we need to clean this room of any evidence that the Hoppers were here,” he said.

“Everything? Even their blood?” Kadee asked with a grimace.

He glanced at the bodies on the floor and the puddle of grey-green ichor that had formed under them.

“No. That’d take too long,” he replied, shaking his head. “The bodies and their tech; that should be enough.”

“I can move it all easily enough,” Paul said. “Where do you want me to put it?”

“If you can get it to the back of the truck, that’ll do for now,” Sergeant Reid replied. “We’ll transport it all back to the Cargomaster and then dump the lot over the middle of the ocean the next chance we get.”

“A much better idea than putting it in a dumpster,” Tolan grinned.

“Dumpster? Do I want to know?” Sergeant Reid asked before shaking his head. “You lot use those abilities of yours to get the job done. I’ll run interference with the police downstairs.”

Instantly, Tolan stepped up. “Vic, Ray, do a sweep over the rest of the penthouse. Paul, Kadee, let’s get everything piled from here to the elevator. Have we still got eyes on that dumpster? We’re going to need to retrieve that Hopper as well.”

“Matt’s down there, keeping watch,” Paul replied.

“Good,” Tolan replied, as he touched his earpiece. “Alana, Corporal Browning, we’re going to need the truck in the lowest carpark under this building.”

CHAPTER 15

The waiting was hard. Seconds felt like hours, minutes like days. As for hours, they seemed to stretch into centuries. Vic didn't know whether it was the place or the reason that they were there that was making the wait so difficult.

Massachusetts General Hospital was big, bigger than any hospital that Vic had ever been in, not that that number was all that impressive. By the time that they'd done what needed to be done and arrived at the hospital, hours had already passed. Then had come the miles half-run through the hospital finding the right wing, floor and department and, finally, this waiting room.

It'd been hours and still there was no news on John at all, whether he was even still alive was an unknown. The fact that no doctor or nurse had come to tell them otherwise, gave Vic hope. Still, it'd been hours, hours that he'd been in surgery.

Their one blessing had been that the waiting room was small and completely empty. It'd allowed them to find their own place to fall into chairs. Mostly, they sat together, filling up two rows of chairs facing each other. Sergeant Reid had disappeared to find answers, while Private Dillan, after telling them what little she knew, sat apart, her back against the wall closest to the door.

As time dragged on, Vic found herself slumping further and further in her chair, a combination of tiredness, adrenaline wearing off and worry mixing together and making her feel almost queasy in her stomach

"What are we doing?"

Vic lifted her head from where it was practically between her knees, her eyes finding Tolan. He, like the rest of them, was seated on one of the plastic seats in the waiting area. But unlike everyone else, his head was up and his back was straight.

"We're waiting for news on John," Matt replied, clearly confused at Tolan's non sequitur.

Tolan's head turned and Vic could see that his eyes were blazing and, now that she looked closer, she could see that the knuckles on both of his hands were white with how tightly they were gripping the arms of his chair.

"That's not what I meant and you know it!" Tolan snapped back.

Vic caught Alana's eye. Her answering shrug told her that she had just as much of an idea of what Tolan was on about as her.

"Sorry, man, I've got no idea what you mean," Matt replied.

"Perhaps if you told us what you're thinking?" Vic suggested cautiously.

"What are we doing here? We're wasting time! Time that we don't have!" he hissed.

Suddenly, he shot out of his chair and stalked down the row. The end wall brought him up short and he spun around. Every muscle in his body looked tense. Vic's eyes narrowed, assessing him. If she didn't know any better, she'd have said that he was getting ready to run or to come out of his corner swinging. Maybe he was.

Tolan's eyes searched out each of them, boring into their eyes and causing Vic to shudder.

"We're losing more and more time here!" Tolan stated forcefully. "You know we are. Most places, we're in and out within a couple of hours tops, the devices in hand. But not here!"

"Tol, everything's different here," Paul reminded him.

"John..." Alana added.

"I know! I know!" Tolan replied, his hands shooting up to run through his hair, pulling it and leaving it standing every which way. "That's my point!"

"I get it, man, I do, really, but we *need* to be here," Matt said. "John had his *arm blown off*! He's in surgery, been there for hours already. We can't leave until we know he's going to be alright."

"That's even assuming we'll be allowed to leave then," Tolan groused. "You heard that cop. He wanted us in a cell somewhere!"

"Detained for questioning, that's what he said, not in jail," Vic corrected.

"Like that makes a difference!" Tolan huffed. "It's time we don't have! When we started, we had fourteen days to scour the world to find and secure five hundred pairs of Hopper devices before the Swarm arrives to activate them and knock out Earth's defences. How many have we actually found? How many are still out there? You all know exactly how many days are left. Not enough! Especially if we're stuck here in a *hospital waiting room* of all places or in a police station!"

"We know Tolan," Matt replied, his voice harder, more annoyed. "But it is what it is."

"He's right," Ray said.

He'd spoken so quietly, that Vic almost missed it.

"Ray?" she asked. "What did you say?"

His head came up from where he was slumped in a chair across from her. He looked at her and Vic gasped. His eyes looked dead. He looked defeated, as though he'd given up.

"Tolan's right," he repeated. "We don't have the time to wait here. Not that it matters."

"Doesn't matter?" Vic repeated.

"What do you mean it doesn't matter?" Tolan snapped, taking an aggressive step forward. "The sooner we get back out there, the sooner we can complete the mission and save the world."

Ray's laugh was hollow.

"Save the world? Not likely. We've all seen what the future looks like," he said, shaking his head, a thumb cocked in Kadee's direction.

"We changed that future!" Paul reminded him. "We went to *space* to make sure that that future wouldn't happen."

"We didn't change a thing!" Ray shrugged. "The world is still poised to go to hell in a handbasket."

"Don't say that!" Kadee whimpered. "I can't. I can't live through that again. Here's so different, so good."

"We're making a difference, Ray, you know we are," Matt stated. "We're saving lives. We're collecting those devices and removing them so that Earth's armies and everyone can fight back with every weapon that we've got."

"It won't make a difference," Ray replied, shaking his head.

"It will if we *get back out there!*" Tolan stated, forcefully jabbing his finger towards the nearby window.

"Come on, Tolan, face it! You know that all we're doing is delaying the inevitable," Ray replied. "And only for the parts of the world that we manage to get to and remove the devices from before the Hoppers gets here. A Swarm of Hoppers! Thousands of aliens in who knows how many spaceships! Earth doesn't stand a chance."

Vic stared at him as he slumped further into his chair after his rant. His arms went slack, falling into his lap. His eyes were the only thing about him moving, flicking about, moving from one to another of them, as though gauging how they might respond to what he'd just said.

"The more of those devices we neutralise, the higher the chance we have," Tolan insisted. "And that means going now!"

"Plus, last time, in that other timeline, the world didn't have *us*! We're a pretty formidable team," Paul stated.

Vic listened to them but her eyes never once left Ray. For him to speak up like this ... it was so out of character for him. Yes, he'd been coming out of his shell, ever since they'd befriended him in the future but, in general, he was still the quietest of them all. And he *never* challenged anyone. Not like this, at least.

"Ray has a point," Vic said slowly.

"Vic?" Tolan said, rounding on her. "Don't tell me you're buying into this 'we don't have a chance' bullshit!"

Ray simply raised an eyebrow but otherwise remained silent. It seemed that, now that he'd said his piece, he was content to draw back into himself and simply wallow in his thoughts. Deeply depressing thoughts, at that.

"Vic?" Kadee asked.

Vic looked at her. The girl from a future-gone-to-hell. A future where a

Swarm of aliens ruled the planet. A world where humans had tried to fight back but had zero chance and were all but exterminated. A world where, if you wanted to live, you had to find the deepest, darkest hole and bury yourself out of the light where the Hoppers lived.

Yes, they'd bought the world more of a chance with their bringing back a warning from the future. They'd even enhanced that chance by stopping the worldwide EMP that would have taken out all advanced weaponry without a shot being fired. They were even buying the world a better chance by gathering up the devices that still lay hidden all over the world and waiting for the activation code as soon as the Swarm arrived.

And yes, Tolan was right. The longer they sat there, sitting on their hands doing nothing, the less chance that they had of getting to and finding all of the devices.

But really, how much chance did they have in the first place? Fourteen days to travel the globe and find over five hundred pairs of these devices? It was an impossible task from the beginning and they were simply fooling themselves if they thought that they had any chance of succeeding.

No, they didn't have the time that they needed.

An extra week or two and they *might* have succeeded. An extra month and it was a sure bet. Hell, if she was going to wish for more time, then why not an extra century or three to give the world a chance to catch up to the Hopper's superior technology?

"Vic?" Kadee prompted again, causing Vic to blink out of her dark thoughts to see Kadee and Alana sharing worried looks.

"Ray has a point," she repeated.

"He f'n doesn't!" Tolan snapped back. "We *are* making a difference. We are going to make sure that the world not only has a chance but can win!"

Vic sighed. This, she knew, was going to be a hard sell.

"We can't win," she replied, hating herself for saying the foul-tasting words.

"I've never seen a Hopper do this!" Paul argued as the row of chairs containing Ray, Kadee and Matt floated into the air.

"That's true," Vic shrugged, "but we're just seven teenagers. Telekinesis. Prediction. Accuracy. Sight. Illusions. Camouflage. And a personal force shield. *Against an alien race that can fly, has advanced laser guns, spaceships and who knows what other tech that we've never seen before!*"

"We're not alone," Matt stated, nodding at Private Dillan sitting over the corner keeping an eye on them even though she was doing her damnedest to pretend otherwise.

"Okay, let's say – just for the sake of argument – that we actually manage to find and remove all of the Hopper EMP devices before the Swarm arrives," she said. Before anyone could say anything, she held up her hand. "I'm not saying that we'll actually achieve that, I'm with Ray with this one, we simply don't have enough time. *But*, for the sake of argument, let's say that we do it."

"Okay," Tolan agreed suspiciously, his arms crossing over his chest.

"Right," she nodded. "No EMP devices means it's just us verses them. How will we win? How will we stop the Swarm from taking the planet?"

"We fight," Matt replied simply.

"We shoot them out of the sky before they can even land," Paul added.

Alana's frown told Vic that she was starting to see the same problem that Vic had just realised.

"We tried that, remember?" Alana said. "With that other Hopper spaceship. The US shot a missile into space. The Hoppers saw it coming and destroyed it before it even got close."

"Then we use jets to shoot them down when they come into the atmosphere," Tolan countered.

"Maybe that'll work, maybe it won't," Vic shrugged. "We don't know if Hopper atmospheric ships like the *Beetle* have shields."

"They do," Kadee nodded. "I've seen them."

"You have?" Matt asked, his eyebrows high. "I didn't think anyone had ever fought back before us?"

"It wasn't humans," Kadee laughed sarcastically. "It was a flock of birds. A *Beetle* flew right into the middle of them. I saw the shield flaring as it hit the birds."

"Right, that answers that question," Vic said. "Which means that, even if we had enough jets up there covering every inch of the planet at all times, it's still a crap shoot as to whether they could even make any difference."

Unexpectedly, Tolan slumped, barely missing the edge of a chair before slipping the rest of the way to the ground.

"We're outgunned," he said. "That Hopper, he told us that."

"What?" Vic blinked.

Tolan looked up at her and then around at all of them. "The Hopper that we captured. When we were interrogating it. Remember? The EMP devices. He said that they hadn't always used them, that they'd conquered other planets before that tech was invented and started being used."

"We are so screwed," Matt stated.

"I hadn't even thought that far ahead," Paul admitted. "I'd just been so focused on us finding all of those EMP devices to give us our edge back."

"We all were," Tolan said.

"Not all of us," Vic argued. "Ray knew. You've always known, haven't you? Just been too damn noble to burst our bubble!"

The sad smile that he gave her told her that she'd gotten it exactly right.

Sergeant Reid returned some time later. Where he'd been or what he'd found out, he never said. He had looked intently at the seven of them, as though there was something that he was picking up but he didn't come and ask, something that Vic was particularly thankful for – she wasn't in the mood for rehashing it right then and there were too many thoughts running through her mind to process without adding to it.

Her eyes followed him as he took a seat beside Private Dillan. Their mouths moved, almost too small of movements to be noticed, but she saw. She knew what was being said.

The door being pushed open had heads darting up like a group of meerkats, especially when it was followed by a pair of doctors, still in their surgical scrubs, paper hats on their heads and face masks dangling from their neck.

The scramble to get across the room caused a minor traffic jam between the seats but it was quickly sorted, made even easier by Matt jumping onto and then stepping over the back of the chairs.

"How's John?" Sergeant Reid asked, having stationed himself front and centre, leaving everyone else to gather to either side of him.

"Corporal Knox is a fighter," the surgeon stated with a ghost of a smile. "The surgery was long and difficult. Apart from the most obvious wound, his arm, which required hours of surgery alone, he also had significant abdominal trauma."

"He was behind a wall when it exploded," Sergeant Reid supplied.

The surgeon nodded. "We were able to repair all of the damage. He's currently in recovery. It will be a long process but he will be okay."

"How long will he be here?" Sergeant Reid asked.

The surgeon shook his head. "I wouldn't want to move him for at least two days and even then, it would be best if it was only within wards within the hospital. If you're asking when he'll be able to travel home to Australia, it could be weeks, possibly months. We'll know more in the next forty-eight to seventy-two hours."

"We understand," Sergeant Reid nodded grimly. "Thank you for all you've done for him."

"Just doing my job," he replied. "I suggest you go home or, at least, to wherever it is that you're staying. Corporal Knox won't wake until tomorrow at the earliest."

Then, after a final nod, the doctors headed back the way that they'd come, a multitude of 'thank yous' following them.

"Right, you heard the doctor, there's nothing more that we can do for John here," Sergeant Reid stated. "I've spoken to the Australian Embassy; they're sending some people, including someone from the Army to be here for John when he wakes. It's time for us to get back to the Cargomaster and plan our next move."

Obediently, the seven of them followed the two soldiers but Vic could see that everyone was feeling exactly as she was and questioning exactly what the point of doing that was.

CHAPTER 16

The Cargomaster took off. They flew, following the predetermined course. They landed, disembarked and used the Hopper Padd to find the next set of EMP devices. Traps were dismantled, secret doors revealed. Cargo was loaded and they moved on. And repeat.

Through it all, little was said. Their normal banter was muted, subdued. Those that could, slept. Those that couldn't, stared into nothingness, trapped within their own thoughts.

They were a man down; Corporal Knox having been left behind and there being no time or opportunity to find a replacement and bring them up to speed. They managed.

"Captain Fuller, we're strapped in and ready, take us up and to cruising altitude," Sergeant Reid ordered even as he himself was still strapping in.

Vic noted the words but otherwise didn't react to them. She didn't even look at him, nor notice the looks that the sergeant was sharing with Corporal Browning and Private Dillan. A nudge on her shoulder had her looking around with a frown. But it was only Kadee, looking at her and tapping her headset.

Vic blinked. Right. Headset. She'd forgotten. After glancing down to ensure that she was belted in correctly – she was, something that had started as needing her full attention to ensure that the clasps to the shoulder straps were buckled into the correct spot, was now second nature and needed no thought at all – she plucked her headset from its hook and placed it on her head.

"Right. Now that everyone can hear me," Sergeant Reid said, sounding annoyed, not that Vic could bring herself to care, *"as soon as Captain Fuller announces that we're at cruising altitude and that it's safe to unbuckle and move around, I want to see everyone in the conference room."*

Vic blinked. A meeting mid-flight? They'd had a couple since they'd first started but they were rare. Those other times had been because they'd taken care of a continent and had needed to plan out their next path. But this one was different, not least because they had not long started this section.

For a second, Vic forgot where they were and where they'd just been. Spain. Majorca. They were still in Europe, not long started in fact. There were still a lot of devices to find and remove.

Her eye was drawn to the rows and rows of alien devices lined up along one side of the Cargomaster. There were what? A hundred already? Something like that. It helped that the Boeing was fast and they could usually get to their next destination within a couple of hours tops and, most often were in and out in an hour. What helped even more was the fact that countries were coordinating around the world based on the data that they were sending ahead, finding the devices, transporting them to hubs and making it a simple matter of them flying in, loading up a dozen or so and flying out again.

Stockpiling all of the devices in the one place may not have been the smartest idea but, at the very least, it got them out and away from countries where they could do so much harm.

"This is Captain Fuller. We have reached altitude; it is safe move around

the plane."

"You heard the man," Sergeant Reid said. *"Meet me in the conference room in five."*

She was obedient, even if she had no clue why there were being summoned there or what use it could be. Vic was very aware that they were simply continuing with the mission because there was no better alternative. They were doomed to failure. They didn't have enough time and they all knew it. Her eyes met those of her friends as they unstrapped and made their way forward; every single pair looked dead inside, completely defeated.

A jolt of turbulence had her grasping the handle of the spiral staircase at the front of the great, cavernous cargo space. She held on tightly, waiting for it to settle. Finally, the plane steadied and she was able to keep climbing.

As expected, she was the last one in; closing the door behind her shut out most of the sound of the engines, giving her ears a reprieve.

The room itself wasn't large as one would expect on an aircraft where space was premium and vehicles, troops, food and supplies, even entire helicopters needed to fit. The best that could be said about the conference room was that it was functional.

A single metal table, large enough for four to sit around on each side filled the middle of the room. The centre of the table was currently in place but she knew that, at the touch of a button, a section would depress slightly and slide away to allow a set of monitors to rise out of the floor for everyone to look at. More monitors lined one wall, while opposite it, a large glass window overlooked the cargo bay.

Vic settled into place between Ray and Kadee, with Matt filling out the last spot on one side of the table. Around the corner from Matt were Paul and Alana, while opposite the couple, adjacent to Ray, was Tolan. Sergeant Reid stood staring at them from opposite Vic; the last two members of their team being seated to either side of him.

Vic waited, watching Sergeant Reid as he glared at each of them, the silence stretching out longer and longer. She felt more than heard her friends starting to shuffle awkwardly in their seats. She glanced to either side of her, trying to gauge if one of them would say something but either no one knew what to say or simply didn't want to.

"Right," Sergeant Reid finally spoke. "I want to know what's going on!"

Again, Vic glanced to either side, waiting, hoping.

"What do you mean?" Tolan finally replied.

"Something happened in Boston," Sergeant Reid stated. "Something that has the lot of you rattled. Yes, you're doing your jobs but you're not focussed. And unfocussed means sloppy. Sloppy equals someone doing something stupid and people getting hurt. Or worse."

"The Hoppers in the penthouse..." Alana tried.

"No. Don't give me that BS," Sergeant Reid cut her off firmly. "I've read the reports, I've seen you in action myself. Every one of you is capable of handling something like that. You're better than this. Try again."

"Corporal Knox..." Vic tried but she knew even before she'd opened her mouth that that excuse wouldn't work either.

"No. Try again," Sergeant Reid replied, a sharp edge to his voice even though it was obvious that he was trying to remain calm.

Vic sighed. She knew what the problem was. They all did. But repeating it out loud again? They'd agreed without any of them saying it that it wasn't to be discussed. Thought about, sure, there was no getting around that, but not spoken, not aloud.

Ray, though, decided to ignore that message.

"We had a ... talk. At the hospital. About what we're doing and where it's leading," he said.

The glance that Sergeant Reid and Private Dillan shared confirmed for Vic that they'd already spoken about it, that she'd filled him in on the entire discussion. Why he was going through this charade to get them to tell him when he already knew, she didn't know. Or perhaps simply didn't want to admit.

"You know the mission briefing as well as I do," Sergeant Reid stated. "'To find all of the alien technological devices that can cause an EMP and to remove them from those places.'"

He stared at them, obviously waiting to see what else any of them would volunteer. None of them did.

Finally, he sighed, pulled out his chair and sat. "Tell me what the problem is with the mission."

From the corner of her eye, she saw Ray drop his head and *knew* that he wouldn't volunteer any other answers. A pressure formed in her gut. It wasn't hot or cold or painful, it simply was. And more than anything, what it was doing was pushing at her. Pushing at her to speak. She resisted it as long as she could. But she knew better than to go against her ability.

Locking her eyes on Sergeant Reid's so that she didn't have see the looks of betrayal or hurt or depression in her friend's eyes, she let it out.

"The mission itself is good. But it's not going to work."

"Why not?" he asked, not that he needed to, she wasn't done, simply taking a breath.

"For one, we don't have enough *time* to get the job done," she continued. "Yes, we're finding and collecting these devices faster than any of us thought possible. Especially now that the world governments are starting to work together enough to get some of the job done ahead of us. But we only started with fourteen days. It was never going to be possible to find them all in time."

"You don't think that we didn't know that before we started?" Sergeant Reid smiled wryly. "Contrary to popular opinion, 'army intelligence' isn't always an oxymoron. We knew the odds. And we accepted them."

"What's the *real* mission here then?" Tolan asked and Vic could hear the suspicion in his voice.

"Same as it's always been. To give the world a chance," Sergeant Reid assured him. "Our job was to find and remove as many of those devices as we could. The more we found the better. Yes, the ones that we couldn't find would be activated and those parts of the world would go dark. But they could be rebuilt! Once we won the war, the planet, the countries that still had working tech could go in and help the ones that suffered."

Shocked silence prevailed as the seven of them stared between each other and then at Sergeant Reid.

"Not a bad plan," Ray admitted. "Just one thing. It won't work."

Sergeant Reid spread his arm, his palms up. "Why?"

"Because even if we found every single one of those things, even if every single army, navy and air force was fully prepared, even if every world government worked together, it still wouldn't be enough," Ray told him flatly.

"I think you're underestimating what the armies of Earth are capable of," Sergeant Reid replied.

"And *you're* underestimating what the Hoppers are capable of," Tolan shot back. "Spaceships with shields. Big-ass ray guns. Tech we can't duplicate or imagine. And they can fly, well short distances anyway."

"You weren't there," Paul added. "Not when we discovered that Hopper ship sitting there in orbit. The US fired one of its most powerful weapons at the thing. And. It. Didn't. Do. Squat! The Hoppers blew it out of the sky without even blinking."

"Maybe you're right," Sergeant Reid allowed. "But maybe you're wrong. This isn't that other timeline that you saw. The world doesn't have to end up like the one you went to in the future. The future's not written, isn't that what you told the brass back home? You've already made a difference just by bringing us back a warning of what's to come. We will keep fighting. We will not stop. And maybe, just maybe, we'll surprise you."

Matt gave a derisive laugh. "Fight all you want. They're decades, centuries ahead of us. Yes, we bought the world some time, but nowhere near enough to matter."

Slowly, Vic's head turned towards him. There was something there. Something *important*. She could feel it. Sense it. And it was something that she'd 'tasted' before. Not that long ago, either.

"I don't care if they are," Sergeant Reid replied. "They haven't faced us before. We might surprise them."

"They've studied us for God knows how long. We won't surprise them," Tolan replied sarcastically.

"We have something that they don't know about," Private Dillan said quietly but intently.

"What's that?" Alana asked.

"You," she replied simply.

"Us? We're not exactly much. Seven teenagers. Big deal," Tolan dismissed with a wave of his hand.

"No! It *is* a big deal. All of you are," she argued. "You can do stuff that we've only ever imagined in comics and movies! *You* can move things with *your mind*! *You* can blend into the background and disappear. *You* can create illusions, make people see or not see thing. Do you get my point? You are all incredibly special with a whole bunch of abilities!"

"She's right," Sergeant Reid said. "I've seen the seven of you do things that my soldiers can't. And you have dealt with it better than a lot of cadets that I've seen, despite being younger. *That* is an advantage that they don't know we have!"

"Maybe," Tolan allowed, still not sounding convinced.

"You've travelled through time! Twice, even! Anyone who can do that when they want is unstoppable," Private Dillan continued.

Vic froze. Her eyes were wide. She'd even stopped breathing. The only part of her that continued was her heart, and that felt like it was about to pound straight out of her chest. Everything in her was screaming at her.

Here!

Here!

Here!

Here was the answer! This was it! What they'd been looking for!

It wasn't completely formed, Vic knew that, but it was so tantalisingly close.

Her eyes were still unfocused when she shot to her feet. Her chair was sent flying behind her, not that she noticed.

"Vic?"

She heard Alana's voice but dismissed it; it was unimportant. All that mattered was capturing that thought, that answer.

Allowing herself to be guided by her instincts, she turned about, away from everyone. And found herself staring right at the big window that looked over the cargo bay. Unconsciously, she walked forward until her nose was all but pressed up against the glass.

"Vic?"

There were multiple voices this time that needed to be ignored, a slightly harder task, causing her to frown.

To distract herself from them, she looked down into the cargo section of the plane. There were the trucks and bikes. There was where they normally sat. And, filling a massive section of the bay, were the hundred or so alien devices. Each were identical, pairs of devices exactly like the ones that they'd first seen in the future, the pair that brought them back to their own time. And, mixed in there somewhere, was the pair that took them to the future in the first place.

A flash caught the corner of her eye and she shifted her head. There it was again. Outside the plane, visible through a window. Lightning. A storm. They were flying near a storm. Another flash lit up the window and, a second later, a further burst of lightning could be seen, streaking across the sky.

Lightning.

Future.

Past.

Those Hopper devices.

They weren't designed to do it, but, under the right conditions, a malfunction could be induced to turn a pair of powerful alien EMP devices into something that would take someone out of their timeline and off to somewhere, some*when* new.

"Time travel," she said, wondering at the answer even if she wasn't sure *exactly* how it could be used.

"Vic?"

"What'd you say?"

She turned back to her friends, taking a moment to look at each of them in turn. Yes, Private Dillan was right. The Hoppers didn't know about them. The Hoppers didn't know what they could do or what they knew. They'd never faced anyone like them before. They might still be young, but that didn't mean that they couldn't cause an alien Swarm of spaceships some trouble.

"Time travel," she repeated.

"What are you talking about?" Ray asked, concern lacing his voice.

She smiled at him. "Time travel!"

"You keep saying that," Matt pointed out. "Care to elaborate?"

Vic frowned at him. She had the answer, even if she didn't know how they were to use it. She'd done her part; it was time for them to do theirs. She just had to motivate them.

"Time travel!" she insisted, this time emphasising the answer by pointing out the window at the cargo bay and the Hopper devices.

"Sweetie, we're going to need a little more than that," Alana told her gently.

"Time travel!" she repeated, harder this time, more urgent.

"This isn't Vic," Tolan stated, then carried on over the top of the scoffing. "Well, it *is* Vic. Sort of. You know her. We've seen this before. It's her premonition ability. She's got something. At least, almost. We just need to put it together. Time travel. And I think she's pointing at the EMP devices."

"Isn't that what I already said?" Private Dillan said. "You lot have travelled through time, more than once. You brought us the warning of what's coming. If you can do that ..."

"But we can't travel through time, not whenever we want," Paul argued.

"Both times were accidents," Matt added.

"Time travel!" Vic insisted.

Suddenly, Ray was up and standing beside her, both his hands resting on her shoulders as he looked intently into her eyes.

"Time travel?" he asked and she nodded eagerly. "The devices?"

He kept staring into her eyes and she willed him to understand to get the missing piece that she couldn't find.

"We went through time, forwards and backwards, because of the devices malfunctioning," Ray said slowly. "And we know how it happened because we *saw* it happen. That second time, at least."

"How does that help?" Tolan asked.

"We know how to time travel," Ray gasped.

Vic smiled wider than she ever had before even as all of the tension in her body that she didn't know that she was holding instantly melted away. If Ray hadn't been there to catch her, she was sure that she would have collapsed to the ground. She allowed him to help her back to her seat and she gave him a grateful smile.

"We know how to time travel," Ray repeated, this time louder, more clearly as he looked around the table.

"I guess we could work out how to recreate the malfunction if we had to," Tolan allowed doubtfully. "But why would we want to? What good would that do?"

"Yeah," Matt agreed. "We'd only be jumping forward to see what happened or backwards to a time when Earth would be even *further* behind in tech than the Hoppers."

"That's true," Ray allowed. "If *we* were the ones jumping through time."

"'We'? You got someone else in mind?" Tolan asked.

Ray glanced at Vic before simply grinning at everyone else.

CHAPTER 17

There was an energy in the air. An excitement. No, Vic decided, that wasn't quite the right word. Expectancy? Better but still not right. Potential? Purpose? Yes, purpose, that fit. Purpose and direction.

Everyone felt it.

Matt and Paul were joking, laughing and smiling and playfully shoving each other even as they all-but jogged across the cargo section of the plane. Alana was almost skipping, a smile on her face, her eyes alight as she watched her boyfriend. Tolan and Ray were happily poring over the largest map that Vic had ever seen, deep in conversation about timelines and tactics up in the conference room. Even Kadee seemed more buoyant, as though a weight had been lifted from her shoulders.

After a day of misery and the darkest of thoughts circulating, never stopping, where everyone was sullen and quiet and staying firmly ensconced within themselves, this felt like a brand-new day. It was akin to the difference between the blackest of night and the first rays of the sun peeking over the horizon.

Vic couldn't help herself, she laughed and revelled at the sound of it echoing about the plane, even above the sound of the engines roaring as they raced across the sky.

"You okay?" Alana asked, her eyes twinkling as she looked at her.

"Yep," Vic replied and stepped closer as they walked so that she could link arms with her best friend.

"This is going to work, isn't it?" Alana asked, sounding positive of what the answer would be.

"No idea!" Vic replied, happy despite the answer she gave.

"It'll work," Kadee stated with a nod.

"How can you be sure?" Alana asked, leaning forward to see past Vic.

"It's obvious, isn't it?" Kadee replied. "Just look at Vic. Have you ever seen her like this? This confident? Her ability wouldn't allow her to feel this way if it had no chance of working."

"Right, how do we do this?" Paul asked, interrupting their conversation.

"Well, somehow, I don't think trial and error is going to cut it," Matt replied sarcastically. "Not unless we want to go for another trip again. Or blow ourselves out of the sky."

Vic frowned, considering the two different pieces of alien machinery that they were standing in front of. One was big and cylindrical; its bottom half, the section under a slightly raised 'belt' was a solid piece of deep orange metal, while its top half rose high into a dome filled with irregular pieces of metal of all lengths, angles and distances from each other. The second piece of Hopper technology was simply a great, big cubic hunk of metal filled with switches and dials.

And there were rows and rows of the two different devices, all identical to the ones that they were standing in front of.

"Let's start with what we remember," Vic suggested. "*Without* touching anything."

"They were powered on," Matt began.

"But we didn't turn them on, remember? There was that live wire hanging down that touched them to get them working," Alana added.

"Right. Thanks to Paul's 'turning off the lights'," Vic grinned and quickly held up a hand to stop his spluttering protest. "Hey, no complaints here; it got us home."

"The question is, did that jolt of electricity just jumpstart them or did it provide a little 'extra' juice to kickstart what was needed for the time jump?" Matt asked.

"I don't remember seeing any wires anywhere in the tunnel when we retrieved the devices that sent you forward to my time," Kadee pointed out.

"You're right," Vic nodded. "So, I think it's safe to say that no extra power is required other than what the devices are capable of providing themselves. What else?"

"The obvious one – they were leaning against each other," Paul replied.

"That should be easy enough so far; we get them turned on and then create a lever or something under one of the devices that we can remote activate to tip one into the other," Matt said.

"Surely it can't be that easy," Alana said. "Turn on and touch? No. If that was it, then the Hoppers would have been jumping all over time for who knows how long."

"Alana's got a point," Vic agreed.

Her eyes roved over the two devices, trying to work out what else was needed. The problem was, they had no idea how the devices were supposed to work, individually or together. All that they knew for certain was that, in conjunction with each other, they created a powerful electro-magnetic pulse that could cripple any tech within its radius.

How though? That was the question. How did any piece of tech work? Input the settings you want and then activate it. Simple. And it worked with anything. Human, alien, the most advanced super tech imaginable or something simple like a computer or phone or even a TV.

"The settings!" she blurted.

"Settings?" Kadee asked, clearly confused.

"But we don't know the settings that the Hoppers use to make these devices work," Matt pointed out.

"That's not the point," Vic replied.

"Wouldn't they already be set, ready to do their thing to make the EMP?" Alana asked.

"Probably," Vic allowed, "but are those the settings that we need? It's *possible* that when the devices were knocked into each other, that they hit a button or a dial or something and changed the settings anyway."

"Great!" Paul replied, throwing his hands in the air. "How are we supposed to work *that* out?"

"Matt did suggest trial and error before," Vic grinned. "But I think that, if we work together and use a combination of what we remember and my ability, we should be able to work it out."

"Let's just make sure that we keep these things apart," Matt stated.

"Right. First things first. How do we turn them on?" Alana asked.

"Please take your seats and strap in for landing," Captain Fuller announced.

Heads shot up to glare at the nearest speaker.

"Really? Now?" Matt asked sarcastically.

A shift in the plane's level sent notebooks, pieces of paper and pens sliding along the floor from where they'd been scattered all around the devices. All were filled with pictures, diagrams and notes about the two Hopper machines. Most of them had been discarded in favour of new ones, the ones being held by Kadee who had the best drawing skills of them all.

"You heard the man, strap in!" Sergeant Reid yelled as he hurried down the spiral staircase.

"Paul!" Vic snapped, waving her hand at the mess.

Instantly, the pieces of paper and notebooks zoomed off the deck and around to land in a neat stack where they hovered right in front of her. Vic shot him a nonplussed look; she hadn't asked him to give them to her, just clean the mess up. Nevertheless, she grabbed them and hurried across to her seat.

As she was doing up the buckles, the wad of paper under her leg, a stampede of boots ringing on the staircase had her looking up to see Ray and Tolan racing down to join them.

"Where are we?" Vic asked the instant that she'd settled her headphones over her head.

"Just outside of Cairo," Sergeant Reid replied.

Egypt? Pyramids and mummies and the Nile and who knew what other kind of wondrous ancient stuff there was to see, the thought flashed through Vic's mind.

If only, she thought bitterly.

"Unfortunately, no sightseeing for us," Ray said, obviously on the same wavelength as her.

"I thought we were heading straight back to Australia?" Tolan asked.

Sergeant Reid shook his head. *"We need to refuel. Besides, we haven't been issued the orders to do so."*

Vic blinked. Orders? They needed orders to go back to the one place that had a spaceship that they could use to make their plan work?

"We need to head straight back home," she stated into her headset. *"We don't have enough time left before the Swarm arrives to keep hopping around the planet first."*

"As much as I agree with you, orders are orders," Sergeant Reid replied.

"We'll see about that!" Tolan stated.

"Right, we don't have enough time to do things the normal way," Tolan stated.

The great Cargomaster was on the ground and the rear ramp was in the process of being lowered. The seven of them had hardly moved after unbuckling, staying together instead of bustling off to get ready for the next mission on the ground like they normally did.

"What's the plan?" Matt asked.

"Divide and conquer," Tolan replied. "How's the devices part coming?"

"I think that we've pretty much got it," Vic replied. "I'd like to go through the sequence again – powering up, adjusting the settings that need it – once or twice more and check my feelings on it. If everything checks out, then it's simply a matter of going through every device here and setting them correctly."

"Good," he nodded. "I *thought* that Ray and I had worked out with Sergeant Reid and Captain Fuller the most efficient route home that would also have us landing to refuel at places where there were extra devices. Cairo wasn't on that list."

"How can we get the plane heading straight home?" Alana asked.

"I could alter its heading?" Paul suggested doubtfully but Alana instantly vetoed that idea.

"Babe, no. You'd put too much strain on yourself fighting the engines. Plus I very much doubt that you know the way."

"We need to get those orders changed," Ray stated.

"Agreed," Tolan replied. "Matt, is there just the one location here?"

Matt already had the Padd powered up and the map centred. "Yep. Fifteen or twenty kilometres south-east."

"Good," Tolan replied and took a deep breath. "Matt, you, Paul, Alana and Kadee. Go with the soldiers and collect those devices. Get back here as quickly as you can."

"And the rest of us?" Vic asked, already suspecting that she knew what was coming.

"We're going to make a phone call," Tolan replied seriously.

Getting permission to call back to Australia was relatively simple. Captain Fuller even went one up and suggested a video conference. The problem was on the other end. Apparently it being three o'clock in the morning was 'inconvenient' for a number of people and they were politely asked if they could try again at a more 'reasonable hour'.

"Listen you f..." Tolan began before being unceremoniously shoved out of view of the screen by Vic and held there by Ray.

"Captain," Vic said sweetly to the officious officer on the other end. "I understand that you have your orders. I even understand that you're not in the habit of being told what to do by a bunch of civilian teenagers. Let me ask you this: do you know who we are and what the mission is that we're on?"

"I have been fully briefed," he replied.

"That's good," Vic said, aware that Tolan had stopped struggling and was now sitting quietly on the ground – although that might be because Ray had perched himself on top of the guy making it impossible for him to move. "One last question, do you know the importance of what we're trying to achieve?"

"As I said, I have been fully briefed," the Captain repeated.

"Excellent," Vic smiled. "Then you'll understand what General White will say when you tell him that we had the timetable all wrong and the Swarm arrives in an hour. Goodnight, Sir."

Quickly, she reached forward and stabbed the button to disconnect the line, vanishing the now-spluttering Captain on the other end.

"What was that?" Ray asked.

"Get off me!" Tolan snapped, heaving at Ray who slid off with a bump onto the floor. "What'd you do that for?"

"Because you were just making things worse," Vic told him. "That guy was enjoying saying no and making life difficult. Let's see how he likes it."

"What?" Tolan asked.

"We're receiving an incoming video transmission from HQ," Captain Fuller reported.

"That didn't take long," Vic grinned. "Put it up please, Captain."

The screen blinked back on, this time revealing a pyjama-clad General White. His hair was standing up, sticking out every which way and Vic was certain that one of the buttons in his shirt was in the wrong hole.

"What's this about the alien invasion starting in an hour?" General White demanded without preamble.

"Sorry General, I don't know what you're talking about," Vic denied.

"Captain Anderson said…" General White began

"Whatever he said was obviously a misinterpretation," Vic stated. "But since we've got you, we need you to order Captain Fuller and Sergeant Reid to fly this plane home ASAP."

General White's eyes narrowed. "Are you telling me that you got me out of bed at this unearthly hour of the night by lying to one of my officers just to ask me to change the orders of the only mission that'll give our planet a chance to survive what's coming?"

"Actually, General, it's not," Tolan said, stepping up beside her, Ray flanking her other side.

"It's not what?" General White asked.

"This mission is not Earth's only chance to survive the Hopper Swarm. In fact, this mission will do nothing more than delay the inevitable," Tolan replied. "However, we have come up with a real plan that *will* give the Earth a true fighting chance."

"How much of a fighting chance?" General White asked.

As confident as Vic was, she wasn't certain exactly what their chances of pulling it off were, let alone it working as intended. Not that she was going to admit to that.

"My premonition ability has never let me down. Our plan *will* work," she replied, putting as much certainty into her voice as she could.

He stared at them for a full minute, not saying a word. Finally, he sighed.

"I'm listening but this had better be good."

The truck pulled to a stop at the bottom of the ramp, just in front of where Tolan, Vic and Ray were waiting for it. The others piled out of the back of it almost before it'd stopped, heading directly for their friends.

"Well?" Tolan asked.

"Well?" Matt asked at the exact same time.

"Everything went smoothly," Alana said. "No hidden surprises, just a simple grab and load."

"Kinda boring, actually. We didn't even get a glimpse of the pyramids," Paul complained.

"How'd things go here? Are we headed home?" Matt asked impatiently.

"We got General White to issue the order," Tolan replied.

"Reluctantly," Ray added.

"Doesn't matter," Vic said. "We're headed home, where we need to be for the real plan."

"I still don't like how evasive he was when we asked about the *Scorpion*," Tolan frowned.

"He was evasive? How?" Paul asked, cocking his head.

"I'm not sure, he didn't seem to want to answer any questions about it," Tolan replied.

"Doesn't matter," Matt said and held up the Padd that never left his sight. "We've got this, we can find the *Scorpion* on our own if we need to."

The rumble of the truck driving up the ramp had them turning and, once it had passed, they followed. Sergeant Reid was waiting for them at the top.

"We've secured the three pairs of devices that were waiting for us and the plane's been refuelled," he told them. "As soon as the truck's in place and strapped down and the devices that you found have been secured, we'll lift off."

"Is it a straight flight home?" Vic asked.

"The Cargomaster doesn't have the range for that distance flight," Sergeant Reid replied with a shake of his head. "We'll stop to refuel in Kolkata, while it's doing so, we can find the device there. After that, it'll be a straight shot home to Brisbane."

"Good," Tolan said. "The sooner the better."

CHAPTER 18

Everything looked decidedly ordinary.

The people out the windows were either driving their cars, going about their usual Friday – Friday? Vic thought, trying to determine if that was, if fact, the right day of the week – yes, Friday morning routine. Many were off to work, others to school or shopping or whatever else was going on in their lives. They had no idea of what was coming. Maybe it was for the best. Vic didn't think their ignorance would last much longer.

Their car turned into the long drive up to the gates to the Army Base where they were stopped, looked over and then waved through. As soon as they'd pulled to a final stop, Vic, Ray, Matt and Kadee were out. Seconds later, the second car pulled up, discharging Tolan, Paul and Alana. After them came the trucks, three of them, all loaded to capacity with alien technology.

Vic watched the trucks drive straight past and she frowned when they didn't even stop at the next intersection, instead heading deeper into the depths of the Base.

"Wonder where they're taking them?" she mused.

"There's a special bunker where hazardous material is stored," Sergeant

Reid replied, appearing behind her. "They'll be stored there safely out of the way until we need them."

"But we'll need them in the next day or so," Tolan frowned. "We've got to find something to load them into so we can take them to space."

"Sir," a Private said, snapping to attention in front of them, his eyes focused on Sergeant Reid. "General White has requested your presence and the presence of your team in Building C."

"His team?" Matt muttered. "Since when did we become his team?"

"I thought that he was here to support us, not the other way around," Paul agreed.

"Leave it, guys, it doesn't matter, just so long as we stop the Hoppers, we can worry about credit later," Tolan told them.

"*I* think it matters," Matt groused.

Vic actually agreed with Matt. If Sergeant Reid – or any of the Army personnel – were seen to be in charge or simply *considered* themselves in charge, then there could be problems with them getting the job done. Not that they'd really let a small thing like 'authority' stand in the way before – the tarp over the hole in the big gymnasium's roof that she could see from where she was standing attested to that.

"Let's go," Sergeant Reid ordered.

Obediently, they fell in line behind him, even if they did look more like a gaggle than anything soldierly.

Sergeant Reid, the Private at his side and with Corporal Browning and Private Dillon bringing up the rear, led them along the path to the correct building before he took the stairs two at a time and straight through the door. Oddly enough, it was a straight line from there, down the main corridor to the fourth door. A double-rap knock was quickly answered and they filed in.

"About time," General White stated. "Take a seat."

A conference table dominated the room, large enough to seat twenty.

"Sergeant Reid, report!" General White ordered once everyone was seated.

"I thought ..." Ray began, only stopping when Vic's hand landed on his knee and squeezed.

She caught his eye and rounded her own. *There'll be time for that later*, she tried to tell him. Whether or not he understood was impossible to say; either way, he remained silent.

"As ordered, Sir, our mission was to locate and collect as many of the alien devices that were capable of producing a powerful electro-magnetic pulse, thus rendering all man-made technology within its sphere of influence inert," Sergeant Reid began. "We utilised the alien Padd to track down said technology.

"A systematic search was conducted of Australia, New Zealand, a number of Pacific Islands, South America and North America to good effect. An alien cell was located in the United States city of Boston. The cell was neutralised with the only casualty being Corporal Knox. When we left the city, he was listed as being in critical but stable condition."

"Corporal Knox is doing well," General White informed them. "He's out of the woods but it will be a long, slow road to recovery."

"Thank you, Sir," Sergeant Reid replied. "After leaving North America, we continued east, tracking into Europe. Our contacts in a number of foreign countries successfully followed the directions that we gave them, managing to find and locate more of the alien devices and moving them to locations where we could pick them up and transport them away."

"You were not due back here until you had completed your mission, Sergeant," General White pointed out. "I know that I approved the order for your return, but I want you to look me in the eye and explain to me why it was necessary."

Sergeant Reid's eyes flicked to each of them before he answered.

"Sir, you and I already knew the futility of the mission, that there was zero chance that we'd be able to find all of the alien devices in the timeframe that we had. That became obvious to the rest of the team to the point that it was becoming detrimental to the mission. Yes, we were continuing with the mission but the psychological factors meant that mistakes were on the verge of being made.

"I attempted to address the problem. In doing so, a different solution to the greater problem that we face was determined. Factors indicated that there was a very good chance that this new solution would deal with the main problem and also subsequently render the current mission moot."

General White stared at him; his eyes narrowed.

"All of which means that you believe that the premonition abilities that Vic had in relation to this 'plan' of theirs, trumped the orders that I gave you."

Vic bristled. "You obviously believe that, too! You wouldn't have issued the order for us to come home otherwise."

"Vic has a point," Tolan agreed. "Sergeant Reid and Captain Fuller were following your orders regardless of what they believed to be the right thing to do was."

This time it was the seven of them being stared at by the General.

"I know what each of you can do," General White eventually allowed. "That doesn't mean that I trust it. However, you have been right so far and I had to take that into account."

"Thank you," Tolan replied.

"Now, tell me again – and this time in a *lot* more detail – exactly what this plan of yours is to deal with the alien fleet that's supposedly heading our way," General White ordered.

"You know that it's coming!" Matt retorted. "You heard the Hopper yourself. It wasn't lying."

Something in the General's face, the way it went blank and rigid, sent a cold shiver up Vic's spine.

"General, where is that Hopper now?" she asked carefully.

"In a safe location," he replied and the tone of his voice screamed that that was the best answer that they were ever going to get about that topic. "Now, this plan of yours. Explain."

"Before we do, General, could you please tell us what happened to our families? I know that we told them to get somewhere safe, to 'run and hide' basically, but we haven't heard anything from them or about them since we left," Alana asked.

At first, the General looked defiant, as though he didn't want to say but then his demeanour changed.

"I guess that there's no harm in telling you. I will preface this with stating that this information has been deemed Top Secret. Where they are will be the fallback position for the Premier, other important people, including scientists and engineers, as well as a contingent of the Armed forces," he said.

"We understand that," Tolan said, looking around at all of his friends. "And believe me, none of us wants to compromise our family's safety. No one will hear about it from us."

"Good," General White nodded. "Your families, along with a number of their closest friends and relatives, were sent to a location in Far North Queensland. They're accompanied by a platoon of soldiers to ensure their safety."

"Where *exactly* in Far North Queensland?" Paul insisted.

"The Undara Lava Tubes. It's remote, not near any major towns or cities and the tubes stretch for a couple of dozen kilometres underground. Much of those tunnels are also quite large, meaning that they can hold quite a sizeable population," the General replied.

"Underground and away from cities sounds right to me," Kadee said. "Hoppers hate the dark and caves and tunnels are easy to defend."

"That was our thinking, too," General White nodded. "Those tubes are some of the longest in the world, something that we can use."

Vic had heard of Undara before but the information that she'd just been given amounted to more than she'd previously known. It sounded like the perfect place. Their families would be safe, even if they were a long, long way away.

"Now. This plan of yours. Let's hear it," General White demanded.

Suddenly, Vic felt as though she was under scrutiny. A glance around the table had her sighing. Every single one of her friends were looking at her. Apparently, she'd been designated as their spokesman. Again!

"What it all boils down to, General, is that we simply don't have enough *time*!" Vic began. "No matter what we do, we're royally screwed. The Hopper Swarm is on its way. It'll be here in a matter of days. I'm actually surprised that our astronomers haven't spotted it yet. But no matter what we do, even if we managed to find and destroy every single one of those EMP devices on the planet – something that is impossible to do – we're still hopelessly, hilariously outgunned. Even combined, the full military presence of every country in the world cannot hope to match the Hoppers."

"We know all that," General White frowned.

"I know you do. That's why you're already created the fall-back position where our parents are," Vic continued. "But what if we had more *time*?

What if the human race had enough time to develop the technological know-how to, at the very least, put up a decent fight, maybe even enough time to make the Hoppers realise that even *thinking* about invading Earth was a very bad idea?"

"Yes, I understood your rationale when you explained it to me over the video conference," General White replied. "It's a good theory. In practice ..."

"It's a theory that we can make a reality!" Vic interrupted.

"We," here she gestured to all seven of them, "we've jumped through time. We even saw how that freak accident happened. And what it was was a malfunction in two of the Hopper EMP devices combining to produce a brand-new effect. *We* saw it happen and *because* we saw how it happened, we know how to recreate it!

"What we're proposing is that we actually recreate that time travel mistake again. We've already collected over a hundred pairs of those devices. We're proposing to reset them, put a timer of some sort on it, drag the lot into space and activate it right in the middle of that great, big Hopper Swarm!"

"A Time Bomb," Tolan grinned. "We send the entire fleet away, to some point in the future giving humans the time that we need to advance."

General White sat back in his chair, his eyes slowly moving from one of them to another as he contemplated the idea.

"You really think this'll work?" he asked.

"My ability says that it will," Vic replied matter-of-factly.

"I like the idea, of getting a fighting chance instead of simply facing a foregone conclusion," General White mused.

"I believe it'll work," Sergeant Reid added. "I've seen what these seven can do and if they're this confident, then we'd be fools to ignore them."

This time it was the Sergeant under scrutiny. Finally, the General sat up in his chair.

“Assuming that I approve this, what will you need to make it happen?” he asked.

Vic shot a grin at her friends, the General was in, he just wasn’t quite willing to admit it yet.

“Obviously all of the Hopper EMP devices,” Tolan began, listing things off on his fingers. “Something to carry them in – maybe a giant box or something? Some mechanical work to get the devices to tip into each other at the right time. Maybe a few other things, but not a lot.”

“We’ll also need the *Scorpion* back,” Matt added.

Again, a sweep of cold rushed over Vic, a feeling of dread settling into her stomach.

“Ah, that might be a problem ...” General White said.

CHAPTER 19

"What do you mean that that could be a problem?" Tolan growled, a dangerous edge to his voice that Vic had never heard before.

General White glared back. "You already know that the *Scorpion* was moved off Base. I am currently unaware of its location."

"Matt?" Tolan asked, his eyes never leaving the General's.

Matt's ever-present backpack was slung off, opened and the Hopper Padd pulled out. They waited, impatient and silent for Matt to turn it on and do his thing.

"Got it," he said. "Still in the same place it was before we left to go traipsing around the world."

"There you go," Tolan said to General White. "We can *give* you the address where our ship is. All you need to do is to do your thing, throw that star you're wearing around or something, and get it back for us."

The battle of wills between the two continued for what felt like hours or days before the General finally gave a short, curt nod.

"I'll make enquires."

"Sir," Vic said, being as polite as possible. "You know what's at stake.

Without the *Scorpion* we don't have a chance."

Again, he simply gave a single nod before standing and striding from the room.

Many had tried to move them along. All had failed. Nothing was going to move them from where they loitered. A group of four military police had been the last to try. They'd marched towards them, grim expressions on their faces that had turned to shock and horror when they'd felt themselves lift from the floor and shoot back down the corridor and out the far door. Not even their scrambling hands at door jambs had halted their progress.

After that, they'd been left alone and supposedly ignored, although the way eyes darted towards them and people veered away or stopped, turned about and found another way around told a different story.

Matt, Tolan and Paul had set themselves leaning against the wall directly opposite the door. Ray and Vic were seated just to the side, so close that their knees were almost – but decidedly *not* – touching. Alana and Kadee had their heads bent together talking quietly.

The second that the doorknob rattled and began turning, the seven of them had shot to their feet and forward.

"What are you lot doing out here?" a startled General White bellowed at them, most likely in a vain attempt to cover his shock at being accosted like that outside his office door.

"Well?" Tolan demanded.

"Well what?" General white growled back. "And you had better have a very good reason for making a nuisance of yourself! I heard about what you did to that squad."

"They shouldn't have tried to get us to move when we need an answer,"

Matt shot back.

"This is an Army Base! You're nothing but civilians. You have no authority here. Do you understand that?" General White blustered.

"You're right, we're not military," Ray replied. "Which also means that we don't have to follow orders."

"If you'll please tell us the good news, then we'll happily head back to our room," Vic said, trying to interpose some calm into the situation.

"Good news? What good news?" General White asked.

"The good news telling us that the *Scorpion* is being moved back here as we speak," Vic replied.

General White's face froze and Vic knew the answer before he said another word.

"Not yet. At this stage, there is no ETA for the ship to be moved here," General White said. "Now, if you'll excuse me, there is real Army business that I need to attend to."

Then, before they could protest or question him more, General White had pushed through them and marched away.

Sergeant Reid strode into the dormitory that they'd been assigned and was standing in the middle of them before they'd even realised that he had, in fact, knocked first.

"Tell me more about what you need for this 'Time Bomb' that you're creating," he said, a pad and pencil in his hand.

"We need some sort of box or container large enough to hold all of the EMP devices that we've gathered," Tolan replied as he rolled off the bed and walked over to him.

"I can work out the minimum size for that, fairly easily," Sergeant Reid nodded, making a note in his pad.

"It's got to be something that we can remotely release," Matt added.

"I don't think that the *Scorpion* has anything that we can attach something to, so she'll probably need something added to her hull," Ray mused.

"That shouldn't be too hard for the engineers and mechanics to work out," Sergeant Reid said.

"And I guess some way to remotely activate the devices when we're ready – we don't want to be caught in the middle of it and sent to who knows when," Alana added.

"Sounds easy enough. Is that all you'll need for the bomb?" he asked.

"Pretty much," Vic replied, "unless you can think of anything else. It doesn't need to be complicated, just work."

"Really, the devices themselves do all the work, all we need is something to transport it all," Tolan agreed.

"Alright, I can work with that. I have a potential idea already. I'll let you know as soon as it's arranged," Sergeant Reid said and glanced at the clock. "It won't be today. Expect the main part here by lunch tomorrow."

Matt waited until the Sergeant had left the room before summing up their thoughts. "It's nice to actually work with someone who knows how to get things done."

General White entered the Mess Hall and paused. The way his head moved and froze, it was easy to see that he was not only looking to see if they were there, but the exact moment when he located them. As planned, not one of them gave any indication that they were also observing him. They kept eating their dinner, shovelling chips into their mouths or cutting into their pie, drinking and talking, all while watching from the corner of their eyes. At least, those that could watch did, Matt, Paul and Alana were forced to fight the urge to turn around.

"He's coming in!" Tolan whispered excitedly.

Their plan had hinged on this one detail. Would the General see them and still come in for dinner like he usually did? Or would he turn tail and run? It'd been even money either way and none had wanted to guess which way he'd fall, not even Vic with her premonition ability.

"He's in the line," Tolan continued giving commentary for those who couldn't see. "He's gone for the pie, potato and corn. Bypassed the peas, apparently our resident General doesn't eat his greens! And, yes, he's picked a large serve of chocolate pudding and ice-cream for dessert – it's no wonder he looks like he's getting a bit of a belly on him. Predictably, he's drinking coffee."

The commentary dried up just then, Tolan's head dropping towards his plate as the General turned to look over the hall. He was watched as he strode across the room, leaving Tolan, Vic, Ray and Kadee to have to fight the urge to turn around to keep track of him.

"He's chosen not to dine alone tonight," Matt stated, picking up the dropped commentary. "Is that Colonel Jorgensen and Captain Straight-Arse he's chosen to sit with? Haven't seen either of them since before we left to go traipsing around the world."

Vic snorted, nearly blowing chunks of pie out of her nose. It was close. *Really* close. Images of the two missing officers appeared before her mind. Neither was particularly friendly, both had been too straight-laced and by-the-book, especially Captain .... Kibble ... Klibby ... whatever his name was. With the benefit of hindsight, she wondered how much their behaviour were their normal personalities and how much was actually the fact that they were so scared with what they were facing – aliens, kids with abilities, the concepts of time travel and imminent invasion – that all they could do was to fall back on their training and what they knew best.

"Looks like the General's half-way through his pie," Matt stated. "Shall we?"

"Let's," Tolan agreed with a predatory smile.

They'd barely risen from their seats and were only a few metres towards the General when he saw them coming. His fork was dropped and he half-rose from his seat. They'd anticipated that reaction. As soon as they were able to, the seven of them spread out in the hall, each taking a different path through the tables, boxing the General in. Seeing their manoeuvre, he gave in, retaking his seat.

"Evening, General," Tolan said as they arrived at his table.

The scowls that Colonel Jorgensen and Captain Klibbe (Vic had taken a second to read his name badge to jog her memory) were both soundly ignored. A couple of middle-aged men scowling at them was *nothing* compared to a facing a cell of Hoppers shooting blasters at them, not to mention the Swarm of aliens intent on subjugating the world and eradicating the human population that was currently heading their way.

"No. No, I have not heard anything about when the alien spaceship you like flying around in will *or indeed if* it even will, be returned to this Base. No, I don't know when I will. No, Prime Minister Donovan has not yet returned my phone call," the General stated adamantly, having anticipated each and every one of their questions.

"We didn't think it would hurt to ask," Vic stated.

The General sat back and contemplated them for a moment. "I understand your impatience. I even share it to some degree. But my hands are tied at the moment. I promise to let you know if anything changes."

"Thank you, General," Tolan replied, "that's all we ask."

"Enjoy your dinner," Alana smiled before the seven of them turned and strode from the room.

The rumble of a truck followed by the squeal of brakes alerted them to the fact that what they'd been waiting for had finally arrived. Almost in unison, they shot towards the door. There was a slight scramble as they sorted themselves out but within a couple of minutes, they were outside, blinking in the sunlight.

What they found wasn't just any sort of truck, it was a massively long flat-bed and, sitting proudly on top of it, was a shipping container. It was old and a little rusty in patches and some of its white paint was peeling off, but that hardly mattered.

"It's bigger than I thought," Ray commented.

"That there is a forty-foot, not your regular twenty-foot. This'n'll hold a lot. And I do mean a *lot*," the truck driver told them, having climbed down from his rig. "Now, I just need to find out who's going to get this monstrosity off'n my truck and I can be heading back home."

Paul and Matt glanced at each other with a grin.

"I know who to ask," Tolan volunteered. "The mess is over that way, I'm sure that you could get something to eat while it's getting unloaded."

"Thanks, kid, I might just go do that," the grizzled man replied. "Make sure that they let me know when they're done. I don't want to be stuck here any longer than I have to be."

"I'll make sure that they do," Ray promised.

They waited until the man had disappeared inside the mess hall before they turned back to the truck and its cargo.

"Right, where do you want me to put this thing?" Paul asked.

"The EMP devices are still in the bunker down that way," Alana suggested. "The closer it is to them, the less we have to move the devices."

"Makes sense to me, Babe," Paul grinned.

Seconds later, the great forty-foot shipping container floated a few feet into the air and then drifted out and away from the flatbed. Then with Paul in the lead, they started walking down the roadway towards the bunker.

It was inevitable that they gathered a crowd. Soldiers stopped what they were doing, some in the middle of a march or an obstacle course, just to stare. Others, who seemed to have no real purpose or destination in mind – at least none that Vic could divine – were drawn along after them like moths to a flame.

The bunker was a long, low building, its roof curved from the ground on one side up and over before ending at the ground on the other, resembling a cylinder cut in half and laid down. The main door was reached by a ramp that descended from the roadway, the ground on either side having been cut away and held back by concrete. They'd never been in there but with how low the main door was, it gave the impression that the bunker extended a long way underground.

"Where should I put this thing?" Paul asked.

"Not on the road," Matt replied quickly.

"We need somewhere flat – don't want the devices tipping against each other before we're ready," Tolan mused, looking around. "What about over there?"

"Looks good enough to me," Paul shrugged, beginning to walk towards the break in the tall gums that dotted this part of the Base.

"That's not going to be easy for trucks or cranes to get to," Alana commented, dodging the rain of falling leaves created by the container brushing through branches.

"So? We don't need trucks or cranes to move it; we've got me!" Paul beamed.

When they'd reached the clearing, Paul had the container rotate slightly to fit better and to give more access to its front before finally lowering it to the ground.

"Any idea how to open this thing?" Ray asked.

"We can do that!" one of their entourage exclaimed.

Then, after slapping his buddy across his chest with the back of his hand, the two quick-stepped forward to the front of the container. Their backs hid the first part of whatever they were doing – presumedly undoing a lock of some sort. Seconds later, both men began walking backwards, two handles in each hand, each of them opening one of the doors.

Eagerly they moved forward and peered inside. It was dark towards the back, not that there was anything to see, but otherwise it was precisely what they expected it to be: a large, empty box.

"That should definitely hold them all," Matt commented.

"It still needs some work done to modify it before we can start loading it up," Tolan said.

"What do you need done to it?" the soldier who had volunteered to open the door asked. "We're part of the engineering corps; we can build whatever you need."

"You can? That'd be great!" Ray exclaimed. "Thanks."

"Has anyone got any paper and a pen?" Vic asked.

"Here," Kadee volunteered, pulling out a small notebook.

"Thanks," Vic smiled at her.

Opening it, her eyebrows rose. The first few pages were filled with rough pencil sketches of buildings, the next few pages with animals. Vic recognised their school, her home, monkeys and a tiger amongst others. Vic had had no idea. Kadee was *good*. Very good, in fact. Which, when Vic thought about it, shouldn't have been a surprise – she'd seen the Hopper that Kadee had sketched that first morning that she'd taken Kadee with her to art class. The most surprising thing was that Vic hadn't noticed Kadee drawing in the notebook at all.

Turning to a blank page, Vic began sketching. On the top half of the page she drew two pairs of the devices sitting beside each other – the width of the shipping container indicated that they should be able to get two rows of pairs inside. Under them was a thick flat line, a square around the lot. On the bottom half of the page, she drew the same four devices, this time with each pair tipped towards each other, the thick lines under each device now in a V-pattern and the square of the shipping container all around it.

"This is what we need," Vic said, showing not just the engineer, but two of his buddies who'd also crowded in to see. "We need some sort of platforms in there that will run the entire length of the container and that can tip up towards each other."

"Some sort of tilt tray?" the engineer asked. "Should be easy enough."

"And we need it to be remote controlled," Vic added quickly.

"Nothing to it," another stated. "When do you need it by?"

"ASAP," Tolan replied. "The sooner the better."

"Right, you heard them boys, that's what we're building, and it needs to be done by yesterday! Let's get to work," the first declared. "Is it alright if we have that?"

"One more thing," Ray said quickly as Vic tore off the page and handed it to the engineer. "Can you make the devices stick to the tilt trays so that they don't move?"

"Sure, we can weld them into place if that works?" the engineering Sergeant replied.

"That would be perfect!" Ray grinned.

"Kadee, those drawings are amazing! You have a lot of talent, I'd love to see more some time," Vic said, returning the notebook to her.

Kadee blushed slightly and ducked her head. "Thanks."

"What was that, Ray?" Tolan asked.

Ray stared at him. "We're going into space. Space. Where there's no gravity."

"*Riiight*," Tolan replied, drawing out the word as comprehension dawned. "Good call."

"Well, that's that underway. What's next on the list?" Matt said, unintentionally interrupting.

"The *Scorpion*. We need the *Scorpion*," Vic stated.

CHAPTER 20

A night spent where most of them tossed and turned and managed little to no sleep did not help their mood. They'd gone to bed frustrated, angry and annoyed at the way they were being blocked at seemingly every turn from the *Scorpion*. They woke up even more frustrated, aggravated and itching to get something done.

There might not be any real proof that the Hopper Swarm was really on its way but none of them doubted it. They'd all heard the Hopper that they'd captured and interrogated. It'd been telling the truth. The fact that there were a large number of military officers that knew about it and believed it but didn't seem to be doing a lot about it was enough to make anyone scream in frustration.

Tolan and Matt had disappeared early, only to reappear not long later, grumbling about how extra military police had been stationed at either end of the corridor to the General's office, barring their entry.

"Guess, if we can't get to him, then we're just going to have to stake out the building and wait until he leaves," Tolan had growled.

Thus, they'd moved in across the roadway from the entrance to the building and taken up residence on the grass. The sun was wonderful and watching the soldiers training and marching was interesting. At least, it was for the first hour, after that, it started to become repetitive.

Not even Matt tossing rocks about, bouncing them off trees, signs, the building, even a passing soldier's boot once and having the rock return to his hand every time lost its appeal.

"Guys," Tolan said, unexpectedly gaining everyone's attention after nearly two hours of waiting. "General White."

Vic looked up from her phone, her finger automatically clicking off the story that she'd been reading.

General White was standing on the top step, his hands on his hips as he glared across at them. He knew why they were there; he probably even knew that they'd been there all morning waiting for him.

They stood; he glowered.

They started towards him; the pair of military police advanced, intending to block their access to the General. Paul dramatically raised his hands, his fingers pointing straight at the soldiers; the General raised his hand, his mouth moving and the soldiers stopped and stepped backwards.

"General," Tolan said, nodding at the man in thanks for him agreeing to talk to them.

"Look, Son, all of you," General White sighed. "I have nothing new to tell you. I don't have access to that alien ship. I'm being blocked and my enquiries are getting nowhere. There is nothing that I can do."

"What about your superiors? Surely there's someone ..." Tolan tried.

"I've appealed to all of them. And gotten nowhere," he said. "I'm sorry, I am trying, that's all I can tell you."

"But why?" Vic asked, desperation in her voice. "Don't they believe us that the Hopper Swarm is coming?"

General White shook his head. "That I cannot tell you. They all have the same information that we do. They've seen the video of the alien and what you can do."

"Is there anything that *we* can do? Anyone that *we* should be talking to?" Ray asked.

"No. If there was, I'd tell you," General White replied. "Now, I have a Base to run and duties to perform. And I need you to stop hounding me for information that I cannot give you! I cannot do any more, please understand that."

Whether they did or not or were willing to accept it, seemed to be of no importance to the General, for, with a final nod, he stepped down, walked through them and away to whatever he considered more important than doing what was necessary to help prevent an alien invasion.

"Excuse me, Sirs, Ma'ams," a fresh-faced Private, who couldn't have been more than a few years older than them said. "I've been instructed to escort you to Sergeant Whitlow."

At first, none of them realised that *they* were the ones being addressed. Sirs? Ma'am? They were sixteen, for crying out loud! The Private, though, seemed adamant that he was speaking to them, apparent by the way he was standing at attention in front of them and that there was no one else in sight.

"Who's Sergeant Whitlow?" Vic asked cautiously.

"Sergeant Whitlow is a senior member of the Corps of Engineers," the Private replied. "He has been in charge of modifying the shipping container as you requested."

"Oh, *that* Sergeant Whitlow," Vic replied, even though she still had no idea who the man was.

“In that case, lead on,” Tolan said, gesturing vaguely towards where Paul had ‘parked’ the container.

The walk wasn’t long but it did feel wonderful to get out of the building. They hadn’t spent a lot of time outside for weeks, not counting their stake out of the General that morning. In the future, they’d needed to stay underground and out of sight; that had continued when they’d been on the run from the military while they’d been tracking down the Hopper hideout; and this last week they’d been mostly cooped up in the Cargomaster flying around the world.

When they arrived, it was to see nearly a dozen soldiers scattered outside the shipping container.

“Excellent! You’re here!” one of the soldiers exclaimed as they approached. “Let me show you what we’ve rigged up and you can tell us whether it’s what you wanted.”

The triple stripes that he wore were the only indication that they’d just met the aforementioned Sergeant Whitlow as he didn’t actually introduce himself, instead simply striding off ahead of them.

“As you can see,” Sergeant Whitlow said, “we’ve laid down four sets of tracks that stretch from the door here all the way to the back.”

Vic didn’t think that it looked like much, other than the fact that the flooring had been raised by around ten centimetres. Leaning over, she could see that there were pieces of machinery between the floor and the new level.

“Do they tilt? And tilt up and in towards each other like two sets of V’s?” Tolan asked. “It’s really important that they do.”

“Let me show you,” Sergeant Whitlow grinned. He turned around, searching and, after obviously not seeing what he was looking for, bellowed, “where’s that remote? I’ve built a remote for you, even put a nice big, shiny blue button on it to make it easy to differentiate from anything else."

"It's on the bonnet of the truck up on the road," someone called out.

"Well, go get it!" Sergeant Whitlow instructed. "Sorry, this could take a few minutes, we couldn't bring the truck down here."

Vic saw Matt bend, pick something up and begin tossing it up and down.

"On the bonnet of the truck with a blue button?" Matt asked. "No worries."

Leaning back, Matt whipped his arm and wrist backwards and forwards. The sound of something hitting trunks and branches and whipping through trees was all that could be heard before the machinery in the container behind them started to *whirr*.

"What the ...?" Sergeant Whitlow exclaimed, just barely managing to stop the rest of what he was about to say.

"You said that the blue button activated the tilt trays," Matt shrugged.

The trays were tilting exactly as designed. Both pairs adjusting up and into the precise angle that they needed.

"That's perfect! Thank you, Sergeant, and thank you to your team as well," Tolan said, holding his hand out to which the Sergeant happily shook.

"Here you go, Sarge!" a soldier said, running up before slowing and stopping, the remote still in his hand and a perplexed expression on his face as he stared at the tilted trays in the container.

"Thank you, Miller," Sergeant Whitlow said accepting the remote.

"But I never pressed the button," a confused Private Miller stated, eliciting a laugh from Matt.

"Don't worry about it," Tolan told him. "Sergeant, the next step is to lower those trays once again and then to load all of the devices that we brought back with us into the container and then secure them in place like we asked. Please make sure that you have one of the cylindrical ones opposite one of the cubic ones so that, when the button is pressed, they'll tip together."

"Just whatever you do, *do not* let them touch if any of those devices even have one light on them lit up," Vic warned.

"Consider it done," Sergeant Whitlow nodded as he pressed the blue button once again to lower the trays.

The pounding of hurried footsteps outside the door had Vic frowning. That wasn't a normal sound.

"Do you guys hear that?" she asked.

"What?" Matt asked, looking up from where he sat staring at the Padd in his hands.

"That sound. There are people in a hurry out there," she elaborated.

Everyone paused, looking towards the door. Another flurry of boots pounding on the floor punctuated Vic's statement

"Should we go look?" Paul suggested, following his own idea by not only getting to his feet but also pulling Alana along with him.

The suggestion seemed to be mutual as, a few moments later, everyone had stood and filed through the door. The fact that there were a number of high-ranking officers power walking up the corridor, all in the same direction had Vic, Tolan and Ray glancing at each other.

By silent, mutual agreement, they followed along.

The door to the command centre was ajar when they got there and, seeing no one there that could try to stop them, they slipped inside.

The room was packed. There were uniformed men bustling about in every direction. It was only by standing back against the wall that a pattern could be discerned. Officers would make a beeline for a console, lean over the operator, read whatever was on the screen, and then move on to the next console. After reading two or three, a group of officers would merge to discuss something before resuming the pattern once again.

"Any idea what's going on?" Ray asked.

"Sir! We have a response!" one of the officers seated at a console called.

"I think we're about to find out," Vic replied.

"Put it up on the big screen," General White ordered.

The screen snapped on to show a familiar scene. The room behind the lab-coated Japanese man was filled with cluttered desks and chairs and screens. A caption at the bottom of the screen was noted but unneeded: National Astronomical Observatory of Japan, Mitaka.

"Good afternoon," Doctor Hiroshi Tanaka said in his heavily accented English.

"Doctor," General White nodded. "Thank you for responding."

"It is my honour," Doctor Tanaka replied, leaning forward in a seated resemblance of a bow.

"Have you been able to confirm what the Hubble telescope detected?" the General asked.

Vic looked at Ray, then Tolan, a sinking feeling filling her. She wasn't the only one, she saw. All of her friends were sharing glances, looks of realising despair on their faces.

"I have," Doctor Tanaka replied. "Using the coordinates that the Hubble telescope supplied, we trained our telescopes on that location. There are indeed multiple unidentified objects that have entered the solar system at that location."

Silence filled the command centre, only broken by the occasional *beeps* of computers and other machines.

"Can you tell if they're natural or ... created?" General White asked.

"Preliminary observations tend to lend themselves to the objects being under some form of power," Doctor Tanaka replied.

"How many are there?" Tolan called out.

Officers all over the room, including the General, turned to look at him, but no one said a word about his speaking out of turn.

"Indeterminate," Doctor Tanaka replied. "At least two dozen, most likely a lot more."

"Is there any way to know how soon they'll reach Earth?" General White asked.

"If, as we suppose, those objects are indeed under power, then there is no definitive answer to that question," Doctor Tanaka replied. "They could speed up, slow down or even alter course."

"We don't have long now," Vic stated grimly to her friends. "Two or three days at most."

"Let's get out of here," Tolan replied. "It's time we decided our next move."

CHAPTER 21

As the last of them entered the dormitory, Tolan carefully shut the door. The fact that he was frowning at the doorknob, made Vic believe that he wasn't happy that there was no lock.

"Vic, Alana? Either of you see or sense anything?" he asked.

Vic closed her eyes, letting her senses expand, her awareness of the room fill her. It was an odd feeling and not a skill that she consciously practiced very often.

"What am I supposed to be looking for?" Alana asked.

Nothing stood out to Vic. There were no sensations of either hot or cold, no goosebumps or knives of dread in the pit of her stomach. Nothing, everything felt completely normal.

"I think Tolan wanted us to check to see if the room was bugged at all," Vic replied, having opened her eyes. "I'm not sensing anything."

She watched as Alana slowly turned completely about, her eyes wondering over everything. When she'd completed her circle, she shrugged.

"I can't see anything. Not that I really know what it is that I'm looking for."

"Good enough," Tolan nodded.

"Why was I looking for something that could be monitoring us?" Alana asked. "We're supposed to be working with the military, we're not prisoners or enemies."

"Supposed to be," Matt snorted. "They haven't exactly been all that helpful since we got back, have they?"

"The container's ready," Kadee pointed out.

"True, not that it'll do much good without a way to deliver the Bomb," Tolan replied. "Which is what we're doing here."

Vic sighed. "We're out of time, you all have to agree with that."

"You know we do," Alana replied.

"What are our options?" Paul asked.

"We go get the *Scorpion* ourselves," Matt replied. "We know where she is."

"I'm not disagreeing with you, I'm actually for it. And I think it's safe to say that everyone here agrees that we don't have much choice left," Ray said, looking around and receiving confirmation. "But I just want to be clear here: we're doing this without telling anyone from the Army?"

"I think that'd be the best idea," Tolan replied.

"But there's a lot here that are on our side. Sergeant Reid, Jo, Corporal Browning, even Sergeant Whitlow and his team. They could be a huge help," Kadee said.

"While true, they're bound by their own rulebook," Tolan replied. "You saw Sergeant Reid and Captain Fuller. Both of them heard our plan and agreed with it but they refused to bring us home without orders. And you know that General White is never going to issue those orders that would allow them to help us infiltrate that facility and get the *Scorpion* back."

"They could get into a lot of trouble if they disobeyed orders and we don't want them getting in trouble," Vic added.

"It's not like we actually need them," Matt scoffed. "We got ourselves off this Base pretty easily once before. We can do it again and get into the other place without their help."

"Having backup never hurts," Kadee pointed out.

"Dude, I doubt it's going to be quite so easy this time," Paul argued.

Vic though, wasn't so sure of that. "I think we've got some surprises up our sleeves still. We've practiced a lot since that last time."

"Matt, how far away is the place where the *Scorpion's* being held?" Tolan asked.

"A twenty-minute drive," Matt replied, not even having to check the Padd.

"We're going to need transport," Tolan replied.

Paul looked at Kadee and nodded at her. "I think we can cover that."

"What about the shipping container with all of the EMP devices in it?" Ray asked. "It's kind of an essential part of the plan."

"We can't exactly take it with us," Alana said. "It'd stick out like a sore thumb."

"I don't think we've got much choice; we're going to have to leave it here until we get the *Scorpion* and then come back for it," Tolan frowned.

"There won't be enough time to get it mounted to the *Scorpion* here without us being captured first and the *Scorpion* returned," Ray pointed out.

"I have an idea about that," Vic said slowly. "You may not like it although there are both good and bad parts that go with it."

"What's the bad points?" Alana asked.

"We're going to need food, something that can give us a lot of energy and keep us going, no matter what. It's going to take a lot out of us, especially Paul, assuming you're up for it," Vic replied.

"I can move something from ground to space with just my mind, I think that I can cope," Paul bragged and Vic just hoped that he really was as strong as he claimed. Alana might just kill her otherwise.

"That shouldn't be too hard; it makes sense to take some supplies anyway," Tolan said.

"What's the good parts?" Ray asked.

Vic just grinned at her friends, her eyes sparkling. There was no doubt in her mind that they were going to *like* those parts.

"Sergeant Reid?"

The man in question looked up from the great table that he was standing at, his hands spread on the edge as he leant over.

"Just the people that I wanted to see," Sergeant Reid replied. "Come in."

Vic and Tolan shared a look of uncertainty. There was no way that he could know what they'd been discussing and planning, was there? They'd been suspicious ever since they'd received word that he'd wanted to see them while they were in the mess gathering supplies for their 'trip'.

"You wanted to see us?" Tolan asked carefully. "Why?"

"I want another look at that Padd of yours. I think I've got it right but there was a lot to remember," he said, gesturing at the table.

It was only as they got closer that they were able to see that it wasn't a normal table at all. In actuality, it was an enormous interactive screen that was currently filled with a map of the world. What made this map interesting were the hundreds of red, yellow and blue twinkling lights spaced all over it. No light was near another and all appeared to be at about the same distance away from another light.

Vic cocked her head at the map, considering it. It was almost as though the lights formed a net or a web that covered the entire surface of the Earth. There was something there, something about it that caused her heart to race and a tingle to wash up her arms.

Her eyes picked out where some of those lights were: Brisbane, Canberra, Perth, Cairns, the middle of New Zealand, Bolivia, the bottom-most tip of Argentina, Mexico, Florida, California, Boston ... all places that they'd recently been to and all with a blue light. But the blue lights only accounted for about twenty percent of the map. There were slightly more red ones and well over half were yellow.

"Hopper EMP devices!" she blurted. "That's where they all are. Or were."

Sergeant Reid looked up at her with a grin. "Knew you'd figure it out. Although, to be honest, my money was on Matt getting there first."

"I was about to say it," the guy in question protested quickly. "I was just being polite."

"Sure, you were," Vic said, giving Matt a pat on his arm while sharing a knowing smirk with Alana and Kadee.

"Can you pull up the map of the world on that Padd to see how accurate I am, please?" Sergeant Reid asked.

"Obviously the blue ones are the ones that we found," Paul said, "but what's the difference between the yellow and the red ones?"

"Isn't that obvious, Babe?" Alana asked. "The yellow ones are mostly in the ocean, they'll pose less of a threat if they're activated then the red ones are where people live."

"Correct," Sergeant Reid replied. "Obviously any ships or aircraft are still vulnerable if they're in the vicinity if one's activated, not to mention any tech that's on any small island nations, but in general, much less of a threat."

"How many yellow ones are there?" Ray asked.

"About three hundred and twenty-five," Sergeant Reid replied. "Helps that Earth is made up of a lot of ocean."

"That would leave what? about eighty or so that are still out there that could cause serious damage?" Vic asked, eyeing the red lights scattered across most of Asia and parts of Europe.

Matt handed over the now activated Padd and they waited while Sergeant Reid compared what he was seeing on it with what he'd built on the giant interactive screen. A few small adjustments later and the Padd was returned.

"Why are you putting this together?" Matt asked.

"I wanted to see how much trouble the world is potentially in," Sergeant Reid replied. "The biggest concern is that we didn't get to Asia. China and Japan especially, losing them and their tech will be a massive blow to the rest of the world."

"The Hopper Swarm isn't here yet," Tolan reminded him.

"I know," Sergeant Reid replied, looking up at them. "But unless something is done – and soon – they will be."

"General White's told us that he has no influence that he can use to get the *Scorpion* back. We're still waiting to hear from Prime Minister Donovan, but we're running out of time," Tolan stated.

"I'm aware of the situation," Sergeant Reid replied.

His eyes flicked to the door and he frowned slightly.

"Have you heard that the Hubble telescope has detected something entering the solar system?" he asked as he walked around the table.

"Yeah. The Mitaka Observatory confirmed it a little while ago. The Swarm's almost here," Vic replied, watching him close the door and walk away from it.

"Your plan. How certain are you that it'll work?" Sergeant Reid asked.

"Very. You know that," Vic replied.

"That Padd of yours shows you exactly where *any* piece of Hopper tech is, doesn't it?" he asked.

"Yep," Matt replied.

"It's a shame that everyone in the military has their hands tied and can't do anything to get the *Scorpion* back so that you can complete your mission," he remarked idly. "*We* aren't allowed to find some way in to wherever it's being held and to take it back. I wish we could. I'm hoping that the right people can get to it in time."

Vic's eyes widened. Did he just?

"Good luck," Sergeant Reid said, then with a final nod, he turned and strode from the room.

The full-body shiver that swept Ray caused everyone to look at him.

"What?" Ray said. "He just reminded me too much of my dad. All that telling me to do something without coming right out and saying it ..."

“Did he just …?” Alana asked, echoing Vic’s own internal question.

“Yeah, he did,” Tolan replied quickly, speaking over the top of the end of her sentence. He looked around the room, particularly up into the corners and frowned. “We’ve already made the decision, seems we’re not the only ones thinking the same thing. I think it’s time we got going.”

Nods from everyone said that they agreed; the serious, even eager faces, said that they were ready. The warm feeling filling her body only enhanced Vic’s feeling of agreement: it was time.

CHAPTER 22

Walking through the Army Base as though everything was normal wasn't as easy it should have been. They had every right to be there. They had even more right to be walking towards the shipping container holding over a hundred pairs of alien devices. But there was an edginess to how not just Vic, but how all of them were feeling, it was as though the very air had a tang of tension, of anticipation, of warning.

Briefly, Vic closed her eyes and tested her ability. Nothing. No warnings or danger signals; no extra feelings that what they were doing was wrong. Just a normal, everyday sort of walk.

Not that this was. Eyes looked at them, then looked away. But that was normal – seven civilian teenagers dressed in everyday clothes would always draw the eye when they were in the middle of an Army Base where everyone wore uniforms. The feeling of being watched that was putting them on edge stemmed from two things. Firstly, the way the General had seemed to have the Military Police keeping an extra eye on them, or more specifically, making sure that they were kept away from him. The second and arguably more potent reason, was what they were not just planning but in the beginning stages of implementing.

There are no mind readers here, Vic kept reminding herself. *No one but us has abilities and mind reading isn't one of those abilities.*

"There it is," Ray said, nodding towards the flash of white that could be seen in the break of trees.

Where once the grass from the roadway down to the break in the trees where Paul had placed the shipping container had been a pristine wave of green, broken only by a fallen stick here and there, there was now a clear path stretching through it. Dozens of feet moving backwards and forwards along the same trajectory would do that.

Obediently, the seven of them turned down the newly made path.

"You were right," Alana stated. "There's a guard."

Tolan merely snorted. He'd claimed that there would be, that it was in the nature of soldiers to want to guard things.

It took a few minutes of extra walking before the rest of them could see what Alana's enhanced vision had warned them of. What surprised Vic was the fact that the soldier chosen for this particular duty was the same baby-faced private that had been sent to bring them down there the day before.

"Sirs, Ma'ams," the Private said.

"Private," Tolan said. "How's things?"

"Good, Sir," he replied. "The container's ready for whenever you need it, just give the word."

"That's excellent," Tolan smiled. "Would Sergeant Whitlow be around at all?"

That was their cue.

The sharp *rap* of noise away in the trees preceded a *thump* in the grass drawing everyone's attention.

"Look! Kangaroos!" Vic exclaimed. "I didn't know that there were any here on the Base."

The Private took a couple of steps in that direction. “Neither did I. We’ve had them in the past, so I’m told, but not for a couple of years.”

The trio of kangaroos stood there, their ears twitching, their heads pointed in their direction. One stood a little taller and scratched its belly. Then they were gone, jumping away between the trees.

“Sergeant Whitlow?” Tolan said, drawing the Private’s attention once again.

“Yes, Sir, sorry Sir,” the Private replied quickly. “I’m not sure where he is. But he asked me to give you this if you came by.”

The Private turned and strode over to the door of the container where he picked up a small, brown and green drawstring bag and brought it back for them. Tolan took it, opened it and looked up with a smile.

“This is great!” he said and Vic knew that the remote for the tilt trays was inside, exactly what they needed from the Sergeant. “Thanks. And please thank the Sergeant for us, too.”

“Make sure those doors stay closed,” Ray said.

“Don’t worry, Sir, that’s why I’m here,” the Private replied.

“Thanks,” Vic smiled as they turned to go. “Hope you see some more kangaroos or something.”

“It’d be nice, make the duty a bit more interesting,” he replied.

How Tolan managed to wait until they were back on the roadway before asking, Vic didn’t know.

“Did you get it?”

“Yep,” Paul replied, showing a brown, leather wallet. “That distraction made it easy.”

Vic, Matt and Kadee grinned in acknowledgement of their parts.

"Right, we have what we need, time to leave," Tolan said.

Their loitering just inside the main gates had drawn attention. They'd known that it would but there was nothing that they could do about it. Strictly speaking, that wasn't true. Kadee *could* have illusioned them out of sight so that the guards had no idea that they were there. But that would have just caused a different set of problems.

"Is that it?" Matt asked, nodding at the vehicle turning into the long drive from the main road.

"It's definitely a minivan," Alan replied, then, "yes! I can read the word 'taxi' on the light thing on its roof."

Instantly, they were up and headed for the main gate, their eyes keeping track of the minivan as it drove alongside the tall fence that marked the edge of the Base.

"Stop! Where do you think you're going?" a soldier demanded, stepping from the gate house to confront them.

Vic ignored the rifle he held diagonally from hip to shoulder across his chest, instead focusing on his face.

"We're going shopping," she lied. "We've been wearing the same clothes for pretty much the last week and need something new."

Considering that the soldier had probably been wearing the same uniform – or at least copies of it – every day for months or possibly years, Vic was fairly certain that he'd understand.

"I will need to check your clearance with Administration," the guard stated.

Vic frowned. Clearly, her assumption had been wrong. No, she decided, internally checking her ability; she still had a warm tingle pulsing through her.

“Let them through, Mike,” the Corporal’s partner called from inside the gatehouse. “They’re just kids and you know the rumours about what they can do; they can look after themselves.”

Clearly, the Corporal that had challenged them wanted to argue but a superior had spoken and, thus, he complied, pivoting to the side.

“Thanks,” Vic smiled at him as she led her friends around the boom that blocked the driveway and out towards where the taxi had pulled up.

“I’ve got a pickup for Groogan,” the taxi driver said, through his lowered window.

“That’s us,” Vic said happily.

Quickly, the side door was opened and they piled into the minivan.

“Where to?” the man asked.

Instead of an address, Matt leant forward and shoved the activated Padd into his face. “We need to go here.”

“You can drop us off here,” Vic blurted, obeying the sudden ice-cold feeling that had her shivering.

As soon as the taxi had rolled to a stop, the driver turned in his chair, an expectant expression on his face.

“How much?” Paul asked, pulling the Private’s wallet from his back pocket.

“Hope the Private forgives us, he was so sweet to us and not that much older than us either,” Alana commented while they waited for Paul.

“Don’t let your boyfriend hear you talking like that,” Vic grinned, bumping her shoulder.

"He'll be fine," Tolan replied. "Besides, in a couple of days either we would have dealt with the Swarm and we'll pay him back. Or we would have failed and it won't matter anyway."

"What now?" Kadee asked.

"Now we find a way in," Matt replied.

"We work our way around the outside, see what sort of defences we can detect that they have in place and also if we can get a better idea of whereabouts in there the *Scorpion* is," Tolan agreed.

"You know she's going to be inside a building or hanger or something, right?" Ray asked.

Vic looked at him and felt the rightness of his statement.

"It just makes sense," he continued with a shrug. "Whoever they are, they're doing an awesome job of stonewalling even the military. There's no way that they'll leave an alien spaceship out in the open for just anyone to fly over in a plane or with a drone to see it."

"That isn't going to stop me from seeing it," Alana grinned.

"What's the plan for circling the perimeter?" Vic asked. "There are a bunch of houses and buildings that jut up against its boundary in places."

"Paul?" Tolan asked.

He nodded, his eyes searching around them. "I can get us up there if you're okay with hiding us, Kadee?"

"I can do that," she nodded.

"Better keep an eye out; this could be a little loud," Paul commented.

Vic watched him curiously as he strode back up the street in the direction that they'd come, her head slightly cocked as she tried to work out what he was planning.

Scrreeech!

The piercing sound of metal ripping had not just Vic but all of them slapping their hands over their ears. Desperately, she looked around, looking to see if anyone else had heard the metal screaming in protest. While she didn't see any, there was no doubt that others had been alerted.

"Kadee! Hide us and Paul and that!" she cried, the last a general wave in the direction of the big sign that, until moments ago, had hung on the side of the road announcing that up ahead the road was private access only under strict government orders. Not to mention that the road was baren with no cover on it at all.

Her nod and brief closure of her eyes was none too soon as movement off to their left caught her attention. Three men and a woman, all wearing crisp business suits, piled out of the door of a building. The way that their heads darted about up and down the street showed that they had no idea where the noise had come from.

Paul must have guessed what Kadee was doing for he simply walked back towards them, a large piece of metal nearly as tall as he was and about the same in width, floating along beside him.

"A little warning next time," Tolan snarked, not that Paul seemed to care, instead just shrugging.

"We're all supposed to fit on that?" Matt asked incredulously as it was laid on the ground.

"Dude, there aren't exactly a lot of options," Paul replied. "Besides, I'm sure that we'll manage."

The fact that he took a seat at one end, wiggled back a little then held his arms open for Alana to join him on his lap said that he was going to manage just fine.

"It's not like we haven't been on a 'magic carpet ride' before," Ray commented.

Vic gave him a decidedly nonplussed look. In what universe was a large, flat piece of metal that had just been torn from a pole akin to a luxurious piece of carpet? Even if the purpose of said piece of metal had been radically altered by the fact that they were going to sit on it while Paul used his ability to make it fly through the air.

Shaking her head, Vic stepped forward and, like she'd done the other times they'd gone on one of these 'limited room rides', settled herself on Ray's lap. Instantly, she felt her face heat up. There was something different about this time and, while she knew *exactly* what that was, she *was not going to think about it*.

"You okay?" Ray whispered in her ear, sending little shivers down her neck.

"Yep," she squeaked before repeating in as normal voice as she could. "Yes, thank you, I'm okay."

"Everyone ready?" Paul asked.

And then the world began falling away as they floated up and away.

The front entrance of the facility was heavily fortified. For a car to enter, they would need to drive up to the first metal gates of a small gate house, be verified by the guards that came out of their room to check that you were approved to be there, then drive forward far enough for the gates that you'd entered through to close fully behind you but before the inner gates would open. While you idled in your car, you would be sitting inside a small structure that had thick concrete walls on either side and an additional concrete roof added for good measure. Only when you were through the second set of gates would a second set of guards appear to direct you to where you needed to go.

If that wasn't enough to deter anyone from even thinking about entering, eight-foot high concrete walls topped with sharpened metal spikes encircled the entire facility, the only breaks being where the property backed up against a warehouse that stretched even higher into the sky. The few house properties that abutted the facility had the concrete wall separating them from what was on the other side.

Before they were even halfway around, having remained floating ten metres out from the wall at all times and an extra six metres in the air to allow them to see over the top of the wall, it was blatantly obvious that there were only two ways in: the gatehouse or by air.

By air was easy for people on the approved list – there was a helicopter pad set to one side, not far from a hanger that was easily large enough to hold a small plane. Or an alien spaceship.

"Alana?" Tolan asked.

"The *Scorpion's* in there alright. I can see her," she replied.

"How do we want to do this?" Ray asked.

"It'll be dark soon," Vic replied, glancing at the sun. "Maybe it'd be best if we wait until night?"

"The middle of the night. Twelve or even two o'clock," Tolan declared. "Should be a lot fewer security guards roaming around then."

"Works for me," Paul said. "Next stop, food!"

The waiting was hard. It was long and boring and time seemed to take ages to pass. They'd experienced it before, this waiting for the right time to move, to begin a mission. Experience didn't make it any easier. They ate. They tried to sleep; and failed. They talked. They rehashed their plan. They watched the clock.

Finally, it was time.

“All aboard!” Paul called, settling onto the flat piece of metal once again.

“That’s never going to be funny,” Matt told him dryly.

“Maybe not to you,” Paul grinned back.

As soon as they were all settled, their ‘flying carpet’ rose into the air and shot off towards the facility where they knew that the *Scorpion* was being held. There wasn’t even a hint of concern that they would be seen flying through the air – firstly because of how late it was and the streets being deserted; and secondly because Kadee had them covered by one of her illusions. Not a sound was made, no words, no shifting about on the metal.

When they approached the wall, Paul took them up until they were high enough to see over it and down into the facility. Most of the buildings were black, as was much of the grounds. A series of light posts followed the roadways between the buildings and up to the helicopter pad, as well as to the huge hanger where they knew that the *Scorpion* was. Additional lights were placed over the doors to each building, obviously to aid anyone entering or exiting them at night.

There was no doubt that there would be guards down there, but whether they were patrolling on foot or by vehicle was impossible to know. Frustratingly, even after hovering up there for five minutes, there was still no sign of where the guards were.

Finally, at Tolan’s signal of tapping Paul’s shoulder, they floated over the wall and towards the hanger. Once again, they remained in the air as they circled the area. The hanger seemed even larger in the dark and up close. What windows the building had were dark and, unless you were Alana with advanced eyesight, impossible to see in. Two regular-sized doors on one side and another at the back complemented the gigantic hanger doors that a craft as big as a plane or spaceship could fit through.

Still, the security guards remained elusive, which was a good thing. Or should be. Vic's sense of warning, of danger had ratcheted up the second they'd crossed the boundary wall and, now that they were dipping lower towards the concrete, had increased once again. Unfortunately, she had nothing to base her feelings on and thus, she remained quiet – after all, everyone already knew the dangers of them being here.

Ray slid from the metal sheet before his feet had even touched the ground. The second that he was off, Paul shot them straight back up again. Of Ray, there was no sign, the darkness and his camouflage ability having swallowed him whole.

Again, the waiting seemed to take forever. Finally, a flicker of light shone – the lighter that Ray had. A collective sigh, no louder than the gentle passing of the wind, swept through those still seated high above him: the ground was clear.

This time when Paul brought the metal sheet in to land, they all disembarked. The smallest of rattles marked the metal meeting concrete, not that there was anything that they could do about that.

"This way," Ray whispered, his voice coming from seemingly thin air.

The hanger hung like a black curtain in front of them, its bulk silent and looming. The only sounds that could be heard were the occasional rumble of a car far in the distance, the drone of cicadas and the flap of wings around the nearby trees, but whether that was a bat, an owl or simply a normal bird having bad dreams was anyone's guess.

On silent feet they ghosted forward until they were within reaching distance of the cool metal of the hanger. Then, in single file, they followed it, aiming for one of the two pools of light that surrounded a door. At the very edge of the light, they stopped and rearranged themselves so that Paul and Alana were nearest the front.

Vic could just make out Paul bent towards his girlfriend, her voice little more than a breath in his ear as she whispered instructions of what she saw. He nodded, straightened and, a few seconds later, stepped forward and opened the door for them.

The instant that Vic stepped through into the big hanger, a bucket of ice-cold dread washed over her. Eyes wide, she spun about, eyes searching up and down, this way and that. A tingling in her arm spun her further around until she was facing back the way they came. A pain under her chin pushed her head backwards, her eyes going up to stare straight at a small glass dome placed right above the door that they'd just come in.

"Camera!" she blurted, pointing.

When next she blinked, there was an arrow buried deep in it, a few sparks testifying to the fact that its electrical connection had been severed.

"Are there any more?" Tolan asked quickly.

Quickly, Vic closed her eyes and turned around, casting wide and listening to her body. A tingle; a shiver of cold; a stab of pain. With each, she followed her ability, her eyes opening to look.

"Above the other door and the main hanger – two there, above and about a third of the way in from either side," she replied.

"Got 'em," Matt stated, drawing an arrow and nocking it to his bow.

She watched as he fired away into the dark three times, the only tell-tale that he'd hit his mark the bright sparks that erupted when a camera went dead.

"They're going to know we're here," Ray pointed out unnecessarily.

"Yep, let's get to the *Scorpion,*" Tolan agreed.

They ran for the big, dark shape sitting in the middle of the hanger. An urgency in her feet had Vic leaping forward; the clatter and yell of surprise and pain from behind her had her stopping and looking back.

"Tripped on something," Kadee groused.

Vic frowned. Her eyesight still wasn't good in this near-pitch blackness, but she was able to make out shapes – there was indeed something on the ground, something that had her frowning.

"Alana? What is it?" she asked.

"Dunno," she replied. "Just looks like some pieces of metal. And there's a length of cable over that way. Spare parts, maybe?"

"I thought the only thing in here was the *Scorpion,*" Ray frowned. "What would they need spare parts for?"

Wooooooop! Wooooooop! Wooooooop!

The siren was loud but it wasn't that that momentarily froze the seven of them, instead it was the great lights that filled the hanger as every light was instantly turned on. They were left blinking and rubbing their eyes, especially Alana who'd just been temporarily blinded.

"Doesn't matter," Tolan snapped. "We need to get out of here!"

The *Scorpion* was a bare few metres in front of them, beckoning. With Tolan in the lead, they raced around to the rear of the ship, only to be brought up short.

"Vic?" Tolan asked, staring at the raised ramp barring their entry.

But she was no longer there, instead she was obeying the impulse to race further along towards the far wall. A table caught her eye and she angled towards it. Her eyes swept it and settled on a black, metal suitcase. Without thinking, she snatched it up and was racing back towards the others even as she tried to work out how to open it.

"Paul!" she called, holding the thing up above her head.

Instantly, it lifted from her hand, vibrated for a moment and then split in two. Her hand snapped forward and she felt the familiar weight of the Hopper control cylinder fall into it. A thump to her thigh turned it on; a press of the right button caused the ramp to start lowering.

All of them were aboard before the ramp had fully descended and Vic pressed the button to raise the ramp after them. Reaching the command centre, she automatically looked out the great window that filled most of the front of the ship and blanched. Men, guards, all carrying some very serious-looking weaponry were in the process of spreading themselves out in a line that stretched from one side of the hanger to the other. Vic had no doubt that there were others that they couldn't see from the window as well. They were surrounded.

"Now what?" Kadee asked.

CHAPTER 23

"Now what?" Kadee asked, staring at the men, their rifles and handguns raised towards the *Scorpion* that the seven of them were inside of.

"We can't let them stop us!" Tolan declared. "Vic, get the engines going."

"Yep, on it," she replied, racing towards the piloting station. "I'm going to need a way out of here."

"Matt?" Tolan asked.

"Blow the door? With pleasure," he replied.

"Just don't hurt anyone!" Alana quickly added.

A muted *bang* snapped their heads up.

"What was that?" Paul asked.

"I think *that* guy just shot at us!" Ray replied incredulously.

"And that man is saying something, at least, I can see his mouth moving," Alana added.

"What's he saying?" Tolan asked.

"Advanced eyesight, not hearing," Alana replied.

"Probably telling us to surrender or some other crap," Matt replied. "Let's see if he takes *this* as a 'no'!"

Vic looked up from where her hand now rested on the thruster control, having uncovered the main lever. What she expected to see was a burst of bright green laser-fire emanating from the top of the window to slam into the hanger doors and blowing it up. What *actually* happened was ... nothing.

"Matt? Any time now," Tolan said.

"I'm trying!" Matt shot back. "It's not working!"

"You sure you're pressing the right buttons?" Paul asked.

"I know how to fire the weapons!" Matt snapped back.

"Is the ship powered up?" Ray asked, "is that the problem?"

"She's all powered and ready to go," Vic reported.

She turned about to watch Matt frowning down at the console, his hands moving. Something was definitely wrong. She'd seen him fire those weapons before. Hell, *she'd* fired the weapons once, albeit accidentally. It wasn't hard, especially not for an expert marksman. Kadee's movement, shifting and leaning down to rub the knee that she'd landed on when she fell caused Vic to gasp.

"Vic?" Alana asked.

"They've removed the weapons!" Vic blurted.

"What?" Matt exploded, pinning her with an incredulous look.

"All those things on the ground out there, they're not spare parts, they're *part of the* Scorpion!" she stated, horror filling her words.

"Shit!" Matt swore, slamming his hands down hard on the useless console.

"Why'd they want to remove the weapons?" Paul asked, shaking his head.

"Probably to understand how they work so that they can make more," Ray replied. "They do seem to like guns."

The muted sound of another gun being fired only emphasised his point.

"Alright, new plan," Tolan stated. "Vic, fly us *through* those doors!"

She swallowed, hard. Somehow, she just *knew* he was going to say that!

Settling herself as best as she could onto the uncomfortable Hopper chair, Vic focussed on what she needed to do. First step was to get the ship airborne. The slightest tap forward on the thruster lever supplied the power; a few careful touches on the right button increased their elevation. The hanger wobbled outside the big window, extra men appearing and disappearing as the ship slewed slightly.

The extra height – even if it was no more than a metre – was enough to allow her to safely tap the four buttons that would raise the landing legs.

The *Scorpion*, she knew, was designed for whatever space could throw at her. Radiation, meteors, space dust, anything and everything. And most of that stuff was deadly, especially at the speeds that the ship was capable of flying at.

"Shields!" she blurted.

"What?" Ray asked and she felt his familiar, comforting presence just behind her left shoulder.

"We need shields!" she repeated.

"I can make a shield around myself but not anyone else and especially not anything as big as the *Scorpion*," Tolan replied.

"No," Vic replied, shaking her head. "The *Scorpion* should have shields of her own."

Another muted *bang* was heard from outside and soundly ignored.

"If I'm reading that guy's mouth right, he's running out of patience," Alana stated.

"Even if the *Scorpion* has shields, we've never found them and don't have time to now," Tolan said. "Vic, just ram the damn ship through those doors!"

Vic glared at him, her eyes narrowed. She was right, she knew it; they needed shields. Unfortunately, Tolan was also right – they didn't have time to find where they were and activate them. Spinning back around, she focused on the console instead.

They were already pointing towards the hanger doors, a big bonus. Straight ahead, hard and fast, she decided.

Her eyes switched from the console to the doors, back and forth multiple times as she steeled herself for what she was about to do. A single touch of a button caused them to drift forward, confirming for her that that was the right one. The fact that the security guards directly in front of them took a step back was a nice bonus.

"Everyone hold on!" she called.

A breath, another, a third, all shallow and quick preceded Vic simultaneous slamming her finger on the button and pushing the thruster forward.

The *Scorpion* shot forward. Vic squeezed her eyes shut. The muted bangs of dozens of guns going off were drowned out by the enormous *crashing* sound of them hitting the doors. There was a brief *shriek* of metal, then nothing.

Opening her eyes, Vic saw that they were out, nothing but clear skies ahead of them.

"Gah!" she cried, throwing a hand over her eyes, blocking out the unexpected light shining straight in through the front window.

A second later it was gone and she was able to blink her eyes back into focus.

"What the hell was that?" Paul yelled.

"Spotlight," Ray replied.

A spotlight? Vic wondered. Curious, she turned the *Scorpion* in an arc, circling back and around the hanger that they'd just burst out of. A beam of intense light shot up into the sky, weaving towards them. Vic simply frowned at it and shot through it. Another appeared moments later; this one she veered around, only to run straight into another.

"How many are there?" Kadee wondered. "If there were Hoppers on this ship, those men would draw them in like moths to a flame."

"A moth that would be shooting back and killing every single one of them," Tolan stated grimly.

"Looks like there's four spotlights," Alana reported.

"We need to get out of sight. If they can see us, they're going to follow us," Ray said.

Vic nodded in agreement and so did the one thing that she hoped they wouldn't think of: she swooped the *Scorpion* straight back down. Her fingers were a blur as she adjusted their altitude on the fly, aiming for something that would keep them just above the rooves of the houses.

The black of night wasn't quite as black as one would hope for, especially at this height. Not only were there streetlights and the lights from the few random cars that were out and about, there were also a number of houses that had lights on. What people were doing up at this hour of the night, Vic had no idea, although she supposed it was possible that they'd been woken by the sirens and all the shouting that had been going on. Not to mention the gunshots – those, she supposed, would have woken anyone nearby.

Unexpectedly, lights snapped on from the house that she was aiming at, lighting up every window before even more burst on, these ones outside showing the house's backyard as clearly as if it had been daylight.

"Ew! Gross!" Alana exclaimed, spinning about so that her back was to *Scorpion's* big front window.

At first, Vic was confused. Then she saw it. If she hadn't been piloting the ship, she'd have tried to claw her eyes out or, at the very least, cover them. Unfortunately, neither was an option, not if they didn't want to plough straight into the house below.

As much as she tried not to look and attempted to focus on anything but ... *that*, her traitorous eyes kept finding it again and again. A man. A fat man. No, not just fat, a morbidly obese man, had waddled outside to stand in the middle of the backyard. It wasn't his weight that was a problem, at least, not ordinarily. No, it was the fact that he was standing there, looking up at them, wearing just the skimpiest, tightest, brightest orange pair of underwear imaginable! And! Nothing! Else!

"Dude! Put some clothes on! No one wants to see that!" Matt yelled at him, not that he would have been heard.

Thankfully, a few seconds later, they'd shot past, flying so fast that that particular house was left behind, never to be seen again.

"Which way?" Vic asked.

"We need to get the shipping container with the Hopper EMP devices,"

Tolan replied.

“Sixty degrees to your right,” Matt added, and Vic knew that he had the Padd out, turned on and was looking at the map that showed where every piece of Hopper tech on the planet was.

“You know that they’ll know exactly where we’re likely to go,” Ray pointed out.

“We don’t have a choice,” Tolan replied. “Paul, be ready as soon as we get there.”

“I’ll be ready,” he promised as he and Alana left the command centre.

Vic glanced up at Ray. “Don’t forget how fast we can go. Even if they do figure out where we’re going – both now and after we’ve got the container – we’ll have a very decent head start and we’ll get there a long time before they can catch up.”

He nodded in agreement but she could read the worry in his eyes.

“We’re coming up on the Army Base,” Matt reported, unnecessarily in Vic’s opinion.

For the past five minutes, she’d abandoned the ‘straight line’ approach, instead adopting the ‘let’s just follow the roads that she knew’ approach, albeit from a height of a hundred metres up instead of driving along them in a car or truck.

It was still long before dawn, a few hours at least, and thus the ground below was quite dark, lit only by the strings of streetlights and the pools of light that each showed. A few taps slowed their speed and Vic frowned. It was right about ...

“There!” Ray exclaimed, his arm shooting forward over her shoulder.

“I see it,” she replied, her fingers quickly stabbing the buttons that would bank the *Scorpion* to the right.

The long driveway was passed in a flash, as was the g[illegible] was just enough time and light to see a pair of guards sc[illegible]n. There their little house; Vic imagined them standing outside, their from tipped back as they scratched their head trying to figure out wh[illegible] y'd just seen.

There was no way to tell if their presence had been reported; not that they intended on sticking around long enough to find out. Instead, Vic made a beeline for the far side of the Base where the bunker was, or, more precisely, the small clearing where they'd 'parked' the shipping container.

It was dark under the trees, almost pitch black and there was only a vague shape and memory to go on. Vic slowed the *Scorpion* minutely. Finally, when it felt right, she paused their forward momentum completely, instead pivoting the ship about so that her rear was facing further into the trees.

"I see it!" Alana called over the internal comms from where she and Paul were stationed in one of the engine rooms and looking out a tiny window at the back of the ship. *"Can you move us down and back to the left a few metres?"*

Moving the ship backwards wasn't something that Vic had ever done before; still, somehow her fingers managed to hit the right sequence of buttons.

"Perfect! Hold us there!" Alana called.

"Lights!" Kadee cried, quickly stepping forward, her arm up and pointing out the front window.

"I see them," Vic and Tolan replied simultaneously.

There was nothing that they could do about them, Paul needed time to secure the container.

A seco ghts was quickly followed by two more and Vic had no doub e were a lot more soldiers heading right their way, not just e but also on foot – this *was* an Army Base, after all.

Paul reported.

“C

ouldn’t see it but she knew that the shipping container would now e hovering right behind them. Instantly, she hit the buttons and pushed the thruster lever forward to shoot them straight up, leaving the ground and the Base falling below to become nothing more than another random cluster of lights below them.

“Don’t forget about radar? They’ll see us this high!” Matt said quickly.

Vic frowned even as she rotated the *Scorpion* and accelerated east.

“I don’t think it’s going to matter too much,” Tolan replied. “We’re in an alien spaceship, people are going to notice us.”

“No, they won’t,” Kadee reminded him. “I’ve got us covered now that we have the container. All they’ll see is a patch of black flying through space.”

“I’m going to take us out over the ocean and then drop us as low as I can,” Vic reported. “Once we’re below radar height, we’ll head north.”

“Just try not to take too long,” Paul said over the comms. *“Holding this thing behind us is fine for now but the longer it takes, the harder it’s going to be.”*

“You have my word,” Vic replied. “I’ll get us there as quickly as I can.”

After all, needs must, she finished to herself.

CHAPTER 24

Below them was a sea of brown and green. Trees and rocks; mountains and forest. Looking out the front window was next to useless.

"You're sure we're still going the right way?" Matt asked doubtfully.

Vic's eyes settled on the only break in the trees – a wiggling line of brown.

"That's the road down there," she said. "The only way in or out."

"Assuming that we're following the right road," Matt muttered, none too quietly.

"We are," Ray stated, his voice sure. "If Vic says we're going the right way, then there's no question."

She glanced up at him and smiled, receiving one back in return.

"How's Paul doing back there?" Tolan asked.

"He's okay but he's getting tired," Alana replied through the comm system. *"How much longer?"*

"There! Look!" Kadee exclaimed, striding forward to stand right beside the front window and pointing at the ground below.

A circular hill rose before them, a slight plateau on the top and, at the very front, what could only be the entrance to a large cave.

"That's it," Vic sighed. "We're here."

"Any sign of pursuit?" Tolan asked.

"I can't see anything on my scanners," Matt replied. "Not that I could do anything about it anyway."

His tone was dark and angry, a sure sign that he was still furious that the *Scorpion*'s weapon system had been completely removed. A cold shiver swept up Vic's spine, just like it did every time that she thought about the fact that they had no way to shoot at anyone who attacked them – here on the planet or out in space. And just like every other time, she pushed it down, hoping that nothing would go wrong.

"There's a clearing off to the right. I'm going to put her down over there," she said.

"Alana, tell Paul to put the container down wherever he can. But make sure he does it *gently!*" Tolan said. "We don't want to accidentally set the Time Bomb off down here."

"I'm not an idiot, Tol, I know what I'm doing," Paul shot back irritably.

Vic tuned them out. The clearing that she was aiming for wasn't large and there were plenty of tall trees almost completely surrounding it. Sliding the lever back slightly, she reduced their speed, even as she began tapping the right buttons to swing them around so that they were lined up with their destination. Happy that they were on course, she took a moment to press the four buttons to lower the landing legs. After that, it was a matter of finding the right balance between keeping their altitude so that she they didn't hit any of the trees while continuing to reduce speed so as not to overshoot their target.

"The container's on the ground," Paul reported, not that Vic paid much attention.

"There's a bunch of people!" Kadee said. "They just appeared out of nowhere!"

"Probably from a cave," Ray replied. "This is the Undara Lava Tubes and there are a whole *bunch* of caves in this area. Which is why this location was picked in the first place."

That conversation caught Vic's ear. People? Maybe even their parents? Her mum and dad and brother and sister. She shook her head. She could find out when they were on the ground; which she still had to safely get them to.

The sensors looked right; they were dead centre of the clearing. Reducing the engines even more, she lowered the altitude controls, allowing them to sink. The tops of trees appeared directly outside the main window, followed by trunks; then smaller trees and bushes. Finally, she felt the *Scorpion* settle and she cut the engines.

"We're down," she announced unnecessarily.

"Well done," Ray said, his hand landing on her shoulder and giving a slight squeeze.

She smiled up at him, her eyes meeting his. "Thanks."

"Okay, everyone, let's go find our parents then get the container hitched up ready for our next ride," Tolan said.

"Tolan," Vic said, standing quickly enough to catch his arm before he could go far. "We need to rest before we do too much. Especially Paul. He just spent the last hour and a half keeping that container in the air and having it follow us all the way here. He'll be exhausted already; I doubt he could do too much more without dropping. Don't push!"

"You know they'll be coming for us!" Tolan argued. "We don't have the luxury of resting."

"We have time," she assured him.

"You're sure?" he asked.

Whatever expression Ray had on his face as he appeared at her side seemed to decide Tolan for he simply gave a curt nod and headed for the exit.

They found Alana and Paul waiting for them near the ramp, Paul leaning heavily on the nearest wall. He looked like he could barely stand and Alana was fussing, extreme worry etched on her face.

"Hey, man, lean on me!" Matt said, striding up to his best friend and, not taking no for answer, simply picked up Paul's arm and slung it over his shoulder while placing his own arm around Paul's side.

Pulling the cylinder from her pocket, Vic thumbed it on and pressed the button to lower the ramp. The crowd of people standing there waiting for them should have been expected – after all, Kadee had told them that she'd seen them as they were landing – but, nevertheless, it caused Vic to take an involuntary step backwards. That was, until she realised who she was seeing.

"Paul!"

"Matt!"

"Victoria!"

Hearing that awful name had Vic half-tempted to immediately raise the ramp once again; somehow, she refrained, instead setting off down the ramp alongside her friends.

"How are you? We didn't think that we'd ever get to see you again," her mother said, folding her into a brief but fierce hug before pushing her back, capturing her arms and holding them out so that she could look Vic up and down.

"You look alright. When was the last time you ate?" her mother continued.

Vic sighed and shared a Look with her father. It wasn't often that her mother went like this but when she did, it was usually best to simply endure it and wait it out. And she definitely knew better than to try to answer any questions until they'd all been asked.

A snicker caught her attention and she looked across to see Ray grinning at her mother's fussing. In reply, she raised an eyebrow at him, which for some strange reason, only caused him to laugh outright.

Suddenly, her arms were yanked and she felt herself jerked forward to land right up close to her mother.

"That's Ray, isn't it? Is there something going on between the two of you that I should know about?" her mother asked in a none-too-low voice.

"MUM!" Vic replied indignantly.

"Well, is there?" her mother asked, a hint of a smile showing.

"Yeah, Vic, is there?" her sister Selina asked, not even trying to hide the grin on her face.

"No. There's nothing going on between me and Ray," she stated in as dignified voice as she could. A cool sensation washed over her left side, the side that Ray was on and it took everything in her not to turn that way; somehow, she knew that she didn't want to see if he'd heard or what his facial expression was. They'd talked about this! No distracting conversations while they were intent on saving the planet. And she definitely wouldn't allow herself to even consider *thinking* about ... possibilities.

Pulling her arms away from her mother, she turned to her father and gave him a brief hug.

"I'm okay, we're all okay. There was no way that we wouldn't come find you as soon as we could. And I ate this morning – a bacon and egg roll, if you must know," she told them, answering all of her mother's earlier questions, even if said roll had been cold and mostly unappetising.

"Are you here for good now?" her father asked and Vic winced at knowing that she was about to dash the hope lacing his voice.

"We can't stay long," Vic replied. "*Stuff* has happened and we're on a tight schedule. There's enough time to have a short catch-up, a rest, then we need to get going again."

"'Stuff'?" he repeated. "Stuff only you can do, I'm assuming. Victoria, *why* can't you just leave others to handle it? You can be safe here, no matter what happens. Just wait until you see what we're building!"

Vic sighed. She understood what he was saying. And why. But they had a job to do. A plan to pull off.

"Dad, needs must," she said quietly.

He stared at her, his entire body gone still before all of his breath was suddenly expelled.

"You're more like your Grandpa than I think I ever gave you credit for," he smiled wistfully. "Very well, what can you tell us and how can we help?"

Vic smiled at him and graciously extended it to Selina and her mother. Needs must. It was her grandpa's phrase before it was hers; they knew, they understood.

"How about you start with giving us a tour of what you've been doing here while I fill you in on our last couple of days?" she suggested.

The Undara Lava Tubes were impressive. There was simply no other word for it. Awe-inspiring, certainly and definitely capable of taking one's breath away. Some of the tunnels, particularly the ones near the surface were so grand – both in width and height – that the *Scorpion* would easily have been able to sit inside of it. Assuming that it could even get there, past the forest and the low-hanging entrance.

Once through the giant cathedral-like entrances, the caves stretched for a dozen or two kilometres underground. Bubbles where the lava had pooled formed rooms now, some gigantic, others only tiny. Best of all, particularly in Kadee's opinion, was that it was all underground, where it was blacker than the night sky – a place that Hoppers would fear to go. People could be safe down there.

In the short time that the group had taken over the caves (much to the grumbling of the park rangers and tourist guides), they'd started to create a base of operations that could potentially hold a few hundred people at least. Rooms were being set up like dormitories; kitchens and storerooms were being created; and an armoury was being assembled made up of not just guns but spears, bows and arrows, swords, knives and more. They were even starting to bring in some animals, including chickens – real chickens, not *bin chickens*, or ibis, despite Kadee's insistence that they tasted good.

"And these people who had the *Scorpion*, you don't know who they are?" Matt's father asked.

"We were never told," Tolan replied, having quickly swallowed a bite of his sandwich.

"We think that they were trying to work out how the Hopper's weapons work, most likely to develop some advanced weapons of our own," Matt said clearly annoyed. "They dismantled my gun!"

"Matt's still upset by that," Paul deadpanned.

"Really, dear, it's nothing to get upset about, it's not exactly like you could really do anything with it," his mother cooed, a sentiment that froze every male as well as a number of the females in the cave and had them staring at her.

Matt's hand found a rock which he picked up and threw it away with a sharp snap of his wrist. Vic tracked it as best as she could but it was simply moving too fast. All she could tell was that it bounced off of at least five surfaces before Matt's hand shot up and he caught the rock as it was about to fly past him.

"I think we're forgetting exactly what our son can do," Matt's father said to his mother.

"And you have a plan?" Tolan's father asked uncertainly. "To stop these aliens from even reaching Earth?"

"We do," Tolan replied with a nod. "Vic even says that it'll work. We just need to get the last few pieces in place and we'll be ready to go."

"A Time Bomb, that's what you're calling it, isn't it?" Vic's mother asked with a frown. "How does it work, exactly?"

"You know what happened to us, how we ended up in the future where we met Kadee?" Vic shrugged, realising that everyone's eyes were on her – all their parents and siblings, not to mention the extras that had joined with them to make this place a haven for after the Hoppers arrived and won included.

There were more people there than they had realised at first. An army squad had been assigned to escort them and to smooth the way and, from what they'd heard, that squad had been needed: the people in charge of the area, the park rangers, guides and tourist operators, had all kicked up quite a fuss. They, of course, were all still there, along with the tourists and personnel that had been staying at and running the nearby resort. Added to all of those people were the couple of dozen extended family and friends that had been convinced to join the make-shift community.

Vic's eyes wandered over the crowd and, while there was a great deal of curiosity, there wasn't nearly as much disbelief as she would have expected. Whatever their parents and the Army personnel had told them had obviously convinced the majority of these people of the truth.

"We worked out how that accident occurred," she continued. "In fact, our mission over the past week and a half was to find and gather up as many of the Hopper devices that we could that would have set off EMPs, crippling our technology. It was a pair of these devices that malfunctioned and sent us forward in time. And the same malfunctioning tech that brought us back. We've worked out how to recreate that effect."

"That's what's in that shipping container that we brought with us," Tolan continued. "All of the devices that we gathered. Our plan is to remote detonate those devices, those *malfunctioning* devices, right in the middle of the Hopper Swarm and send them ... else*when."*

"What good will that do? They could end up anywhere?" an obese, balding man asked. "You could even make them arrive last year and we wouldn't have any idea ... of ... what's ... coming?"

He trailed off and Vic only just managed to smother her laugh. The guy had just fallen into the perils of talking about time travel as if it made sense. Which it did. Kind of. But only after you got used to the idea.

"Assuming it works at all," another man muttered sourly.

"It'll work," Vic stated, putting as much confidence into her voice as she could.

"As for the idea that they might end up in the past, I guess that's possible, but we don't think so," Tolan shrugged. "We have a bit of experience with the timeline now as we've seen it shift and veer away from what it once was to something new. *If* we somehow *did* send that Swarm back in time, then the timeline would have already changed and we wouldn't be having this conversation."

"Not if we're stuck in a causality loop," a middle-aged man argued, looked around at the confused group and continued. "A causality loop is where an event can only happen if certain other events happen which loop around, usually because of time travel. It's a theoretical idea that's never been tested. What it basically means is that setting off that Time Bomb could send them to the past but they'd only be in the past if we were here to set off the Time Bomb in the first place so whatever the aliens changed in the past caused us to be here so that we can set off the Time Bomb and send them back in time. You see? It loops around itself."

Ray shook his head. "No, it doesn't work that way. We've seen evidence of changes here that mean that the future isn't written that way. What we've done prevented it, made it so that the future *can't* be the same as the one that Kadee's from."

"So, what you're saying is that you believe that – assuming that it all works the way you think – you'll be sending the aliens, what? into the future?" Vic's father asked.

"Yes, exactly," Tolan replied.

"What good will that do?" Matt's father asked. "That just means that they're still coming and that we'll have to deal with them then instead of now."

"That's true," Vic nodded. "However, you're forgetting one very important thing. We'll know what's coming. Yes, it might only be an extra year but it could just as easily be a decade or a century or more, we don't know exactly *when* the Time Bomb will send them to. What we do know is that we'll have between now and then to prepare. Just imagine what we could achieve or invent between now and then."

"Our hope is that when they do reappear, they'll find us ready and a force that they decide they don't want to tangle with and thus, they'll simply turn around and go home," Alana said.

"Or at least that we're much more prepared and able put up a much better fight to make winning this planet a lot more costly," Matt added.

"Well, it sounds like you've got this plan all thought out," Vic's mother said. "Mind you, I still don't understand why it has to be you."

"You know why," Vic replied.

"What do you need from us?" her father asked, interrupting what had the potential to become an argument. "I imagine that we don't have long before the aliens arrive."

"Not just them," Ray muttered but only loud enough for Vic to hear.

"We need to get that shipping container attached to the *Scorpion* so that we can tow it into space, remotely release it and then detonate it," Tolan replied.

"I hope you brought a truck or a crane or something in that fancy airplane of yours," an elderly man said with a shake of his head. "'Cause otherwise, that thing ain't going nowhere."

"Leave that to me," Paul told him with a grin.

The old man standing there gobsmacked, his mouth open, jaw slack, eyes wide and his head tilted back as he watched the shipping container float through the air by itself was incredibly satisfying. Vic was sure that she wasn't the only one to agree, not the way that Matt, Alana and Ray were all grinning exactly as she was. She was certain that she even caught a hint of that smile on Paul's face.

Instead of weaving the container through the trees, Paul took it straight up and over them, making it float along far above them as they walked back down the path to reach the clearing where they'd parked the *Scorpion*. Finally, he set it down behind the ship, as far back as the clearing would allow.

"Right, what is it that you need?" Lieutenant Fuller asked, coming up to them, a team of half a dozen soldiers arrayed behind him.

"We need to attach the container to the *Scorpion* in a way that we can remotely release it later," Tolan replied, pointing from one to the other.

The Lieutenant considered both for a moment before turning to his team.

"Perkins, Jeffries, get the welding gear. Watkins, get me some C4 and a detonator. The rest of you, scrounge up some cable. We're going to need at least a hundred metres of it," he ordered.

Instantly, the soldiers scattered, jogging back the way that they'd come.

"C4?" Ray asked warily.

"Yes," Lieutenant Fuller nodded. "We'll use the brackets on each of the four top corners of the container to attach some cable to. They'll meet in the middle where they'll join together to another cable that we'll attach to the underside of your ship there – once we put a bracket in place to hold it. Where all of the cables meet, we'll plant the C4. You'll be able to remotely detonate it from inside your ship which will break the coupling and allow your container to float off into space. I'm assuming that's where you're planning on detonating it?"

"That's right," Tolan replied.

"Won't the C4 detonate on our way up into space? The heat from the speed as we travel through the atmosphere..." Matt pointed out.

"What about putting that whole thing in a box of some kind?" Paul's father asked eagerly. "We could fill it with some fire-suppressing foam from a fire extinguisher."

"Would that work?" Paul asked.

"Would it stop the C4 from detonating?" Tolan asked at the same time.

"I don't think it'll hurt it," Lieutenant Fuller frowned. "At least, it won't stop the charge from firing. The box should be enough on its own but adding the foam should help."

"I'll go find what we need," Paul's father said, grabbing Matt's father's arm as he passed. "Come on, Nev."

"Is there anything else that needs to be done to make your plan work?" Lieutenant Fuller asked.

"We should probably double check the settings on the devices, make sure that none shifted in the flight here," Alana suggested.

"And make sure that the tilt trays are still in working order," Paul added. "Other than that, I think we're ready."

"Yeah, put all that together then all we need to do is fly up into space and straight at a Swarm of alien ships heading right for us, release the bomb, detonate it and get out of its range as fast as we can," Tolan stated sarcastically. "No worries at all."

The work proceeded faster than any of them thought was possible. It was almost as though they'd kicked over an ant nest with how many people turned up and began scurrying about, getting everything done.

Lines of cables were laid out – one from each corner of the shipping container, another leading straight out from underneath the *Scorpion's* belly. Sparks flew and flashes of white lit up the shadow under the ship as the soldiers welded a bracket into place. Men swarmed up the sides of the container, while others lifted one end of the cable up to them to secure it in place.

Inside the container itself, Alana, Kadee, Vic and Paul walked slowly up and down the lines of devices, checking and re-checking that every setting was correct. Meanwhile, Matt, Tolan and Ray were often on their backs or sides as they examined the tilt trays set onto the floor under the devices, making sure that they would work when needed.

When all seemed ready inside, the tilt trays were tested and found to be good. Paul nodded at them, as he had the trays moved back to level.

"Right, time to power them up," Vic said.

"And hope that they don't shift and fall against each other when we're flying up into space," Matt pointed out.

"They won't," Paul promised. "I'll do the 'heavy lifting', make sure that they stay level. Once we're up there and moving, the container's momentum will do the rest and we can rely on the remotes."

"Besides, they're all welded into place on the trays," Ray added.

The clatter of boots on the roof above their heads had them looking up, not that they could see anything. An echoing *bang* sent them hurrying out of the container.

"Careful with that!" Lieutenant Fuller shouted.

"Sorry. Slipped," a man replied sheepishly.

"Idiot. He had no reason to pick it up in the first place," the Lieutenant muttered darkly.

"What'd he drop?" Vic asked, a cold feeling sweeping over her in anticipation of the answer as she exited the container.

"The box of C4."

Vic's eyes bulged and she swung around to stare up at the box now sitting innocently by itself on top of the shipping container.

"That could have been bad," Tolan deadpanned.

Lieutenant Fuller grunted before continuing with, "all that's left is to attach the five cables to the O-ring, place the C4, build the box around it and fill that box with the fire-suppressing foam."

"How long?" Vic asked quickly.

"An hour, maybe a little less," he replied.

"Vic?" Ray asked, laying a hand on her shoulder.

She shook her head. Whatever feeling had come over her had washed by incredibly quickly, almost too quickly to register. Uneasiness with a hint of danger but that was all that she was able to discern.

"Before I forget, this is the remote to detonate the C4 that will blow the coupling that's being built now. Don't lose it," Lieutenant Fuller said, handing over a box that fit easily into the palm of his hand. There was a simple, clear cover in the centre of it, underneath which, Vic could see a Big Red Button.

"This'll go well with the Big Blue Button that the engineers made for us to lift and lower the tilt trays inside the container," Paul laughed, taking the box.

"I'll put it inside the *Scorpion* if you like," Kadee offered.

How long she was gone, Vic never knew, distracted as she was with what was happening on the roof of the shipping container. She had no idea that it could fit that many people on top of it. There were two for each of the four cables attached to its corners; another holding the cable that snaked down, along the ground and under the *Scorpion*; and another two holding the big O-ring that would tie them all together. Three more were waiting on the ground ready for their turn: to place the explosives, fit the box around the entire contraption and then with a fire extinguisher to fill the box up.

A sound or a feeling had Vic turning to see Kadee running down the ramp and straight for them.

"Kadee?" she asked. "What's wrong?"

"There was a message from Sergeant Reid," she replied, breathing hard, her eyes wide. “The Army! They’ll be here in less than an hour!”

CHAPTER 25

"There was a message from Sergeant Reid. The Army! They'll be here in less than an hour!"

Kadee's words rang over the clearing and all who heard them froze, their heads swivelling to stare at her. Everyone knew what those words meant. The Army would be hell-bent on getting the *Scorpion* back and without her, their entire plan would fail.

"I thought that the Army was smarter than that," Lieutenant Fuller groused. "From everything that you lot have told me, this could be our one chance to survive, to make what we've been doing here unnecessary."

"It's not the Army," Matt stated, then continued, clarifying. "Well, it is. But they're just following orders. Whoever that other group was that had the *Scorpion* has some pretty big pull. They blocked General White's requests about the *Scorpion* at every turn. And if they can stop an Army General like that, then I'm betting that they can also *order* the Army to find their missing ship and to return it to them."

"We can't let that happen!" Vic gasped.

Her arm was thrown across her middle; her lungs desperate for air. Stabs of pain, unlike anything she'd ever felt before filled her stomach and her chest felt like the weight of the world was resting on it, crushing the air out of her.

"Vic!" Ray exclaimed, panic in his voice.

Instantly, he was there, one arm around her back, the other finding her hand. She grasped it like it was the only thing that could keep her alive; she knew that she was crushing it, squeezing too tightly, but he didn't make a sound.

"We're not going to," Tolan told her defiantly. "Kadee, you said less than an hour?"

"That's what Sergeant Reid said," she replied. "He couldn't be any more precise."

Tolan nodded and spun to face Lieutenant Fuller. "How long?"

"We'll be ready," he promised. "Make sure you are."

And then he was gone, striding away towards the container, barking orders at the men, his arms pointing to reinforce what he was saying.

"Vic? Sweety?" Alana asked.

Vic looked around and up to see her best friend there, concern on her face and she realised that the second hand that she could now feel on her back had to be Alana's. The pain in her stomach eased slightly, as did the weight in her chest and she slowly eased herself upright.

"I'll be alright," she said before looking at Ray and smiling at him. "Thanks. And, uh, sorry."

"It's okay," he grinned back but he wasn't hiding the way he was shaking life back into his hand as well as he thought he was.

"What's the odds that they'll be finished and we'll be out of here before the Army gets here?" Paul asked.

Vic shook her head. "With the way my premonition ability is going off? It's going to be close."

"There's not much we can do out here," Tolan said. "That's for that lot."

The men that were standing on top of the shipping container seemed to be working hard at getting the cables all coupled together. As they watched, two men gave another a boost up the side of it before a box, a couple of fire extinguishers and a welding machine were passed up.

"What can we do?" Alana asked.

"We can say goodbye to our families. Again," Vic replied, frowning at the thought that it seemed to be becoming a habit.

They found most of their families deep inside the Lave Tubes.

What they'd built in such a short time was astonishing. With places to sleep, a huge kitchen and dining chamber, plus a bunch of animals and punnets of seedlings that just needed to be planted, it was obvious that, no matter what happened, that they'd all be safe. It helped that this place was a long way off the beaten track and even further away from civilization. If the worst came about and the Hoppers did invade the planet and subjugate it, they'd survive here, especially with the darkness of the tubes to hide in.

"My sunset melons!" Ray exclaimed.

"Well, you said to look after them and to grow them, so I'm doing just that," his father smiled.

"Will they grow down here?" Paul asked doubtfully, looking at the pots lining the table at the side of the cave.

"Not here, none of the plants will grow here," Ray's father replied. "It's too dark; plants need sunlight. But there's a cave about a kilometre down that way that has a hole in the roof, it's not big but it's big enough to get sunlight most of the day and there's a small depression in the middle of it where water has pooled. I think that they'll grow okay there."

"Thanks, Dad," Ray said, and stepped forward to hug him.

"You're here to tell us that you're about to go, aren't you?" Vic's mother asked.

"Yes," Vic replied. "As soon as they're finished outside, we need to take off. The Army's on its way and we can't let them get the *Scorpion*."

Instantly, her mother was there, wrapping her arms around her and Vic sighed into it, letting the warmth of her ease her tension.

"You be careful and come back to us," her mother whispered in her ear.

"We will. I promise," Vic replied. "You look after yourself, too."

She stepped back then and looked at Ray who was just finishing saying goodbye to his father.

"Ready?" she asked.

He nodded and stepped up beside her for the walk out of the cave. The fact that their families followed was expected; the others that fell into line around them, less so. As they emerged into the sunlight, they looked towards the shipping container. It was now devoid of men scurrying about on top of it and all of the equipment that had been scattered around was in the process of being removed.

Lieutenant Fuller marched towards them and Vic could see the satisfied look on his face. The *Scorpion* was good to go.

"Vic!" Alana suddenly screamed, her hand shooting out to point away through the trees.

"What is it? The Army?" Vic asked quickly, knowing that Alana's advanced eyesight could see things that no one else could.

"Yes," she replied, her head nodding enthusiastically. "Trucks. Three ... no *four* of them."

"Let's go!" Tolan snapped.

There was no time for any more goodbyes, just a simple squeeze of her mother's hand before she was off, racing across the clearing towards the rear of the *Scorpion.* As she ran, she pulled the metal cylinder from her pocket and slammed it against her thigh and thumbed the right button. Obediently, the rear ramp lowered.

Matt didn't even wait for it to fully reach the ground before he was up and in, the others right on his heels. The second that Tolan – the last of them up the ramp – was aboard, Vic pressed the button again to raise the ramp.

"Be ready!" Tolan snapped at Paul and Alana as they peeled off at the first side corridor, headed for one of the engine bays and its rear window.

"I will be, don't worry about me," Paul shot back.

The second that Vic entered the command centre, she made a beeline for the piloting console. The first button, the one that revealed the thruster handle was pressed before she'd even taken her seat.

"I don't have any weapons," Matt reminded them. "I can't shoot back or defend us."

"Won't be a problem," Vic promised him, hoping that that would be true.

The rumble of the engines told her that the *Scorpion* was ready to fly and she hit the final set of buttons. Her hand found the thruster lever and she pushed it forward. Obediently, the *Scorpion* lifted off, the trees out the front window sinking away. For a few seconds, they could see the gathered cluster of their families and new friends before the sight was taken from them.

"We're clear," Vic announced as the last of the treetops fell away.

"Paul, have you got that container?" Tolan asked.

"I've got it. Don't worry about it," Paul replied through the comm system.

"No, worry about the two helicopters following us!" Alana yelled.

"Shit! How fast can you get us into space?" Tolan asked.

Vic's eyes narrowed on her console. "Let's find out!"

With one hand, she pushed forward on the lever, with the other, she adjusted their heading and then their altitude.

The view in the front window shifted, showing them pointing upwards, wisps of white clouds floating across the blue. Thankfully, whatever alien technology was put into the *Scorpion* included something that kept the deck feeling level no matter how hard she pushed them or how steep their climb.

"Alana?" Tolan asked.

"They're still there but falling behind," she replied. *"I don't think they're going to catch us."*

The fact that the blue before them deepened and darkened told Vic the same thing. *They* were designed for space; helicopters had a maximum altitude.

And then they were there. In space. White dots of stars appeared even as the sky lost any hint of blue, becoming a solid black. At the very side of the window, a crescent of the moon appeared, shining brightly. Vic wondered what it'd be like to go there, to a place where only twelve men had ever walked. Not that they had any spacesuits in this thing.

Nor did they have the time. They had a mission, a Swarm of alien ships to find and a Bomb to detonate in the middle of them.

Preferably all without getting themselves killed in the process.

CHAPTER 26

Space was big. And black. And infinite. It also had more than just two dimensions. Which, when all added together, meant that finding something in it wasn't an easy task. Ordinarily. Thankfully, the *Scorpion* had some extremely advanced sensors.

"Any sign of the Swarm?" Tolan asked.

Vic examined each screen on her console carefully, looking for anything that might indicate that an alien fleet was in range. There! Her eyes focused in on one screen where, right on the very edge of it, a group of purple dots were starting to appear.

"Got 'em!" she called.

"Me too!" Matt echoed, not that he could do anything with the information even when they were in range.

Once again, Vic wondered what the people who had the *Scorpion* were thinking, dismantling the weapon's system.

"Adjusting heading," Vic announced, tapping the right buttons to bring them around and heading towards the alien fleet intent on invading and subjugating Earth.

"Anyone else agree that this is a crazy plan?" Ray asked.

"Yes."

"Yes."

"Yep."

"Completely out of our minds," Paul added as he as Alana entered the command centre.

"Good, just checking that I wasn't the only one," Ray said.

Silence descended and felt like it was smothering everything and everyone. Even the small sounds that the ship normally made felt muted. But, Vic supposed, that might just be because of the pounding of blood in her ears. With every minute that passed, with every minute that they flew closer to the Hopper Swarm, the number of purple dots on her screen increased.

One dozen.

Two dozen.

Four.

And still they kept coming.

"So, what is the plan here?" Matt asked.

"We've been over this," Tolan replied. "We fly up to the Swarm, release the container, then get the hell out of there, detonating it when it's in the middle of the Swarm."

"Sounds simple when you put it like that," Matt replied. "Um, I know that this is probably a stupid question, but why won't they shoot us out of the sky the second that they see us?"

"Or the container?" Ray added.

"They won't shoot us because we're in one of their ships," Tolan replied patiently. "Just like with that other big Hopper ship that we blew up."

Vic's eyebrow rose as she realised that there'd been no answer in regards to the container. Which made sense. There were no guarantees. Any one of the Hopper ships could see it and blow it up before they had a chance to set off the Time Bomb hidden inside it. All they could do was to hope for the best.

Taking some of her concentration off her console for a moment, Vic considered her body. No goosebumps or extreme feelings of pain. A slight chill in her arms and spine. A glance confirmed that the hairs on her arm were standing up. Caution. Potential danger. Nothing she wasn't already aware of. Crossing her fingers, she hoped it'd stay like that.

"I can see them," Alana whispered.

Vic wasn't surprised. The mass of purple dots representing the Hopper Swarm was getting closer and closer to their own orange dot in the centre of the screen with each passing second.

"How big?" Kadee asked.

"Big," was Alana's only reply.

Suddenly, the speakers burst into life, a *scritching* sound emanating from them.

"I'm guessing that they're asking who we are and what we're doing," Matt said.

"Maintain radio silence," Tolan instructed and Vic couldn't help but look around at him. If that wasn't the dumbest thing he'd ever said ...

"Wasn't planning on talking to them," Matt replied.

"How close do we need to be?" Paul asked.

"A lot closer," Vic replied, shaking her head.

Sweat appeared on her forehead but whether that was from her premonition ability or simply the fact that they were racing headlong towards dozens and dozens of alien spaceships was impossible to say.

Again, that *scritching* sound erupted from their speakers. There was an added edge to it this time, a hardness.

"I don't think they like it that we aren't responding," Matt pointed out.

"Nothing we can do about it. Vic said we need to be closer," Ray said.

"Vic! Four of them have accelerated towards us!" Alana called.

"I see them," she replied, her eyes glued to the screen.

It'd taken a second to be sure but there were indeed four purple dots separating themselves from the rest of the Swarm. She bit her lip, trying to decide what they should do. They needed to be closer, much much closer before they could release the container. But getting shot at or blown up wasn't part of the plan.

Suddenly, she slammed her fingers against the buttons, furiously adjusting their heading. The stars wobbled out the front window, distorted with the speed that they were turning about. As soon as they'd finished spinning, the stars settled once again and Vic slammed the lever forward, shooting them back the way that they'd come.

A single glance at the screen was enough to show exactly what she expected to see: the mass of purple dots behind them with the four smaller dots of their pursuers rapidly closing.

"What's the plan now?" Matt asked.

"We run!" Vic shot back.

"What about the container?" Paul asked.

"We'll release it, don't worry," she replied, not sure exactly when that would be.

Ray's presence at her shoulder was both a comfort and a distraction.

"They're gaining!" he announced

Nope, definitely a distraction, she decided.

"I'm pushing us as fast as we can go!" she snapped back, her hand already beginning to ache with how hard she was pushing the lever forward.

"Vic! The container!" Tolan yelled.

"Not yet!" she shot back.

Her eyes flicked back to the screen, not that she really wanted to see how close those four Hopper ships were getting but needing to know anyway.

"Alana, I need your eyes," Vic said.

"You want me looking out the back window?" she asked. "Going."

The sound of her racing away was enough for Vic to allow her concentration to focus completely on flying the *Scorpion* away from danger. Well, that and trying to determine when the best time to release the container and blow the Time Bomb were.

"Move it! Move it! Move it!"

Vic frowned but didn't otherwise respond to Paul's mutter. Her entire concentration was on the console under her hands. Her fingers moved faster than they ever had before. Buttons were tapped continuously even as she pushed the lever as far forward as it would go and held it there.

"We're not going to make it!" Kadee stated.

Again, Vic ignored it. She was doing the best that she could already.

"Matt?" Tolan asked.

"They're not in range but they're getting close," he replied.

"Vic?" Tolan asked, a hint of desperation in his voice.

"Doing the best I can," she snapped.

"I know that," he replied. "But not what I was asking."

She spared a fraction of her concentration, diverting it to her own body, examining it. No different than it was before, she decided. Not that that was much of a help.

"Not yet," she stated.

"When?" Tolan insisted.

"Soon!" It was the same answer that she'd already given. And no, she couldn't be any more precise. All she could do was trust her gut, her ability to tell her when.

"Paul?" Tolan asked and Vic grimaced – she was getting tired of his one-word questions, even if every single one of them knew exactly what he was asking with each of them.

"I'm ready; just need the word," he replied.

She flew on, continuing to push the *Scorpion* as hard as she could through space. The four Hopper ships that were tailing them were getting close, the scanners on the console confirmed that. Still, she was sure that she could stay ahead of them. And if they could do that, then the main Hopper Swarm wouldn't be a worry.

Thinking of the Swarm had her checking the scanner once again. Orange dot that was them; four purple dots not that far behind; a much, much larger grouping of purple lights right behind them. And gaining. There were far too many to count, especially in the quick glance which was all the time she had. But there was no doubt – they were all there, more than sixty Hopper ships. And every single one of them far, far bigger than their own *Scorpion.*

A sharp, intense heat sped from her fingers to her shoulder. It didn't hurt, in fact it felt more comforting. And urgent.

"Now!" she bellowed.

She didn't turn around to watch, despite how tempting it was. She didn't need to. They'd talked it through so much that she could picture Paul pressing the Big Red Button on the hand-held device that he'd been holding for the past few hours. Sure, it was cliché, but it seemed appropriate.

The device, she knew, would trigger the explosives around the coupling that held the cargo container that they were currently dragging in their wake.

Instantly after pressing the Big Red Button that would blow the box and O-ring holding the container to them, Paul would count to ten before pressing the Big Blue Button, tipping the devices into each other and, hopefully, creating the Time Bomb.

Unfortunately, the container was too tiny for the scanner to pick up; that was where Alana came in.

"I see it!" she reported over the comm where she was stationed in the very back of the ship looking out a viewport. *"The lead Hopper ships missed it, flew right past it!"*

A collective sigh sped through the room; that was the one variable that they couldn't account for. If even one of the Hoppe ships had collided with it or simply shot it to smithereens, their plan was done for. There would be no second chances.

"We need to move, Vic!" Tolan ordered, not that she needed the reminder or that she could do any more than she already was.

They flew on. Silence sat heavily in the control room as each of them counted down in their heads.

Vic was up to a count of twenty-two when Alana's scream of pain burst over the speakers.

"My eyes! My eyes! I can't see!"

"Alana!" Paul yelled back, the quick, heavy thump of boots on the deck telling Vic that he was up and racing back through the ship.

"I was looking right at it when it exploded!" Alana sobbed over the comms.

The wait was excruciating. Vic's eyes may have been focussed on the console in front of her and what her hands were doing, but her mind was firmly at the rear of the ship with her best friend.

A burst of purple flared in front of the *Scorpion*, its intensity so bright that it lit up the entire command centre, washing over everything.

"That's not good," Matt deadpanned.

Another flash, this one green bathed the ship and Vic grimaced. This was *exactly* what they didn't want to happen! They were supposed to be far enough away from the multicoloured lightning storm when it went off.

The fact that the Time Storm was there, flashing around them, was a good thing – it meant that their Time Bomb had worked. Exactly how good or what the results were going to be, well, they all knew that that was a crapshoot.

"She's okay!" Paul's voice filled the command centre. *"It wasn't bad, her sight is already starting to come back."*

Vic breathed a sigh of relief. *That* was one less thing to worry about. Now to just get away from the lightning and the Time Storm. Assuming that they had, in fact, created a *Time Storm*.

Despite the fact that she was already pushing the *Scorpion* as hard and as fast as it would go, she pushed harder at the lever. It didn't budge. They were already at maximum velocity. There was no use, she knew, in attempting to alter their course – a straight line out and away was what they needed. They weren't exactly headed back towards Earth, more of a parallel course, but that didn't matter either.

"Vic?" Tolan demanded.

Her eyes dropped to the screen, her bottom lip held between her teeth. *Something* had happened, that much was certain, now it was just a case of trying to interpret it.

"The sensors are picking up the explosion," she stated, staring at the staticky black and white blob just to the left of centre.

Even as she watched, she could see it growing, beginning to take up more and more of the screen. And spreading directly towards them.

"The Swarm?" Matt asked.

Vic shook her head. "Can't see them. Well, the main fleet. The sensors can't penetrate where they are; it's all one big messy blob. The four that were chasing us are still there."

"We didn't get them all?" Kadee asked.

"No," she replied before amending her statement. "Maybe not. Hard to tell right now."

"We either did or we didn't," Tolan countered. "Which is it?"

"I don't know," Vic snapped back. "Whatever we did, the explosion has blinded the sensors and that area is growing. It might overtake those Hopper ships."

"Might?" Paul asked, causing her to glance back to see him stumbling in, one arm around and supporting Alana, her arm over his shoulders.

"Might," she replied. "It's growing fast."

And it was. The staticky blob looked to be expanding rapidly. Where it'd been about the size of her fingernail when she'd first looked at the screen, it was now easily double that and still growing. She *thought* that it'd overtake the four Hopper ships and her gut concurred. What really worried her was the cold sweat that had developed, warning her that they were also in danger.

Yes, there'd been that initial purple burst of lightning when they'd first set off the explosion, but other than that, no indication that what they'd done would affect them. Other than her feelings starting to point that way, of course. Still, no need to scare the others. At least, not yet.

"Alana? How are your eyes now?" Paul asked.

"Better," she replied. "Still massive white spots every time I blink but it's getting better."

"What'd you see?" Tolan asked.

"The container exploded," she replied simply. "It was just an intense flare of white that lit up the whole of space."

Vic glanced back down at the sensor screen, swallowing heavily at the size of the staticky blob before looking back up again.

"Actually, it might not have just been white," Alana continued, and Vic could hear the frown in her voice. "There might have been every colour mixed in there, just packed so tightly that it was near-impossible to separate them all."

Every colour. And they'd seen a flare of purple lightning in front of them when it'd exploded. Something like a million ants crawled up Vic's spine, neck and into her head. She gasped, it was so intense.

"Vic?" Ray asked, appearing at her side.

"It's nothing," she replied shaking her head.

"No, it's not," he replied flatly.

"Vic, if there's something we should know, just tell us," Tolan added.

Her eyes dropped to the screen again.

"They're gone!" she exclaimed.

"What are? The Hopper ships?" Matt demanded.

"Yeah, those last four are gone. The static on the screen's swallowed them," she replied.

"Good," Kadee said. "I hope they're dead!"

The staticky blob had grown again. It was now pressing hard up beside the exact centre of the screen. Right where they were.

A flare of blue flashed across the screen.

The black of space reappeared for a moment before a streak of green raced across in front of them.

Red.

Purple.

Yellow.

Purple.

The flares of multicoloured lightning were coming thick and fast, almost too fast to identify, leaving less and less time for the black of normal space to be seen.

Thump

“Paul!” Alana screamed.

“What happened?” Vic demanded, too focussed on flying the *Scorpion* to have time to look back.

“He just fainted!” Alana replied.

“Vic? What’s going on?” Tolan demanded.

“Matt?” Ray asked. Then, “he’s collapsed, too!”

“Shit!” Vic swore. Her eyes were glued to the screen, every sense focused on the static that was about to overtake them. “Everyone hold on!”

CHAPTER 27

Streaks of green, blue, red and purple crisscrossed in front of them. Vic refused to look, instead keeping her head firmly down and her eyes fixed on the console. But she knew that they were there. How could she not? With each flash, the command centre flared with colour, let in by the great glass window in their bow.

"Vic?" Tolan's voice seemed to have raised another octave from the last time that she'd heard it.

"Doing my best!" she snapped.

And she was. Her hand was almost outstretched where it was pushing the handle controlling their speed all the way forward. She'd given up tapping at any of the buttons that altered their trajectory – everyone knew that the shortest distance between any two points was a straight line, altering it would only slow them down.

"I think the lightning's getting less," Kadee stated.

"Does that mean that we're nearly out?" Alana asked.

The worry in her best friend's voice caused her to glance around and down. Paul was still flat out where he'd fallen, only now he had his head resting in Alana's lap. Beyond them, she could see Ray struggling to climb back to his feet using the consoles on either side of him as leverage. The lack of anything from Matt had her concerned; the *thump* that she'd heard from his direction when the world, space went haywire had not sounded good.

The room flaring purple, quickly followed by red told her that, even if the lightning storm was lessening, they weren't out of it yet. The fact that they were *in* it at all was worrying. Very worrying.

They'd discussed it, what might happen if they were caught in the blast radius. They knew the risks. How could they not? They'd all been inside this type of storm before, most of them twice. But that was when a single pair of Hopper EMP devices malfunctioned. This time, there'd been a hundred pairs, all rigged to blow at the exact same time. And blown by them, no less.

The fact that only a few of them had been rendered unconscious was promising, but all the same, raised questions.

"Is that it?" Kadee asked a minute or so later.

It was probable, Vic thought, especially considering the last flare of lightning – a burst of yellow – had been half a minute beforehand.

"I think so," Tolan replied.

A groan indicated that Paul was waking up.

"What the hell was that?" Matt's slurred voice asked. "Did something hit us?"

"We were caught on the edge of the shockwave," Ray replied. "At least, I think so."

"What happened to the Hoppers? Are they still there?" Kadee asked anxiously.

"Vic?" Tolan prompted.

She stared at the screen, blinking at it as she tried to understand what it was showing.

"Nothing!" she blurted. "The sensors aren't picking up anything!"

"They're gone? It worked?" Ray asked excitedly, his steps announcing that he was approaching Vic's console.

"They're gone from my screen," Vic confirmed. "Whether that means that they're *really* gone...?"

Her shrug was apparently enough to get Alana moving.

"I guess that's my cue to go look out the rear window again," she sighed. "I just hope that *this* time, I don't get temporarily blinded!"

The wait for her report seemed to stretch. Seconds felt like minutes, minutes like days.

"I'm back here," Alana called over the communication system. *"I'm not seeing anything in any direction. They're gone!"*

"We did it!" Vic whispered.

"We did it!" Matt whooped.

"We did it!" Ray exclaimed before unexpectedly wrapping his arms around her and kissing her cheek in excitement.

Vic felt her neck and face flush. This thing between them, one of these days, they needed to sit down and work out what it was. But not with everyone else there.

"Vic, set a course for Earth," Tolan ordered. "It's time to go home."

"Yeah, but *when* are we going to?" Kadee muttered

Vic glanced at her but didn't have an answer. All she, all any of them could do, was hope for the best.

“Um, Vic? We’ve got company,” Alana stated.

Vic took note of her words but otherwise didn’t really pay attention. Flying an alien spaceship through space was hard enough; flying through atmosphere was a lot harder.

Wisps of blue appeared in the white and Vic knew that they were almost through the clouds. A couple of light taps of a button eased the nose further down. And then they were through.

Blue burst all around them, accompanied by even more blue and swathes of green and brown far below.

“Where are we?” she asked.

“Nearly three hundred kilometres to the north of where we were aiming for,” Paul replied.

“Vic! Company!” Alana insisted.

Company? the phrase didn’t make sense. They were in a spaceship in the air, still dozens of kilometres straight up.

Suddenly, a fighter jet rocketed in from the right, crossed in front of them and shot away out of sight. Vic stared, her fingers stuttering across the control board and making the *Scorpion* drop a couple of metres straight down before she could right it.

“Right. Company,” she stated. “How many?”

“Two,” Alana replied. “At least, that’s how many I saw when we were still in the cloud.”

“Matt, can you work the communication system?” Tolan asked.

“Maybe,” he replied after a pause.

A longer pause and complete silence filled the *Scorpion* as they waited. Meanwhile, Vic flew on, her eyes darting about out the front window in an effort to see the fighter jets. Seeing nothing, she tried the screens set in the console in front of her, unfortunately to no avail.

A squark of static burst from the speakers and Vic winced at the loudness of the sound. It cut out, burst back in and disappeared once more.

“Base *this is* Taipan One. *Bogey isn’t any sort of plane that I’ve ever seen before. Definitely of unknown origins. Over.”*

“Taipan One. Base. *Approved for a flyby with belly cam. Get us a visual of bogey. Over.”*

“Copy Base. *Alright* Taipan Two*, let’s buzz us a UFO and see what she looks like up close and personal.”*

“Taipan One. Base. *Be advised that* Taipans Three *and* Four *are inbound to your position. ETA three minutes.”*

“What is that? Where’s it coming from and what does it mean?” Kadee asked.

“That’s the communications from those two jets that Alana saw,” Matt explained. “Sounds like they’re shadowing us and trying to work out what we are.”

“If there are two more heading this way, does that mean that they’re getting ready to shoot us out of the sky?” Paul asked.

“We need to talk to them, tell them who we are!” Tolan stated urgently. “Can we talk back to them?”

Vic glanced back to see Matt frowning down at his console. He seemed to be tentatively picking at the buttons. Part of her wanted to rush back there and use her ability to guide his hands. The problem was that she was currently busy flying the ship.

Once again, a jet rocketed across their bows and away, this time being quickly followed by a second one, its wings tipped up at a sixty-degree angle allowing them to see its belly.

"I think I've got it!" Matt exclaimed.

"Well, talk to them!" Ray snapped.

"Those other planes should be here any moment," Paul added.

"Um, okay," Matt said, paused, then began. "*Taipan* jets flying near us, this is the *Scorpion*, can you hear us?"

A burst of static filled the air and Vic was sure that she wasn't the only one holding their breath.

"*Taipan* jets..." Matt began only to be interrupted.

"This is Taipan One, *please identify yourself."*

"My name is Matthew Goldstein and I am aboard the spaceship *Scorpion*. We are currently on a trajectory that will have us landing near Cairns."

"Scorpion. Taipan One. *Please repeat. Did you say 'spaceship'?"*

"That is an affirmative. The *Scorpion* is a spaceship," Matt replied. "She's not from around here, even though I and my friends are."

"I can see the other two jets," Alana said, from where she stood at the very front of the deck.

"Scorpion. Taipan One. *We will form up around you. You are expected to follow us down to Base."*

"Tolan? Vic?" Matt asked.

"We've got to land her somewhere," Tolan shrugged. "And if following them stops them from shooting at us, then we might as well."

"I vote for not being shot at!" Paul agreed and Vic looked back in time to see him with his hand raised.

"I'm pretty sure that I can fly with them well enough to keep them happy," Vic said.

"*Taipan One*, this is the *Scorpion*. We will comply and follow you to your Base," Matt stated. "Be advised that our pilot is a little inexperienced so would appreciate no unexpected manoeuvres."

Vic grimaced. He didn't have to tell them *that*! She was doing perfectly fine, thank you very much.

"Scorpion. Taipan One. *Message understood. Tell your pilot to expect an easy ride home. Out."*

"Well, you heard the man, let's enjoy the easy ride home," Ray said and Vic could hear the smile on his face.

Rolling her eyes, she focussed firstly on her board and then out the front window to the two jets soaring ahead of them. With luck, they'd be down and parked in time for dinner.

The airfield that they were led to wasn't in the direction that they'd been going, but it was close. Not that any of them greatly cared; they had to park the *Scorpion* somewhere and what better spot than an Air Force Base.

"I'm putting her down over there," Vic said, pointing from the pilot's seat out the front window.

"Good idea," Ray nodded, having come to stand right behind her, his hand resting lightly on her shoulder. "Probably not a good idea to park on a runway and hold up traffic."

The jets peeled off, not that she was paying them any attention. Yes, she'd landed this thing before; didn't mean she was an expert at it. Her fingers tapped away, altering the *Scorpion's* trajectory and altitude with every touch. It took longer than she thought it should – but probably not as long as it really did – before she felt the jolt of the ship hitting the ground harder than it should have.

"We're down," she announced unnecessarily as she began the process of shutting down the engines and the console.

"Now what?" Paul asked.

"Now we find out whether what we did worked," Tolan said.

"And how badly everyone wants to yell at us," Alana added grimly.

"I'm pretty sure that we got rid of an alien fleet," Matt put in. "That's got to earn us major kudos and a whole heap of slack."

While they'd been talking, the seven of them walked through the ship. Without being asked, Vic touched the button that would lower the ramp before tucking the cylinder in the back of her jeans and pulling her shirt down over it.

"Why is it that there are always soldiers pointing guns at us every time we walk down this ramp?" Ray asked.

"Come out of there with your hands up!" a deep voice ordered.

Vic rolled her eyes and complied, just as the others did. Slowly, they walked down the ramp and spread out in a line.

"Who are you? Where'd you come from? And what the hell kind of aircraft is that?" the same voice asked.

The officer – Vic wasn't sure of his rank and was too far away to read his name badge – was completely bald, except for the thick moustache under his nose. His uniform was Airforce blue with a number of silver medals on his epaulettes.

"We're humans, if that's what you're asking," Tolan replied. "And that's not an aircraft, it's a spaceship, just not man-made."

The officer glared and Vic wondered if he was trying to decide what to do with them next.

"My name's Vic. That's Tolan, Ray, Kadee, Matt, Alana and Paul," Vic said, introducing them since Tolan had failed to do so. "If it's okay with you, could we make one phone call? I promise that everything will be cleared up and explained to you if you do."

"Who do you plan on calling?" the officer asked suspiciously.

"Prime Minister Donovan," Vic replied.

"Oh, *good* plan," Ray whispered. "For a second, I thought you were wanting to call that idiot White."

The officer, meanwhile, was chuckling. "You honestly think the Prime Minister of Australia would take your call?"

"One way to find out," Tolan challenged. "If he doesn't, then we won't protest when you throw us in the brig."

"That's the Navy," the officer stated blandly. "Very well. *One* phone call. After that, all bets are off and you'll be answering any and all questions that I have for you more fully than you've ever answered a question before in your life."

"Do any of you guys actually have the phone number for the Prime Minister?" Ray whispered once they'd been escorted inside, through a series of rooms and to a windowless office that contained a desk, a phone, a couple of chairs and nothing else.

"I think that I can get us through to him," Vic replied.

"You remember the number?" Alana asked, clearly surprised.

"Nope," Vic smiled.

Then, after taking a deep breath, she picked up the receiver on the phone, held her hand so that it was hovering over the keypad and closed her eyes. A series of *beeps* later was followed by the sound of the phone ringing on the other end.

"This is the Office of the Prime Minister, how may I direct your call?" a professional-sounding female voice asked.

Vic punched the air, letting the others know that, once again, her ability had come through.

"Yes, hi, my name is Victoria Groogan," she said. "I would like to speak to Prime Minister Donovan."

"I'm sorry but only authorised persons with an appointment can speak to the Prime Minister," the woman replied.

"If you look up my name – Victoria Groogan – you'll find that I'm an authorised person," she said.

There was a brief pause, then, *"could you please spell your surname?"*

"G. R. O. O. G. A. N. Groogan," Vic replied, glad that she didn't have to spell that most-hated part of her name as well.

"Miss Groogan!" the surprised-sounding woman said. *"Yes, I see that you on the authorised persons list. But I'm sorry to tell you that Prime Minister Donovan is currently unavailable."*

"When *will* he be available?" she asked, gritting her teeth. This wasn't supposed to happen! The man had assured them that they'd have a direct line to him at any time, day or night.

"No earlier than the day after tomorrow," the woman replied. *"I can take a message and pass it along to him, if you'd like?"*

Not that they had much choice, Vic thought.

"Please tell him that Victoria Groogan and her friends – Tolan, Ray, Matt, Kadee, Paul and Alana – are at ..."

She cast around, moving the receiver to her chest. Finding an Air Force officer standing at ease just inside the door, she focused on him.

"Where are we?" she asked.

The man looked at her, seemed to consider whether he should answer or not, then decided that it wouldn't cause any harm.

"RAAF Base Scherger," he replied.

"RAAF Base Scherger," Vic repeated into the phone.

"Thank you, I will ensure that Prime Minister Donovan gets the message at the first opportunity," the woman promised.

With nothing more to say, Vic finished the call and replaced the receiver back into its cradle.

"Well?" Tolan demanded.

"She'll pass on the message," Vic shrugged.

"Which means that we're back to waiting again," a thoroughly unimpressed-sounding Matt summed up.

The scrape of a chair preceded Paul sitting and pulling Alana down onto his lap. "Guess we might as well get comfortable. Who knows how long we'll be waiting *this* time?"

CHAPTER 28

They were left alone for the rest of the day. Only the bare minimum of food had been brought to them, although they had plenty of water. The small office where they'd made the phone call to the Prime Minister's office had been exchanged for a large room, more like a conference room. At the very least, there were enough chairs for all of them, plus a few spares. Unsurprisingly, there were still no windows.

The following day was when the questions began. Vic had been given the honour of going first, whether that was because she'd been the one to make the phone call or because, as the smallest, they thought that she'd be the one most likely to crack first or some other completely random reason, was anyone's guess.

A pair of guards led her to a small room, not unlike the room where, what felt like months or years ago, they'd interrogated the captured Hopper. Inside, she found a Captain already seated, a closed folder on the desk in front of him alongside a pad and a pen.

"What's your name?" Vic asked, even before she'd taken a seat.

"My name is Captain Jonathon Brady," he replied.

"And your role here?" Vic continued.

"To ask you some questions."

The fact that *she* was the one doing the asking and *him* the answering amused her, not that she let it show. Liking the feel for how this questioning had started, Vic decided to keep going.

"We're at RAAF Base Scherger. Where exactly is that?" she asked, tipping her head in curiosity.

"On the western side of Cape York Peninsula, near Weipa," he replied. "I thought you'd know that?"

Vic ignored the question. "Why have you been keeping us isolated?"

"This is an Air Force Base. You were detained here for flying that ... *whatever* it is from what appeared to be space. We're not exactly going to allow you to have free run of our Base now, are we?"

Vic shrugged. The Army had tried that. Not that it did them much good. Really, it was only because they *chose* to remain where they were and to wait for the Prime Minister to come through that they hadn't tried to make a break for it. But now that she knew where they were, that might change things. Especially being so far from civilization.

"How long do you intend on keeping us here?" Vic asked.

"That depends," the Captain replied, sitting back in his seat. "I think that's enough of my answering your questions. It's time for you to answer mine."

This time, Vic simply smiled sweetly at him.

"Your name is Victoria Groogan," he began. "Born in Brisbane, seventeen years of age. Parents, Geoffrey and Catherine, one sister and one brother."

"Mostly right," she allowed. She was *sixteen*, not seventeen, not that she felt the need to correct him.

"How about you start by telling me what that aircraft is that you flew in on?" he suggested.

"You don't know?" Vic asked, grinning at him. "I thought that this was an *Air Force* Base. Shouldn't you already know about every type of aircraft?"

"Yours is something that we've never seen before. I'm guessing experimental? Which then begs the question of how you came to be aboard it. Teenagers aren't usually allowed near normal aircraft, let alone something experimental."

A prickling down her side had Vic looking expectantly at the door. As predicted, it opened.

"Excuse me, Sir," the Sergeant said. "There are some people here requesting to see her and her friends."

"About time," Vic grumbled.

The Captain stared at her for a full minute before suddenly pushing away from the desk and standing.

"Escort her back to her friends," he ordered. "I'm going to go see who our visitors are."

"Why are they looking at us like that?" Alana whispered to Vic.

Vic's eyes narrowed. "I don't know."

General White, Sergeant Reid and Private Dillan had burst into the room and stopped dead. Only their eyes were moving, flicking from one to another and back. What was worse was when General White's jaw *dropped open*! It was so uncharacteristic of the man that it had alarms bells not just ringing, but *shrilling*.

"General? Are you okay?" Tolan asked. "Sergeant? Jo?"

Jo seemed to come out of whatever had gripped the three of them the quickest.

"You're here!" she blurted then blanched at the fact that she'd just spoken before either of her commanding officers.

"Where else would we be?" Kadee asked.

Slowly, Sergeant Reid seemed to reboot and he stepped further into the room, bypassing the General. "Are you alone? Did the Hoppers follow you?"

"Hoppers?" Matt asked. "They're here?"

"I thought we got rid of them all," Paul added.

"No Hoppers?" Sergeant Reid asked.

"No," Tolan replied firmly. "Our plan worked. We detonated the bomb right in the middle of their Swarm. It created a wonderful little Time Storm and swallowed the lot of them whole. Mind you, it nearly swallowed *us* as well – only just made it out."

General White's eyes narrowed and his jaw snapped shut. "Are you telling us that you think you made it out of that weird lightning space storm without it affecting you?"

A cold shiver rushed down Vic's spine and goosebumps rose on her arms and the back of her neck.

"Are you saying we're wrong? That it *did* affect us?" Ray asked.

Seeing the General, Sergeant and Private all share what could only be called 'guilty looks' only reinforced the feeling of dread that had settled in the pit of Vic's stomach.

"How long?" she asked woodenly.

"Six months," General White replied.

"Six months and nine days," Private Dillon correctly quietly, looking sadly at them.

"We were gone for six months!" Paul exclaimed. "No! I don't believe it!"

"That's impossible!" Matt added. "We got out of that Time Storm unscathed. It didn't affect us!"

Vic's eyes had never left General White's. Suddenly, her legs gave out from under her and she fell heavily, luckily into a chair.

"No! No! No!" Alana wailed, both arms coming up over her head. "Our parents! They must think we're dead."

"You've got to be wrong. This is a joke, isn't it?" Tolan asked.

Vic didn't even bother looking up from where her head had fallen forward. It was no joke. She could *feel* it. General White was telling the truth – how could he not be, the man didn't have a sense of humour.

"Vic?" Ray asked quietly.

She looked up then, seeing the plea in his eyes for her to tell her that this was wrong.

"He's right," she replied. "You know he is. We didn't get out of the lightning storm in time, you all saw the flashes all around us. Hell, Paul and Matt collapsed, just like the other times that we've travelled through time."

"But the rest of us didn't," Tolan argued but Vic could hear the doubt in his voice.

"True," she replied. "But that might have been because we were so far from the epicentre, when the other times we were right in the middle of it."

"If ... *if* ... they're telling the truth and we did get pulled into the Time Bomb and travelled through time, then what happened to the

Hoppers?" Matt asked.

"Do you have any sort of proof that we travelled through time again?" Kadee asked.

Of all of them, she was the calmest. Which made sense. She'd already been pulled from her home, from everything that she knew. Six months either way in this timeline wouldn't make much difference to her.

"Here," Sergeant Reid said, handing over a paper that he'd had tucked under his arm. "That's todays."

None of the others seemed to want to touch it, so it was left to Vic to reach out and take it. One look at the date – May twenty-four – was enough to seal it.

"He was right," she muttered, surprised.

"What? Who was right?" Ray asked.

She dropped the paper and looked up at him. "The Captain before. When he was asking me questions. He read out some info about me, said I was seventeen. He was right. I missed my birthday."

"You're not the only one," Paul groaned. "And we missed Christmas."

"Okay. Okay. We jumped forward in time. As hard as it is, I'll accept that. Six months," Tolan said, shaking his head. "That still doesn't explain what happened to the Hoppers."

"The container was pretty much right in the middle of them when we detonated it, they would have been caught in the main effects," Alana said.

"Whereas we just caught, what? a glancing blow?" Matt asked.

"Pretty much," Vic replied. "The Hoppers are still out there, just lost in time. They'll reappear."

"When?" General White demanded.

"No idea," Vic replied. "We set off a hundred pairs of those things, there's no telling what the effects were. They might turn up tomorrow or next week or next year or next century! There is simply no way to know."

"I was afraid you'd say that," General White groused.

"What's happened to our parents? Where are they?" Alana asked.

"When we detected that lightning storm out in space and saw that you'd completed the mission, that there were no more aliens headed our way, they went home," General White said gently.

"We've been keeping an eye on them," Sergeant Reid added. "They're all well and simply slipped back into their old life as though nothing happened."

"But something *did* happen: we disappeared! They must have thought that we'd died!" Ray shouted.

"They did. We all did or at least, that you'd been displaced in time," Private Dillon replied. "There were memorials for you all."

"The world thinks that we died saving the planet? That's cool, macabre but cool, I guess," Tolan said.

But General White was already shaking his head and the pit in Vic's stomach grew once again.

"No. It was decided that the world didn't need to know how close we came to being invaded and eradicated," General White stated.

"Who decided that?" Tolan and Matt demanded simultaneously.

"What did you do?" Vic asked and, even though her voice was the quietest, it seemed to cut through everything.

"There was a meeting, a closed session of the United Nations," General White replied. "Prime Minister Donovan, Premier Jorgensen, United States General McKenzie, not to mention the top politician from every country in the world and quite a number of scientists and military officers were there. The debate lasted for a couple of days. In the end, the decision was made: all references to the Hoppers, their potential invasion, time travel, you ... all of it was classified as Top Secret at the highest levels. No one in the world can talk about it. No one has. Or will. Ever. The penalties for doing so are extreme."

"But ... that's impossible!" Tolan spluttered. "There were so many people around the world who saw us. We gathered all of those EMP devices!"

"There were too many people who saw the Hoppers and us and the *Scorpion*! The soldiers at your Base for a start," Paul protested.

"Not to mention all those people at Undara," Ray added.

"It's done!" General White declared with finality. "It was all written off as a movie that was being made. Special effects and modified aircraft and what not. No one questioned it."

"What did you do?" Vic asked again.

There was no doubt in her mind that everything that he'd said was true. The way that the Air Force personnel reacted to the *Scorpion* told that story. But General White still hadn't answered her question.

"I just told you," the General replied.

She looked up at him, staring him in the eye. "No. With us. With our parents. The ... the memorials. Everyone thinks we're dead! If not because we died saving the planet, then what *do* they think?"

Again, she saw the military officers all looking sheepish, their eyes darting anywhere and everywhere but to any of them.

"Answer Vic's question!" Ray shouted.

She watched as General White's Adam's apple raised and lowered. Finally, he gathered himself and stood a little straighter.

"The world thinks that the six of you died in a plane accident," he said quickly.

The room was dead silent and Vic's eyes shifted from Ray to Alana to Paul to Matt to Tolan to Kadee. Kadee. Six?

"You said six," she pointed out. "There are *seven* of us!"

"No one knows about Kadee," Sergeant Reid replied. "She never existed."

"I'm standing right here!" the girl in question stated.

"Yes, but without birth records or schooling records, it was just easier to omit your existence," Sergeant Reid replied.

Vic stood, drawing all eyes to her. "You will fix that. Kadee exists. She's right here! And we will *not* leave her behind. Now, you're going to fix things. You bring us back to life and you do the same for Kadee as well!"

"I do not take orders from you!" General White bristled.

"You will if you want the world to keep thinking the lies that you've been telling," Tolan said, backing Vic up. "We have a spaceship sitting right outside. You know what we can do. Exactly how long do you think it'll take us to get out of here and fly straight to the biggest city in the world and tell everyone what's been going on?"

"There are some very severe penalties for doing what you're threatening," General White retorted.

"We're dead! What more can you do to us?" Matt asked.

Sergeant Reid broke protocol and probably a regulation or two by stepping forward and placing a hand on General White's shoulder to keep him quiet.

"If we 'fix things' as you want, will you stay silent? Will you keep quiet about the Hoppers and what went on?" he asked.

"Yes," Tolan replied.

"No!" Vic countered. "We came back, jumped forward in time six months. But *we weren't the only ones caught in that Time Bomb!* The Hopper Swarm was, too. And one day, they're going to re-emerge. Earth needs to be ready for that day or what we sacrificed, what we went through to buy everyone that chance will have been for nothing!"

"She's right. And you know it," Ray said, standing by her shoulder.

One by one, the others, her friends, stood, turning defiant faces on the three Army officers. The grin on Sergeant Reid's face was completely unexpected.

"I did tell you, General," he said.

"No one likes a 'know it all'," the General groused.

"I think we're missing something," Alana said.

"You are. Or perhaps, it's more accurate to say that you saw the problem a lot faster than the rest of us did," Sergeant Reid replied.

"After the United Nations' meeting, smarter heads than ours saw the same problem," General White said. "That one day, some unknown time in the future, the Hopper Swarm would be back and we needed to be ready. But we couldn't just go out and tell the world that we had a limited window of opportunity to prepare. So, an organisation was formed."

"An organisation?" Vic asked, her excitement fuelled by the warmth rapidly spreading from her feet all the way up to the top of her head.

Goosebumps were forming as well, but unlike normal ones, these felt *good*, right.

"The Apollo Foundation," Sergeant Reid smiled. "We've been recruiting some of the top scientists and engineers on the planet."

"To do what? Build bigger and more powerful weapons and spaceships?" Matt asked.

"Not as such," Sergeant Reid replied. "Our aim is to advance mankind's technology, to make us better. Yes, the ultimate aim is to construct spaceships, to go out and explore our own solar system and then, eventually, further. We envision colonies and fleets and man's understanding of the universe expanding exponentially."

"How soon?" Paul asked eagerly. "How soon until we have better spaceships that can travel that far?"

"Ten or twenty years, maybe? But with the *Scorpion*, if we study her, we could maybe halve that time," Sergeant Reid replied.

"You keep saying 'we'," Ray pointed out.

Sergeant Reid laughed. "I've got a new posting. Private Dillon, too. We're a part of the Apollo Foundation's Security Division."

"The seven of you," General White said, drawing everyone's attention back to him, "would be prime candidates for the Foundation. Your knowledge of the aliens, their tech and what they can do would be invaluable."

"Not to mention our abilities," Alana deadpanned.

"To some extent, sure," Sergeant Reid shrugged, "but it's your knowledge that would be most valuable. Ray, for example. Those sunset melons that you had your dad growing. They're showing incredible potential. Easy to grow in a lot of diverse conditions. It's still early days but we think that they could be used to help underdeveloped countries.

But that was only possible because you recognised it. The rest of us didn't."

"I can guarantee that the seven of you would have jobs with Apollo for life," Private Dillon said.

"But we're still only teenagers," Paul pointed out.

"Doesn't matter. The choice will be yours. But the option's there," General White replied.

"None of which can happen until *after* you *bring us back from the dead*!" Vic pointed out.

"True," General White nodded. "You understand that it's going to take a couple of days to iron out the details? There's nothing that I can do about that."

Vic could see the protest forming, particularly in Alana, Paul and Ray's eyes. But her gut was telling her that it had to happen that way.

"Alright, just get it done as fast as possible," she said.

General White nodded to her, to all of them and strode from the room, his subordinates following in his wake.

"Vic?" Tolan asked.

"It has to happen this way. I can feel it," she replied.

"What's your take on this Apollo Foundation?" Matt asked.

Once again, that warm, fuzzy feeling enveloped her. "It's the right call. The Hoppers are coming back. There's no doubt about that. The only question is 'when?' This Foundation will help us be ready to face that day."

"Will it be enough?" Ray asked quietly.

“Yes. Yes, I think it will,” she smiled.

Now all that was left was waiting to see how right she was.

A shift in time, then to now…

EPILOGUE

Unlike every other morning, Vic woke suddenly. One moment she was asleep, the next wide awake. Her eyes snapped open and darted about the room even before she sat up.

The deep forest green drapes were still closed over the window, a hint of gold around the edges. It was morning, but obviously still early if her alarm had yet to go off. The door was closed, as it should be and there was no sign or sound that anyone had entered her room – not that they would if they knew what was good for them.

Slowly she sat up, doing her best to ignore the stiff muscles in her back and legs. They were old companions these days and ones that she'd gotten used to too many long years ago. Reflectively, she glanced at the other side of her bed but it was empty – something else that she'd grown used to seeing. That didn't mean that she didn't miss him dearly every day and still expected to see him lying there, or at least the indent in the covers where he was supposed to be, just that she was used to this new reality.

Still, something had woken her. Her dresser looked as it should, the base of the holo sitting to one side of the mirror, her jewellery tree on the other and her hairbrush in the middle. She couldn't detect any unusual sounds; there was only the constant ticking of the clock in the other room and the twitterings of some birds outside her window.

No, nothing in here had woken her. But then what had?

And then she felt it. A slight lifting of her hairs at the base of her neck and a tingling running up and down her arms. Looking down, she ran one hand over her arm, feeling the slight goosebumps mixed in amongst the wrinkles that now covered her body.

A premonition?

It'd been a long, long time since she'd had one this strong. Over the years she'd learnt to almost ignore the signs, instead simply allowing her mind and body to lead her through life. Oh, it'd gotten her into trouble more than a few times but in general, it'd helped more than hindered.

Swinging her legs over the side of the bed, Vic slowly stood, using the headboard to help steady herself. She took a tentative step forward and smiled as her legs held; no need for her cane today. Or at least, not yet.

Her eyes fixed on the dozens of frames on the wall, she felt a pull and obeyed, stepping carefully across the room. As she did, she cast her mind back, trying to remember the last time that she'd felt a premonition so strong. More than a decade, even a decade and a half, she decided, but not much more than that.

And then she had it.

A smile graced her face and her eyes sought out one particular picture. Kadee. A Kadee full of life and energy and fun in the prime of her life. There were more recent ones, of course. Well, recent in a manner of speaking. The premonition that she was thinking about had taken place decades after that particular photo had been taken. It'd taken most of the day to work out exactly what she was feeling. And when she did, she'd laughed and toasted one of her best friends on her birthday. Or, more precisely, on the day of her birth. Or what would have been her birth.

Even after all this time, the notion of time and time travel was still confusing. Not that she thought about it all that much. But now that her mind was thinking along those lines, Vic's eyes sought out photo after photo.

Paul and Alana surrounded by their children, grandchildren and even a great-grandchild as they celebrated their fiftieth wedding anniversary.

Tolan standing straight and proud, one arm raised. He'd been the guest speaker at the General Assembly of the United Nations that day and his passion was clear to see even in the captured image.

There was Matt, lolling in his favourite chair at his house, his feet splayed out in front of him, a glass in his hand and a wide grin on his face.

Vic's eyes moistened at the next image. Her and Ray strolling arm in arm through his beloved field of sunset melons. They'd danced around each other for years before finally deciding to give being a couple a go. Wasted years, Ray had always claimed, although Vic was more of the opinion that they'd needed time to grow into themselves before they were ready to find their other half. Who was right, it hardly mattered. All that counted were the decades that they'd had together and the family that they'd cultivated before it'd just become her again.

Her eyes slipped to the picture of that day, nearly a century before. There she was dressed in white, her veil flipped to reveal her smiling face, her eyes filled with love for the tuxedoed man standing beside her. Of course, they weren't alone. All seven of them were there, grouped together with their arms around each other.

Her friends. Her best friends. Alana. Paul. Tolan. Matt. Kadee. And Ray. She was the last of them, now.

"I miss you. I miss you all so much," she whispered, her hand reaching out to touch each of their faces but finding only glass.

From that picture, her eyes sought out all of them, glossing over her children and her children's children and the rest of her descendants just then to fix on her friends. She held each one and cherished the memories that each photo brought.

Her premonition jolted full force into her once again as her eyes landed on the oldest of all the pictures and she gasped.

It was of the seven of them again, back when they were still teenagers, proud smiles on their faces having accomplished the impossible. What made it so special was the fact that they were standing in front of the *Scorpion*.

Now, *there* was something that she hadn't thought about in a long time – her time piloting the Hopper spaceship. Vic's eyes narrowed. Hoppers. It felt right, *tasted* right.

Surely not ...

But the timing... a little more than sixteen years since she'd felt when Kadee should or would have been born. Which would make it about the right time, perhaps even to the day?

As fast as her legs would carry her, Vic moved back across towards her bed before touching the communicator on her bedside table.

"Apollo Foundation. This is Yvette."

"Good morning, Yvette. This is Victoria Thompson," Vic replied, internally suppressing her distaste for having to use her full name, even if she was old enough with enough authority to order everyone to call her whatever she wanted. Still, the protocols had to be maintained.

"Good morning, Mrs Thompson. What can I do for you today?"

"Please put out a fleet-wide directive," Vic ordered. "I want all ships within the solar system stationed in orbit around Earth within the hour and to maintain position until further notice. Send the message to the ships at Pictor as well."

Vic could hear Yvette's uncertainty in her pause, which was, of course, completely understandable. Vic didn't actually hold a rank within the Foundation but paradoxically, she also did hold the authority to give the order that she'd just issued.

"Of course, Mrs Thompson. Will there be anything else?" Yvette asked.

"Yes, please have a car sent for me," Vic replied.

"It will be there within half an hour," Yvette assured her.

Vic nodded. Half an hour would be fine. Having closed the connection, she picked up her dressing gown and headed for the shower.

Vic could feel the curiosity around her. It was as understandable as Yvette's confusion over her issuing such a drastic order to the Apollo Foundation fleet had been earlier. It didn't help that she sat in a chair on the upper level of the Command Centre, sipping her coffee and looking down on everyone. At least it amused her and gave her something to do while she waited.

And that was the big problem. The waiting. She'd been there for over five hours already and the order to assemble the fleet had gone out even earlier than that. The only deviation in that time had been when she'd been brought a particular metal briefcase that had been locked away in storage years ago and that she'd hoped would never be needed.

Pushing her glasses more firmly into place, Vic looked up at the big monitor once again.

In the very centre was a brilliant blue and white ball, not unlike a marble: Earth. Surrounding it were sixty-seven small golden icons: the fleet that she'd had assembled. Well, most of them.

"Has there been any word from Pictor?" she asked.

The lieutenant that had been assigned to her stepped forward from where he'd been trying not to hover, a data pad in his hand.

"We received a message from Captain Lornicaan. *Star Runner* is leading the combined Jellican and Mamoan fleets to Earth," he said. "They're expected to arrive in seven hours."

Vic grimaced. Too long. Of that, she was sure. Whatever was going to happen would be well and truly over by then. At least, that's what her gut was telling her. Still, the fact that it was now considered common knowledge that people from other planets existed would help when what was to happen happened.

Honestly, Vic had no idea how the secret had been kept for so long. It was a decision that she'd never agreed with but it'd been made while she and her friends had been time travelling and once they'd arrived, it'd just seemed easier to go with the flow rather than rocking the boat. Only the fact that humans had encountered aliens by venturing out into space themselves – even if the encounter had only happened the year before – gave her hope that things would turn out okay.

"Ma'am, is there anything that you need? Would you like the car brought around?" the Lieutenant asked.

A commotion at one of the science consoles caught Vic's attention. Ignoring the lieutenant, she leant forward, her gaze intent.

"I'm detecting some strange readings approximately one and a half AU from Earth! Is anyone else seeing this?" a sandy-haired officer stated.

Vic levered herself to her feet, both hands resting on the rail, her gaze fixed.

"What sort of readings?" the Operations Commander demanded.

"Tachyons, a number of different forms of radiation including x-rays, gamma and delta. And a bunch of things that the computer can't identify," the Science Officer replied.

This was it! Vic was sure of it. She could *feel* it.

"Is it possible to get an image of that part of space on the screen?" she asked.

The Commander barely spared a glance in her direction before issuing the order. "Do it!"

It took a surprisingly short time before the big monitor switched to a view of space.

"This is taken from the *Antiquity*," an officer announced. "It's the closest ship that we have to the anomaly. She's currently on course, rendezvous in nine minutes."

"No!" Vic shouted. "Tell them to keep their distance!"

The Commander's look at her was longer this time before he reinforced the order. Not that Vic was paying attention, instead, her eyes were fixed on the screen.

A flash of something caught her eye. Green in space? It came again and was quickly followed by a bolt of purple.

Vic held her breath, her mind flying back to the last time she'd seen something like this.

And then space lit up.

Bolts of green.

Flashes of purple.

Shooting yellow and white.

The darkest of blue that was almost impossible to see.

A cloud of red, orange interspersed amongst it.

And then that entire section of space erupted in a light show, an electric storm unlike anything anyone else in the room had seen. It covered an area dozens of kilometres across, 'lightning strikes' bursting out in every direction.

"What the hell is that?"

Whoever'd asked the question obviously didn't expect an answer. They got one anyway.

"That is what happens when hundreds of alien devices are caused to deliberately malfunction all at once in the exact same place," Vic stated.

"Alien?" the Commander asked.

Vic tore her gaze from the screen to look down at him.

"Yes. Alien. And not the nice kind, either," she stated grimly. "Have the fleet prepare to engage."

"Engage what?" the Commander demanded.

"The alien fleet that's about to come out of that lightning storm," Vic replied.

"*What* alien fleet?" the Commander snapped. "I'm going to need more information than that!"

"One hundred and nine years ago, Earth was threatened by an alien invasion," Vic replied, her eyes back on the screen but her mind reliving those events once again. "My friends and I got caught up in it and managed to prevent it. There was time travel involved and a lot of events that you wouldn't believe. *Part* of the solution we found was to shift the alien fleet out of time, to today it seems."

"Time travel? Alien invasion?" the Commander repeated, clearly sceptical.

Vic looked down at him to see him looking past her, obviously at the lieutenant that had been assigned to her.

"I'm not crazy or senile or whatever you're thinking, Commander," Vic assured him. "Yes, I'm old, too old maybe – a side effect of getting caught up in *three* of those phenomena when I was a lot younger."

"Sir! Ships!"

And there were. At first there were only a handful, all emerging from within the lightning storm. But as the multitude of colours began to dissipate, more and more ships appeared.

Four.

A dozen.

Two dozen.

Fifty.

And still more.

Even the first time that Vic had seen them, all those years ago, she'd never known exactly how many Hopper ships there had been in the invasion fleet. And it was that fleet. All the ships that she remembered. Ones as small as the *Scorpion*; others the same class as the one that they'd destroyed; while many, many more were even larger.

"Lieutenant, bring me that case," Vic ordered. "Commander, have the fleet stand ready but make sure that they do not approach too closely."

Taking the case that was handed to her, she balanced it on the railing and used her thumbprint to unlock it. Inside, cushioned in foam, was a modified Hopper translator collar. Carefully, she picked it up and nodded at the lieutenant when he took the case away.

Almost automatically, her hands found the tiny catch that allowed the collar to be opened. With a grimace, she placed it around her neck and closed it up. The smallest of twists was needed to place the extra rectangular box against her chest before she pulled up the built-in microphone.

"Commander, open a communication line; it's time to try something that would never have worked last time," Vic stated.

A nod from the Commander preceded an answering nod from a lieutenant seated on the far side of the room.

"Alien fleet approaching the planet Earth," Vic began before pausing.

Hearing your own words echoed in an alien language, one filled with hisses and clicks and guttural sounds, a language that you couldn't understand, was quite disconcerting. As far as she was aware, the English to Hopper translator had never been tested. She was flying blind here. All she had to go on was the fact that her premonition feelings were all warm and tingly, telling her that she was on the right track.

"Alien fleet approaching the planet Earth," Vic began again. "You will have noticed the strange effect that you just emerged from. This was a warning of what you will be facing if you continue on your path towards us. We are not defenceless. We are prepared to resist. If necessary, we are prepared to retaliate with every means at our disposal.

"Your intelligence on us said that we were weak, unable to stand against you, that we had no weapons that could hurt you. You even believe that we have no spaceships to oppose your invasion. Take a good, long, hard look at what you are flying towards. Our fleet is ready for you and we have more ships on the way from outside this solar system.

"I urge you to do the smart thing. Think again. Earth is not ripe for your pickings. We are not worth your time. You will not win here. Turn around. Go home. And when you get there, stay there. Find other ways to solve your food and housing problems that doesn't involve you attacking other peoples and planets.

Vic paused, not only to allow the translator collar to finish its work but also to allow herself to catch her breath.

She'd been working towards this moment for a long, long time, it was why she'd stayed with the Apollo Foundation even after she'd officially retired years before. Ships had been built. Humans had spread out, exploring, seeing what was out there. A fleet had been prepared, even if its true purpose had never been known, not before now, at least. But was it enough? They were outnumbered. There was no mincing that fact. Nor was there any doubt over which fleet had more experience in battle.

"Is there a response?" the Commander asked.

"No, Commander," the Communications Lieutenant replied. "The line is open and the message is being received by them, but no response."

"Status of the alien Fleet?" the Commander demanded.

"Hopper," Vic corrected, not that he seemed to pay any attention to it.

"Still on course for Earth."

"Our fleet is gathering and moving to intercept," a different officer supplied.

"Alien fleet, I urge you to reconsider your course," Vic tried again. "Do not do this. There will be too many lives lost on both sides. We will stop you. Turn around. Go home. This fight is not one that you can win, not like any of the other dozen planets that you've conquered. We are not easy prey. We will not surrender. Take your Swarm and leave!"

Her eyes fixed on the screen and the Hopper Swarm, Vic willed them to do the smart thing. Unexpectedly, a warm flush travelled from her fingers and toes up her arms and legs to settle in her chest. She let out a breath, a smile appearing on her face.

"The alien fleet is changing course!" an excited sounding Lieutenant exclaimed. "They're moving away, heading out of the system."

Whoops and cheers filled the Command Centre, a sense of relief at the diverted disaster permeated the air.

"Close the channel," the Commander ordered.

"No!" Vic countermanded. She still had one last message to send before that was to happen. It was one that she knew Ray would want her to send, one that he'd advocated for his whole life and one that she knew he'd been right about.

"Alien Swarm, please take this message back to your leaders. There is another way. Attacking other planets does not have to be the only way for you to survive. If you need help, if you find that you cannot survive on your own due to lack of space to grow food or lack of resources, consider working in partnership with others. Talk. Be diplomatic. Two or more peoples can be stronger together. If your leaders want to open a dialogue with Earth, we will be ready to listen and potentially offer assistance. We do not have to be your enemy. We do not want to be your enemy. Let us be something more, something different."

"The alien fleet just jumped to hyperlight speeds. They're gone," the Lieutenant at tactical announced.

"Was there any response on communications?" Vic asked.

"No, Ma'am, I'm sorry," she was told.

Vic's head dropped. If she was honest, she hadn't expected one. But at least she'd tried. Ray, she knew, would be proud.

"Ma'am? Did you mean what you said? You'd really want humans to help some aliens that nearly attacked us?" the Commander asked.

Vic looked up at him. "Yes. While it's true that they intended to invade Earth and subjugate the planet – and believe me when I say that I know exactly what that would have looked like – *it never happened*! In the end, they did not attack us. They chose the smart option. Are humans ready to open diplomatic relations with people from other planets? Yes! We're already doing that with the Mamoan and Jellican refugees at Pictor. Who's to say that the Hoppers won't be next? We, at least, have done the right thing. We've extended the olive branch, admittedly alongside a rather large stick, but still. The ball's in their court now and I've seen stranger things happen."

The Commander nodded, obviously deep in thought at her words. And that was enough.

She turned and caught the eye of the young lieutenant that had been assigned as her aide. "Please have the car brought around, it's time I went home."

As she stepped into the elevator, her eyes closed and for the briefest of moments, she felt all of her friends around her once again. Tolan, Alana and Paul, Matt, Kadee and Ray. It'd taken a long, long time but finally, their job was done. What once could have been had now shifted away, veered onto a new path, a better path.

What the future would bring was anyone's guess. She'd done her part; it was time to rest.

The End.

Want more?

This story is just one of many. To find out more of what has already been written or what is planned, go to the website –

https://stargonbooks.wordpress.com

or Facebook page –

https://www.facebook.com/StargonBooks

Other Books by Mark McDonough

The Star Runner Series

1. Star Runner
2. Little Red Men
3. Gravity Well
4. Journey's End?

The Star Runner Series Accompanying Stories

The Flight of the Myserink
Fractured Gem
Smuggler's Run
The Phantom of Krashnoa Station
Bubble Burst
The Black Hole Mythdemeanour

The Phoenix Chronicles

1. Mud Grave
2. Kettlan's Box
3. Blackbeard's Rest

Stand Alone Stories

Saint George and the Dinosaur
Radelae's Scheme

Boxed Sets

The Star Runner Omnibus Edition
Space Lanes
The Phoenix Chronicles

Continuance Cycle 1

Shift

Aliens and Adventure.

Costumes and Superpowers.

Crazy future worlds full of danger.

These are the things you expect going to a Comic-Con. And while Vic and her friends' expectations were met, it wasn't quite how they'd envisioned.

A Shift in Time saw to that.

Now, with a few extra abilities

and a new friend alongside them, they have two choices: accept this new reality or try to find a way home.

Continuance Cycle 2

The future: Dark. Destroyed. Ruined.
A place where humans are almost extinct.
And filled with aliens.

A freak accident sent Vic and her friends there.

But the Shift in time wasn't their only change. Each of them also developed powers, powers that allowed them to fight back and to find a way home.

Now, they're back. They know what's coming.
But is the future set or can they change it?

Either way, it's time to find out.

Made in the USA
Columbia, SC
17 November 2022

71490031R00185